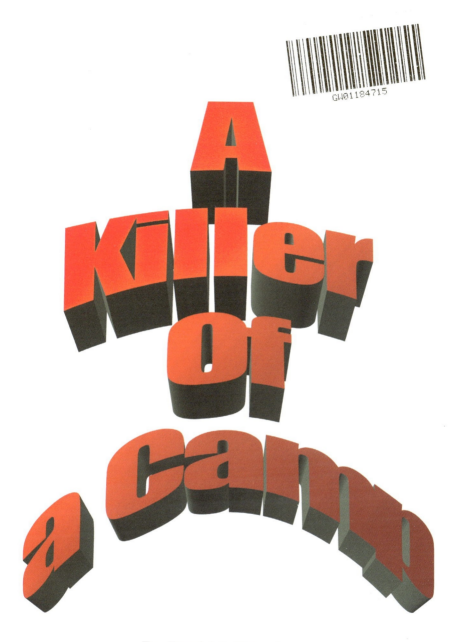

By David J. Dougherty

David J. Dougherty

Now don't let the photo of David above fool you, because his hair isn't always like the style above. As it was thanks to his regular hairdresser, Leo Mgrail, who came up with the idea for David to go **ahead** with it and get a crazy haircut instead of his usual zero baldy cut. Where doing so it thankfully managed to raise money for The Encephalitis Society, who are an organization that provide people who've contracted Encephalitis the professional information and support they and their families need. For those who aren't familiar with what Encephalitis is, Encephalitis means inflammation of the brain. The inflammation is caused either by an infection invading the brain (infectious Encephalitis): or through the immune system attacking the brain in error (autoimmune Encephalitis). Their website can be found at www.encephalitis.info for more information, where some of the stories are near enough as scary as to what you're about to read, due to some of the experiences ones have had to go through.

Now I hope you're all sitting safe, strapped into your settee's, have got all your drinks, goodies, handkerchiefs and torches by your side, as when you start reading 'A Killer of a Camp' you won't be able to stop and your heart will be racing 100mph. As with the four students, Paul, Alan, Ryan and Chris, who head on a camping spree, they are unaware Alan has been given the fake identification of a killer, who's closer than one ever wishes to imagine when they set up camp.

We hope you enjoy the novel and leave feedback on the website - www.akillerofacamp.com

A Killer of a Camp
FH: - Thriller/suspense
Copyright © David J. Dougherty 2013
Copyright protected through the IP Lab
Visit: - www.akillerofacamp.com

The right of David J. Dougherty to be identified as the author of this work has been asserted by him in accordance with the Copyright, Design and Patents Act 1988.

All rights reserved. No part of this publication may be reproduced, stored in or introduced into a retrieval system, or transmitted, in any form, or by any means (electronic, mechanical, photocopying, recording or otherwise) without the prior written permission of the author. Any person who does any unauthorized act in relation to this publication may be liable to criminal prosecution and civil claims for damages.

Based in Boston, MA, USA, A Killer of a Camp is a work of complete fiction. Therefore the names, characters, places and incidents throughout the novel are of the author's imagination or are used fictitiously. Any resemblance to locales, events or persons living or dead, are of entire coincidence.

Publisher
The Print Project, Unit G1, Dundonald,
Enterprise Park, Dundonald, BT16 1QT

Very special thanks to David's wife, Diane E. Dougherty, who did the photography to the front cover of the novel and has supported and encouraged David throughout his writing.

"A Killer of a Camp is specifically set out for to have you feel like you're actually watching a movie. As I want the vibes to literally shiver from the lower part of your spine and all the way up to your neck, as if everything's happening right in front of you, so that you're closer to the story than you could ever possibly imagine."

"Enjoy, 'A Killer of a Camp.'"

1.

Gliding through the country morning sky looking down at the trees to the woods, all looks so still and peaceful, but gliding into the woods and dodging all the trees one by one with ease, the speed starts getting faster and faster and faster, then suddenly stops. Strait ahead is an abandoned house.

Inside the abandoned house, which seems to be one big room, there's a worn-out settee, table and chairs toppled over, newspapers ripped to pieces, photographs torn up, but sitting on the floor in the corner of the room as white as a ghost is a girl, Naomi Layne, looking down at the floor with her lifeless frozen eyes.

Quickly sitting up appearing from under her bed covers, Samantha Molar intently looks around the room with an alarming scared facial expression, until she suddenly catches on where she is ..., her bedroom.

Falling back into the lying position with a sigh of relief wrote all over her face as she shakes her head side to side, the smirk on Samantha's face is more of a relieved happy one than a funny one.

Peeling the bedcovers from herself, that seem to be stuffed with a mountain of feathers due to the flimsiness of it, her legs still remain hid under the covers as she rolls onto her side like she's struggling to get up, as with the tiredness in her eyes it's plain to see her head hadn't hit the pillow to early.

Eventually managing to get herself up into the sitting position, with her legs, completely exposed, dangling over the edge of the bed, her soft skin has a bit of light shining on it, which seems to be coming from the morning sky that's gleaming through a little gap in the curtains that haven't been closed over fully.

Slowly sliding into her slippers Samantha stands up from sitting on the bed, where doing so the bottom half of her night dress slides down towards her ankles slowly covering the bareness of her legs as she walks on into her shower room, closing the door behind her.

Above the headboard to Samantha's bed, hanging on the wall is a calendar, where under the title of the month, which is July, there is writing in big block capitals reading, '**WORK HOURS FOR MIXTURES**', where under each day of the week there are timings wrote under certain days of the month, though most of them seem to fall on the weekends. Also on the bottom part of the calendar, which would usually be part of the blank white border that covers the whole page, there's some more artistic writing done with a permanent marker reading, **_Samantha Loves Mr. ?????_**.

Walking back out of the shower room with her tired eyes being that little bit heavier as the sound of the toilet is flushing in the background, Samantha looks at her alarm clock that reads 08:30, where grabbing hold of her bed covers Samantha just falls face first onto the mattress, slips off her slippers and throws the bed covers over her perfectly as she takes a big deep breath and lets out a long relieving sigh.

Heading towards the little gap in Samantha's curtains and looking out of the window, at the end of her driveway which is on the right hand side of Samantha's bedroom, it leads onto a single filed country road that is roughly 20 meters from the house. Where quickly appearing out of nowhere and having a dog bark its head off like there's no tomorrow, the little female figure which can be seen cycling away from behind, starts increasing her speed something crazily in the event to get away.

Though heading around to the back of Samantha's house from where the dog barks are coming from, the dog is seen barking in a complete different direction altogether.

Even from Samantha's window, to where the cyclist vanishes out of sight altogether, the dog continues barking like crazy, where back in Samantha's bedroom she quickly grabs hold of her pillow whilst shouting, "**OH, JACK!**" Then she fires the pillow over her head and lets off what sounds like mumbling words of spite as she throws the covers over her head in the process.

Drifting out through Samantha's bedroom window and heading in the direction of the loud angry dog barks that are coming from the back garden and getting angrier, Jack being all tied up to his kennel is looking in the direction of the woods that surround Samantha's house, where heading in the direction that Jack is barking towards and skimming past the trees with speed. After a minute of travelling in the direction that Jack was barking towards and passing a big thick tree, strait ahead is the old worn-out abandoned house again, but this time being seen from the front.

With the rundown entrance door to the abandoned house being slightly open, heading on in through the door it causes a bit of brightness to shine in on it, which behind the door in comparison to the rest of the house it seems to be the only part of the house that has been kept half clean. Even a picture on the wall of what looks like a little boy and his Mum has barely got an ounce of dust on it too.

With the smile on the little boys face being so happy, as the hand to the motherly figure behind him rests on his shoulder, getting closer to the two of them and only having the little boys face in view, it starts to get all bleary and out of focus altogether.

With a close up of the hand reappearing, it suddenly moves and lets go of the little boys shoulder as he starts to walk depressingly slow towards a bus, where as the door opens he slowly walks up the steps and gets stared at from all the directions as he tries to find a seat in the process of keeping his head low.

"Yo, Robbie, Mark, check it out, look at the shit that's just slithered on the bus."

"No way, uh, no way, look at it Sam, look at the slime on it man, is it actually alive?" Robbie says as he puts on an obnoxious forsaken exaggerated facial expression as he looks in the same direction as Sam and Mark with their evil eyes.

"I wonder what the feeble excuses are gonna be this time for bunking off school, huh?" Mark says as he chews on his chewing gum. Then as he gets himself into a crouched up sitting position with his knees leaning up against the seat in front of him, Mark starts to twist the chewing gum he's chewing around his thumb and forefinger.

"Ah, who knows, hay Jo?" Sam says with a silent questionable voice as he looks at Jo, whose head has not lifted up an inch from looking at the floor.

Taking a seat on the same side of the bus to Sam, Robbie and Mark, where there's a gap of a few empty chairs in between, Jo raises his head a bit as he has his back turned on the bullies. Where looking out the window Jo's eyes start to turn very watery looking.

THE DAY BEFORE

Being swung around in the air as the water splashes all over them, Jo's face is smiling like crazy as he looks into his Mum's eyes, to which both look like they're recovering from having been blackened, as she spins him around whilst standing in the shallow end of the water to the seaside. Though Jo's facial expression turns into an unimpressed look as he takes his eyes away from looking at his Mum whilst the spinning around slows down, and looking over towards the bar that his Dad, Jamie-Lee Walters is sitting at, his Dad is trying to start an argument with the barman.

Noticing what's starting to occur, Veronica takes hold of Jo's hand. "I think we better head on home babe," Veronica says to Jo as they walk towards their towels that are lying on the sand in front of Jamie-Lee.

Arriving through their front door with Jamie-Lee barely being able to stand, Jo tries his hardest to assist his Mum on hauling his Dad into the living room. Where eventually managing to get him seated in the centre of their three seat settee, Jamie-Lee takes hold of both of their hands unwittingly and pulls them towards him to sit on either side of him.

"Isn't this the life, having a family that can stick together?" Jamie-Lee drunkenly says. Where becoming quite uncomfortable as Jamie-Lee throws his arms around them and pulls them towards him for a squeezable drunken cuddle, Jo and Veronica remain silent as Jamie-Lee eventually knocks out for the count.

With a few hours having past and Jamie-Lee being all alone, he sits up from his drunkenness and gives his head a little shake as he stands up, then exiting the living room he heads strait for the front door.

"I'm headin' on down to the bar Veronica, don't bother cookin' for me, I'm sure I'll get somethin' when I'm out." Jamie-Lee quickly says as he opens the front door and closes it behind him not even waiting for a response, though in the process of closing the door he nearly loses his balance altogether.

Up the stairs in his bedroom, busy reading away as to what appears to be a school book, Jo's body figure seems to have come to an ease as the sound of the front door is heard closing, as his shoulders drop down from a stressful position and seem to be that little bit more relaxed as he continues on with his reading.

Fast asleep in his bed, with his homework set on his bedside unit and school bag placed on the floor below it, Jo seems to be in his own little perfect world as he sleeps with not being a single bit overwrought.

Though in at Jo's Mum and Dad's room, the only figure that's under the covers is his Mum, to who looks like she's in the middle of a nightmare due to the appearance on her facial expression and body movement, which is quite nerve racking to see.

Down the stairs with all being quiet, in at the living room it's completely empty, though going into the hall the front door which is on the right hand side suddenly opens with Jamie-Lee staggering in, being a lot more worse for wear than he was earlier.

Very unsteadily making his way into the kitchen, Jamie-Lee opens his fridge door.

"Ah, bitch how come she's left me nothin' to fuckin' eat, huh?" Jamie-Lee says, nearly stuttering with his words. "She won't forget the next time after I'm finished with her!" Jamie-Lee says as he starts to march drunkenly up the stairs.

In at Jo's room his eyes suddenly open as he starts to get all worked up due to hearing the bad temperedness of his Dad's tramping up the stairs, where he quickly sits himself up as if his Dad's just about to enter the room.

"Where's my fuckin' food bitch," Jamie-Lee angrily spurts out to Veronica, who all startled tries to protect herself with the covers.

"You, you, told me not to bother makin' you anythin'." Veronica says all shook up.

"Don't gimme your crappy excuses bitch." Jamie-Lee says. "And where is that little thick piece of shit we made, huh, how come he didn't make his Pop anythin' to eat?" Jamie-Lee says with his voice getting much angrier.

"Uh, he's, uh, stayin' at a, uh, uh, friend's house for the night." Veronica quickly says with a little bit of a stutter.

"Don't talk the biggest pile of shit, like what fuckin' friends does he have, huh? I'll teach the little ass wipe some manners." Jamie-Lee says as he infuriatingly grabs hold of a belt and charges for Jo's bedroom.

"*I'll make you somethin', I'll make you somethin'!*" Veronica terrifyingly says as she jumps out from under the covers busy racing after Jamie-Lee.

Inside Jo's bedroom, Jamie-Lee swings the mettle part of the belt strait towards the direction of Jo's pillow.

"I'LL MAKE YOU SOMETHIN', *I'LL MAKE YOU SOMETHIN'*!" Veronica hysterically shouts as the tears are rolling down her cheeks. Where as Jamie-Lee turns around to look at Veronica, behind him there is no sign of Jo.

"And where is the little fucker, huh?" Jamie-Lee says.

"Uh, like I said, he's stayin' at his friend's house for the night." Veronica says, barely being able to get a word out of her mouth due to trying to hold her tears back.

"Without askin' me," Jamie-Lee says as he holds the belt in the shape of a speech bubble and gives Veronica a slap around the face with it.

"Without askin' me," Jamie-Lee repeats as he pushes Veronica out of Jo's bedroom with force. Where continuously asking Veronica the same question as he pushes her out of sight altogether, all that can be heard are continuous forceful slapping noises making their way down the stairs, followed with what sounds like Veronica being pushed down the last few steps.

Behind Jo's bedroom door which slightly overlaps the right hand side of his miniature walk in wardrobe, the right-hand side door is seen opening slowly, approximately no more than three inches, where with a little bit of light shining in from the hall through the gap to his bedroom door, Jo's beetroot face slowly appears as he stands there shaking like a leaf, trying his upmost hardest not to make any noise at all.

BACK ON THE BUS

As the bus moves off slowly gradually picking up speed, Jo is seen looking in the direction of his mother, whose face has cuts and bruises all over it, where to top it all off it looks like it's been accompanied by two very brand new looking black eyes. Furthermore, Jo's Mum looks like she hardly has the energy to move, though raising her head very minor and managing to look in the direction of Jo as the bus drives off, she manages to move her lips slightly and send Jo a powerless kiss, though in the process of doing so the rest of her body remains completely still.

With a tear rolling down the right hand side of Jo's nose and his eyes getting very watery, Jo only has the ability to move his lips ever so vaguely as he sends his Mum a silent kiss back.

"Hay Jo, is that new makeup your Mom's got on?" Sam says.

"That's not what she was wearin' last night," Mark says.

"In fact was she wearin' anythin' the whore?" Robbie says, busy laughing away at his own ruthless remark.

Wiping a tear out of the way, then giving both of his eyes a little rub, Jo doesn't even look like he's paying any attention to the slagging off that he's getting from Sam, Mark and Robbie. As his eyes and thoughts are completely focused on his Mum, who fades away as the bus turns the corner.

Arriving at school and the bus coming to a halt Jo stands up ready to get off the bus, but hastily pushing him back into his chair is Sam.

"Where do you think you're going Mr. Shit-For-Brains? I think you'll find it'll be us guys getting off before your kind of slime." Sam says as he looks at Jo, to whose head drops down in ignominy as Robbie and Mark follow Sam off the bus.

Eventually being the last person to get off the bus and stepping off the last step, as Jo puts both of his feet on solid ground a football rolls up to him as the bus behind him drives off.

"Hay, throw us the ball man!" A polite mannered male student shouts over to Jo as he stands outside a basketball court with his friends to the right hand side of Jo, though looking in at the basketball court it's empty due to the door being locked.

"Sure bring it on over and join us before it's time to head on into school, huh?" The nicely mannered young boy says.

Though as Jo bends down to pick the ball up, before his hands even get a chance to make contact with it, his body plummets sideways to the floor forcefully as he gets pushed out of the way by Sam.

"Oh, my apologies is this a non-contact sport?" Sam says all cocky mannered.

"I think it would be a little bit to rough for him anyway, huh? Plus, uh, just think of all the slimy remainders that might get left all over the ball, uh!" Robbie says as he takes a heroic look at Jo as if he's a germ.

Then walking towards the basketball court Sam and Mark bounce the ball back and forth to each other, where as Mark passes the ball back to the polite mannered student who asked Jo to pass the ball back to him, the bell rings.

Not even paying any attention to Jo being on the floor, students charge on into school passing him in their dozens like he's not even there. Then Jo, only on his hands and knees still struggling to get up, has Mark, Robbie and Sam, being what looks like the last few remaining students to head on into school, looking at him.

"Has your Mom been giving you lessons?" Sam says.

"Yeah, cuz that looks like the exact same position she was in last night when I seen her roaming the streets." Mark Says. Then clicking his thumb and forefinger together he points at Jo. "She was on all fours the bitch, yeah that's right." Mark says finishing his nauseating sentence.

"Now come on guys seriously, look at it. It skives, it's last in register, it probably knows it's not gonna make it anywhere in life. And just outta curiosity, is it not supposed to be like father like son? ...," Jo looks at Robbie angrily then Robbie continues his sentence, "..., or like mother like daughter?"

As the word 'mother' leaves Robbie's lips the angry look on Jo's face slowly disappears.

"Yeah, but in this case it would be the like mother like daughter kinda thing." Sam says.

"Whatta you mean?" Mark says.

"Cuz its Mom's nothin' but a waste of space, and it's nothin' but a pussy on all fours as well." Sam says as they all turn their backs on Jo and walk off towards the school.

As the doors to the classes close and the hallway turns as quiet as can be, as Jo being the only one in sight arriving in front of his locker, looking a little worse for wear, it's plain to see it's not from a tired form, it's more of an 'I don't want to be here' kind of manner. But suddenly out of nowhere and as fast as lightening Jo grabs hold of his bag with both hands and slams it to the ground sending echoes up and down the hallway from the force of the bags landing, then continuing to let all his anger out Jo gives the bag a major kick, which is plain to see he's picturing someone in the process. Then turning towards his locker and putting both of his hands on his forehead, Jo's elbows and hands supporting his forehead keep banging against the locker continuously as if he's going insane, but with a good few forceful hits against the locker, Jo starts to slow down. Then with force, running his left hand through his hair as if he's trying to wipe out all the problems he has on his mind, Jo's right hand is turning into a very angry looking fist, looking like it's pointing straight for the locker, but with his fist unfolding slowly he reaches down into his pocket and takes out a key that ends up aiming towards his lockers keyhole.

As the locker door opens steadily, red dots that look like blood start dropping to the floor, then as Jo lifts his head up slowly from looking at the floor, he opens his locker door that bit wider and on the inside of the locker door there's a photo of Jo's Mum with ketchup rolling down a good sized piece of the photo, covering half of her face. Then looking at the three little air vents that are at the top of the locker door, a small ketchup sachet that is dangling from the top of the air vent has been squeezed from the outside to have the ketchup run down the inside of the locker door and have it end up where it is, all over the photo of Jo's Mum, who doesn't half take a lovely picture when her face hasn't been beaten up.

Getting a loose piece of plain paper from the inside of his locker, Jo wipes what ketchup he can from the photo, but doing so more of the ketchup falls to the floor, having Jo needing to quickly bend down after it and try and clean it up. But as he attempts to do so, arriving right in front of him is a tall, well built man, late fifties looking, with a badge pinned on the front of his top left hand blazer pocket reading, "**Headmaster – Mr. Connery**".

"How come you're not in class yet, huh?" Mr. Connery says thunderously with his loud voice, while he looks at Jo angrily.

Jo doesn't answer, "Well?" Mr. Connery says looking for a reply. But as Jo lifts his head up and looks at Mr. Connery revealing his watery blood shot eyes and bruised face from his push to the ground earlier over a basketball, the words that Jo looks like he's wanting to express don't seem to be coming out.

"I want to see you back here at lunch time giving this place a clean over, okay?" Mr. Connery says. Where with Jo still not answering Mr. Connery says, "Or would you prefer after school detention?"

"No Sir," Jo says answering Mr. Connery silently.

"WELL, COME ON GET TO IT, HAVE YOU NOT GOT CLASSES TO GET TO?" Mr. Connery hastily shouts. To which Jo quickly grabbing a couple of books from his locker, closes the door over, picks up his rucksack and turns around to head in the direction of his class.

Arriving close to the entrance door to his class with no sign of Mr. Connery about anymore, Jo quickly takes a step back to where he can't be seen through a small semicircular window that is built into the door and shakes his head side to side knowing rightly he doesn't want to go on in, but taking a step back to the door that has a sign on it reading, **"English – Miss Jarden**" and pushing down the handle, as he enters on in, all heads lift up, pens and pencils stop writing and Sam, Mark and Robbie, with their evil looks wave at Jo as he enters, with the door closing over freely behind him causing a bang and making Jo jump a bit.

"And what's took you so long to get into class?" Miss Jarden asks, but not even giving Jo a chance to answer her question, she follows up with a quick closure, "In fact explain it at lunch time, I'm not wasting anymore class time. Now take a seat."

"But, but....,"

"*I said take a seat*." Miss Jarden says butting in demandingly. Though heading for his seat Jo already knows he has a booking with Mr. Connery at the same time, lunch.

- -

As the locker door closes, Sam, Robbie and Mark's evil faces appear. "Yo Jo, you fancy a sandwich." Mark says waving a sandwich in front of Jo's face.

"Sure here, here's a Pepsi on the house too." Robbie says busy teasing as he takes a slurp.

"I'd love to of offered you this ....," Sam says as he shows Jo an opened chocolate bar, "...., but I believe you've a date to be heading to, huh, with a, uh, Miss Jarden." He says as he takes a bite of his chocolate bar.

With Jo closing his locker door over, he faces at Sam in disgust for a few seconds, then turns around and walks off.

"Now don't forget about the lessons your Mommy was explaining to you now." Robbie says putting on a baby voice as Jo opens the English classroom door to Miss Jarden and walks on in, closing the door behind him.

With Jo out of sight the entrance door to the hallway opens up unveiling Mr. Connery, who starts walking towards Sam, Mark and Robbie, who are still standing next to Jo's locker.

"Have any of you seen Jo Walters?" Mr. Connery asks, busy looking at each of them individually for a reply.

"Yes sir, uh, he's just took his lunch with him to head off and meet up with a lady friend, for a date I suppose," Sam says.

"What, a date?" Mr. Connery says questioningly unimpressed.

"Yeah, he met up with her earlier and they arranged to meet each other again at lunch time, it's true love Sir, I'm tellin' you, it's just true love." Sam says, knowing rightly he's putting Jo into quick sinking sand.

"Right, just wait until ....," Mr. Connery says angrily as he turns around and storms off, charging through the hallway doors he came through and disappearing out of sight.

"Oh, I hope I haven't put Jo in trouble." Sam says pretending to care.

"**NOT**." Mark and Robbie answer together.

"Aw, look guys," Sam says pointing at Jo's locker. "At least he did get somethin' to eat. He looks like he's cleaned that ketchup up rightly that we gave him earlier out of the kindness of our hearts."

"Gee's, he looks like he's licked it clean." Robbie says.

"Like I told you, he's definitely taking in those lessons his Mom's been givin' him. Cuz she'd lick anythin' clean." Sam says.

- -

As the bell rings, looking down the hallway, all of the class doors burst open with students of all age, height, race and build, busy galloping their way down the hallway as they head for the exit door. Although trying to keep his balance from nearly getting knocked over and only just making it safely to the exit door, Jo has a hand grab hold of his shoulder.

"It's detention for you I think you'll find." Mr. Connery says busy escorting Jo back into school, due to not being impressed with Jo's absence over his lunch time detention.

"But, Sir, I ....," Jo says, looking all worried as he looks towards a car with a manly figure in it.

"No more excuses. And if this continues I'll be making an appointment with your parents to inform them of the non-stop unacceptable behavior you've been carrying out, okay?" Mr. Connery angrily says as he still has hold of Jo's shoulder as he escorts Jo back into school again.

Passing by the gymnasium door that is open as they walk down the hallway, Mr. Connery and Jo are being watched by Sam, Mark and Robbie, who are bouncing the basketball back and forth to each other as Mr. Connery brings Jo to the detention room.

"Now how do you think he could've ended up on detention like that, huh?" Sam says as if he doesn't know about it.

"I think he's done it on purpose." Robbie says, busy bouncing the basketball to Mark.

"Why on earth would he wanna do that now, huh? It was us you stupid dripzoid!" Mark says as he bounces the basketball to Sam.

"Are you sure? Cuz look what little birdies just arrived to take charge of those on detention." Robbie says as he receives the basketball from Sam.

"Why paint my basketball socks pink! It's Miss Jarden." Mark says as he throws the basketball towards the net.

Walking out of the detention room Mr. Connery shakes his head in disgust over what he's seen. Though looking into the detention room with everyone being silent, Jo who is sitting at the desk next to the window not looking happy at all, watches the car he seen earlier with a manly figure in it, drive off.

Having finished detention and getting ready to walk out of the school, all Jo can see as he opens the exit door to leave school, is a dark, miserable and very wet evening with the rain coming down in the bucket loads. So putting his jacket over his head, Jo heads down the stairs to make his way home, where being forced to walk on the side of the road due to there being no path, he's getting an unaccountable amount of muck fired at him from passing vehicles, along with his pair of very wet and dirty looking sneakers getting wrecked.

Back at school, Sam, Mark and Robbie come running out from a sheltered space they're hiding under and head towards a land rover that's just pulled over.
"Thanks a lot for the lift Trevor." Mark says as he jumps into the back of the land rover with Robbie.
"Yeah, thanks a lot." Robbie says as he also takes a seat in the back and gives his head a shake.
"Ah, no worries," Trevor says. "Sure I was coming down to pick up my little baby boy Sam anyway." Trevor says as he strokes Sam on the back of the head like he's a baby as he get's into the front of the car, "Ain't that right my little prince?" Trevor says finishing his sentence and showing Sam up.

"Dad, are you feelin' okay?" Sam says trying to move his head out of the way from getting stroked by his Dad's hand.

"Oh, it's okay. We'll be home soon for some dinner my little baby," Trevor says still messing about as he drives off the school property.

"Yeah, I think you'll be gettin' those extra happy pills you'll be needin' too." Sam says as he looks at his Dad weirdly.

"Hay," Trevor says, acting a little bit more serious.

"What?" Sam says.

"Ain't that little dude on the side of the road from your school, and in the same year as you guys?" Trevor says.

"Yeah, that's Jo and he's nothin' but a jerk, we can't stand him." Sam says, with Robbie and Mark also seeing Jo on the side of the road getting drenched.

"Oh, come on let's give the little dude a lift, huh?" Trevor says.

"Oh, Dad, no way please!" Sam Says.

"Come on, he can't be that much further up the road from here." Trevor says as he pulls his land rover over in front of Jo and winds his window down.

"Hay Jo, you wanna lift? You look like you're gettin' drenched out there man." Trevor says to Jo as Jo lands inline with the driver's window. "Come on, jump in and I'll drop you off near your place." Trevor says.

"Uh, only if you're sure though." Jo says as if he's getting in the way.

"Yeah, jump on in there." Trevor says.

But as Jo opens the back passenger door he surprisingly watches Mark move into the middle seat to make room for him, to which he's thinking twice about getting in now.

"Come on, what's the hold up?" Trevor says as he watches Mark and Robbie having to place their rucksacks on their laps whilst Jo takes a seat beside Mark.

"Right are we ready to move?" Trevor says. Where with none of them replying he quickly says, "Well, let's get movin'."

Picking up a good bit of speed as he drives off the mucky hard shoulder, Sam notices his Dad isn't paying much attention as to what he's up to due to keeping his eyes on the road, so quickly taking the advantage of it Sam slips something back to Robbie. Where with Robbie taking a look at it he passes it onto Mark, who happily after reading what seems to be a note, passes it to Jo after reading it. Then as Jo opens the note, it reads: -

> **You're DEAD. When we get you into School, we're gonna kick the ten ton Crap out of your Mr. Waste-of-Space Ass.**

Quickly folding the note up, Jo puts it into his pocket looking scared stiff less. Though the worries on his face look like they're more over the fact that he's sitting next to the devils other than the note he's been given.

"Well, here's your place isn't it Jo?" Trevor says whilst indicating and pulling over.

"Uh, yeah, uh, thanks." Jo says busy looking over his shoulder as he gets out of the land rover, making sure there's going to be no more surprised mischief coming his way.

"Well, take it easy." Trevor says.

"Okay." Jo replies as if it's an order as he closes the door behind him and heads for his front door.

"He's a bit of a strange guy isn't he?" Trevor says in an unsure manner.

"We told you, he's nothin' but a jerk." Sam says.

"No, I mean, he's just like strange, huh?" Trevor says confusingly.

"Don't worry Pop, we're nearly home. I'll get you your happy pills then, okay?" Sam says as he places his hand on his Dad's forehead busy acting like a nurse as they all drive off.

As Jo arrives at the front door and takes his keys out of his pocket, he's still looking over his shoulder continuously as if someone's about to bounce on him. Then as the door opens, he quickly takes his key out of the keyhole and heads into the house that is pitch black, where closing the door behind him and putting the bolt on, as he turns the light on and hangs his bag on a peg on the wall, Jo notices a couple of letters on the floor next to the door, one which is addressed to his Mum, Mrs. Veronica Walters and the other addressed to his Dad, Mr. Jamie-Lee Walters. So setting the two of them on the hall table, as Jo turns around, lying on the floor straight in front of him is his Mum, whose forehead is poring with blood.

"*Mom, Mom. Are you okay?*" Jo says hysterically as the tears start to emerge from his eyes as he kneels down next to his Mum and takes hold of her hand that rests powerlessly on her belly.

"What's happened Mom, what's happened?" Jo says struggling with his words as he gently strokes his Mum's hair with his other hand then cries uncontrollably on her shoulder.

"It's, it's, okay ..., baby." Veronica says barely able to catch her breath.

"We've gotta do somethin' Mom, we've gotta do somethin'!" Jo angrily cries as he cuddles her looking like he doesn't want to let go.

"Oh, it's alright now my angel." Veronica slowly says.

"It's not Mom, it's not!" Jo says with a heated temper whilst the tears flood from his eyes.

There's a knock coming from the front door, and looking through the peep-hole a man can be seen with his back turned.

As the door opens he turns around.

"Jamie-Lee, I wasn't expectin' you at the door."

"Well Charlotte, I just couldn't stay away." Jamie-Lee says as he takes hold of Charlotte and slips his tongue into her mouth while they drift into her house with Jamie-Lee kicking the door over behind him.

"Jamie-Lee, there's somethin' I've gotta tell you." Charlotte says as

Jamie-Lee has her up against the wall in the hall licking her neck whilst rubbing his right hand up and down her thigh.

"Can't we just have a little bitta fun first babe?" Jamie-Lee says as he licks Charlotte's lips that follows up with a French kiss as he takes hold of her right boob. Then as he starts licking her on the neck again he begins to undress the top half of her clothing.

"But, oh, I wanna get it out in the open now," Charlotte breathlessly says as she enjoys getting her neck licked like crazy, whilst even assisting Jamie-Lee on taking her clothes off.

"What baby?" Jamie-Lee says whilst busy licking her from her neck all the way up to her lips and looking her in the eyes as she tries to catch her breath and bring herself back to reality.

"I, I'm, uh, I'm pregnant!" Charlotte says eventually managing to get her words out.

"No!" Jamie-Lee says in disbelief.

"Yeah, I was at my Doc's earlier on today, due to not being able to keep any food down whatsoever yesterday or this morning, and he ran a few tests on me and told me it was, uh, like I'm sayin', I'm pregnant." Charlotte says as she goes to cuddle up to Jamie-Lee for a bit of comfort and support.

"Get off me bitch, don't fuckin' touch me, okay?" Jamie-Lee says looking all uneasy.

"But it's your baby too." Charlotte says. "I mean, do you not remember the amount've times we've made out now, huh? I'm three months gone." Charlotte says.

"Are you sure it's mine?" Jamie-Lee says.

"Of course I'm fuckin' sure." Charlotte answers as she watches Jamie-Lee walk around all worked up.

"Get an abortion. That's the answer, right? Get an abortion." Jamie-Lee says.

"I'm not killin' a kid." Charlotte says, "Especially if it's mine."

"Did you not fuckin' hear me bitch?" Jamie-Lee says as he takes hold of Charlotte's upper arms with force and shakes her back and forth forcefully. "GET AND ABORTION," Jamie-Lee shouts as he throws Charlotte up against the wall behind her with an almighty shove, making her drop to the floor in a crouched up sitting position all scared and shook up.

"Cuz if you don't bitch, I'm tellin' you, I won't be able to control my actions." Jamie-Lee says. Where turning around Jamie-Lee storms out of the house slamming the door behind him, leaving Charlotte shivering with scarceness on the floor.

Walking towards the entrance door to a bar that has cigarette smoke palling out of it, Jamie-Lee, looking so outraged fires the door open as he enters. Then as the door behind him closes, a poster on the door reads, "Crazy Cards Night - Every Night."

"Well, what'll it be?" The bar person asks.

"Gimme a double vodka, cuz for what I'm just after hearing I'll be needing more than a few of those this night." Jamie-Lee says.

"I've a little suggestion man," a man at the card table behind Jamie-Lee says, "How about joinin' us guys for a game of cards? It'll help you relax and unwind and take all the worries off the mind."

"Ah, what the heck," Jamie-Lee says, "Why not, it's not like this night could get any worse, huh?"

"Yeah, that's the spirit, I'm Willy." Willy says as he watches Jamie-Lee walk towards them, "Take a seat, take the weight off the feet, relax, unwind and let's play poker," Willy says smoothly.

Walking up to his Mum who's in the kitchen getting a bit of food sorted out for the two of them, Jo takes hold of her hand, then as she turns around he puts his arms around her so affectionately, it's as if he doesn't want to let go. "Mom, are you okay?" Jo says.

"I'm okay baby, but more to the point what's happened to you today?" Veronica says as she gently strokes Jo's bruised face.

"I'm scared he's gonna do somethin' to you Mom." Jo says busy ignoring his Mum's question as he closes his eyes like he's trying to keep his tears from appearing.

"So, you wanna start packin' now for the two of us to move off to the big Boston City?" Veronica says holding Jo as tight as can be.

"Are you serious Mom?" Jo says like he's overwhelmed with happiness.

"It's about time, huh?" Veronica says trying to be strong for both of their sakes.

"I love you with all my heart Mom." Jo affectionately says.

"I love you too baby." Veronica says. "Now come on, let's get to it, huh?" Veronica says as she puts her hand out for Jo to take hold of, to which he does in a flash, where they both head out of the kitchen closing the door behind them.

- -

"Well, it looks like this'll be your last round, huh?" Willy says as Jamie-Lee searches his pockets inside out for more money so he can continue playing poker.

"No, no, wait up, sure I'll head back to mine and get a few bucks and be back in a few minutes, huh?" Jamie-Lee says as he looks at each player individually for a response.

"Hmmm, I dunno what do you guys think?" Willy says waiting for a response from the others, to who are either shrugging their shoulders or tilting their heads a little bit.

"Right, we'll give you ten minutes, how's that?" Willy says to Jamie-Lee, "But if you're not back in time we're carrying on without you, okay?"

"I'll be back in ten." Jamie-Lee says as he runs for the door.

"And here, if you're back in ten, the next rounds on you, okay?" Willy says, but Jamie-Lee has already flown out the door.

"Right, you guys wanna look at his cards while he's gone?" Willy says busy looking at the other players who don't seem to be replying to his question. Then suddenly they all reply at the same time and take a look at his cards one by one, busy expressing their thoughts over the hand he has.

Heading up to the living room entrance and taking a look inside, Jo is fast asleep on the settee leaning up against his Mum, Veronica, who has her arm around him with the side of her head resting on top of his head while she also sleeps comfortably too. Though looking down the back of the settee, a suitcase that is bulging has a small rucksack on top of it that can be seen poking out.

Suddenly loud banging noises come from the front door that are getting noisier by the second, where followed with a big powerful snapping noise the door is heard banging forcefully against the wall, with what sounds like the latch rattling against the door in the process, startling Veronica and Jo out of their sleep. Then unexpectedly with all the noise, Jamie-Lee storms swiftly into the living room appearing a lot more worse for wear, more than likely due to the air hitting him as he walked out of the bar, which seems to have changed his form of manner into being one very angry tipsy individual.

"**I need money**." Jamie-Lee angrily informs Veronica in a desperately drunken shook up manner. Then storming up to Veronica and Jo, with his temper running high, violence is getting the better of him as he grabs a tight grip to Veronica's coat, pulls her up from the settee, shakes her back and forth like crazy, then throws her back onto the settee beside Jo, who is shocked over witnessing what's happening in front of him.

"I NEED MONEY! NOW WHERE IS IT BITCH?" Jamie-Lee shouts, nearly coming in nose to nose contact with her.

"I don't have any." Veronica replies, scared lifeless.

"Don't gimme that shit lady, now where's the fuckin' money?" Jamie-Lee says furiously as he grabs hold of Veronica and pulls her up from the settee.

"You took the last of the money with you." Veronica replies with tears rolling down her battered and bruised face. Where looking at Jo as Jamie-Lee has hold of Veronica, he gets up from the settee and sprints to the entrance of the kitchen that's connected to the living room, busy looking at his Mum helplessly in despair.

Slapping Veronica around the face vehemently, to which some blood from her recent beating is seen landing on the wall behind her, Jamie-Lee shouts, "YOU'RE HIDING IT FROM ME BITCH, YOU'RE HIDING IT FROM ME." Then suddenly noticing the suitcase poking out from the back of the settee, Jamie-Lee's head drops and shakes side to side slowly, to which there is complete silence for a few seconds. Though quickly breaking the silence, Jamie-Lee throws an unsuspected uppercut towards the right hand side of Veronica's jaw bone, causing her to plummet to the floor.

"YOU AIN'T GOT ANY MONEY. YOU AIN'T GOT MONEY, SO WHAT THE FUCK'S THE MEANIN' OF THESE THEN, HUH, HUH?" Jamie-Lee angrily shouts as he takes hold of the suitcase and fires it at Veronica.

"NOW LESS OF THE LYING BITCH, I NEED SOME MONEY NOW, NOW WHERE IS IT?" Jamie-Lee shouts as he grabs Veronica by the hair and pulls her up to the sitting position then fires her back onto the settee. Where looking behind Jamie-Lee, Jo's face is drowning with tears as he stands at the kitchens entrance scared silly.

"I haven't got any," Veronica chokingly says, "I swear." She says like it's her last gasp of breath being used.

Then Jamie-Lee looking towards a stereo system notices an empty bottle of beer. Where grabbing hold of it he walks over to Veronica and waves it in front of her face that is poring with blood.

"You see this." Jamie-Lee says pointing at the label stuck on the bottle, "This is the only thing worth fuckin' living for, but without money I can't get any. **CAN YOU NOT DRILL THAT INTO YOUR FUCKIN' HEAD**?" Jamie-Lee shouts as he smashes the hefty glass bottle over Veronica's head, where with the glass shattering everywhere, in slow motion Veronica plummets sideways to the floor with no sign of eye movement at all as her body crushes to the ground, where Jo is literally in shock watching everything happen right in front of him.

Kicking her in the belly while she's down, Jamie-Lee waves the remainder of the smashed bottle at Veronica's dead eyes and says, "You'll never fuckin' change, will you?"

The roars of thunder can be heard in the background as Veronica's face is as still as can be, with the rain raining down on it. Then suddenly small heaps of muck start getting thrown on top of her body bit by bit as the rain gets heavier, with lightning and thunderous noises getting closer, where drifting back a little bit, a small figure being covered by the darkness is seen shoveling muck that disappears as it leaves the spade.

As the engine to the land rover is running, all the doors are closed as the rain pelts down on it. Where sitting inside on the front passenger seat facing towards the drivers side, Jo's eyes are poring with tears as his body shakes unstoppably. Soaking wet from top to bottom, his clothes are also plastered in an unaccountable amount of muck, with bloodied patches all around his clothing too. Where looking away from the drivers side Jo lowers his head in shame and starts crying, "What've we done, w, w, w, what've we done," Jo struggles to say as his tears uncontrollably surge from his eyes.

Outside the land rover the rain is getting heavier by the second. Then suddenly the land rover starts moving at a crazy pace as the rear wheels spin like mad, literally burning the wheels before it zooms off.

Flying down the country road like there's no tomorrow the land rover's barely driving strait, as with it speeding down the hill and getting faster beyond belief, it's narrowly missing oncoming traffic by millimeters, plus the window screen wipers aren't even on either, where as the rain pelts down on the land rovers front window as the lightning suddenly strikes, Jo and Jamie-Lee's faces can't even be made out due to the blurriness.

With the lightning striking again and brightening up the edge of the mountain, a lorry can be seen coming around the corner. But not even slowing down, the right hand side of Jamie-Lee's land rover has the front of a lorry crashing into it with force, literally tossing it over the metal barrier and having it tumble down the side of the steep mountain as the lightning strikes again, but upon landing upside down with force, the land rover suddenly explodes, making the lightning look like a little match stick.

----

18 LONG YEARS PASS BY

2.

Fashionably up-to-date in a San Francisco kind of style, the living room is very nicely laid out with a three-seat reclining settee, two one-seat recliners, a glass table with a shelf underneath it, an electric fire place, though on the wall above the fire place is a 60 inch flat TV screen. Then finally on either side of the fire place are some more San Francisco styled built in units containing ornaments, wine glasses, wine bottles, candles and a photo in a large photo frame of what seems to be a representation of a mother, father and daughter, who are smiling away.

On the box, to which the sound is very low, a news reporter's lips can near enough be read due to the size of the TV screen. Where taking hold of her notes for the next part of the news, she looks into the camera as she holds up a photo and says, "As you can see this picture was sent in a few days ago for….,"

Over towards the settee a man all dressed up in postman uniform isn't paying any attention to the television being on as he walks on through the living room and into the kitchen.

"Well Mrs. Waterson, any appointments for the beauty business today?" He says as he walks up to her as she stands at the kitchens work surface holding what looks like an appointment book in her hands as he kisses her on the neck.

"Oh, hi Pete, enough to keep me goin' anyway."

Up on the kitchen windowsill Pete strokes a picture frame containing the same photo that's on the built in units in the living room.

"Uh, Barbara just outta curiosity, where's our little angel Amy for our morning race, huh?" Pete says as he gently rests his hand on the back of Barbara's head, where as she turns around they both look into each others eyes.

"Bad news you lost ages ago, she sure as hell wasn't waitin' around, not now she's on her summer holidays anyway." Barbara says as she follows up with a kiss.

"Oh!" Pete says as his face droops down after the kiss, "If only I hadda known!" Where holding his forehead he shakes it side to side in a shameful manner as he looks towards the ground.

"Whatta you mean?" Barbara says all concerned.

"She could've done the deliveries for me." Pete says busy lifting his head up and showing his cheeky facial expression.

"Yeah, you wish!" Barbara says as she strokes down Pete's shoulder with her forefinger as if she's trying to get rid of a piece of fluff. Then placing her arms around Pete as she looks into his eyes with love wrote all over her face, their lips start getting closer and closer, where as their lips gently collide, their eyes automatically close.

"You want another cuppa before you head?" Barbara quietly whispers into Pete's ear as they slowly release from their kiss. Where standing back as if he's a western cowboy, Pete pretends to withdraw a gun from an invisible side pouch on his right hand side and twizzles his imaginary gun around his forefinger, sliding it back into his invisible side pouch again.

"If it means gettin' more of those kisses, tea me up lady I say tea me up!" Pete crazily replies with an attempted cowboy accent.

Circling slowly with the mettle bars of the bicycles tire going around and around, at the bottom part of the tire which is compressed to the floor and completely flat whilst being pushed over some hefty bumps, holding onto the handle bar and the bicycles seat is Amy, who is not one little bit amused at all, as the look on her face as she looks towards her bike looks more like she would rather be bringing it to a car crusher other than home, where either way she's nowhere near both locations.

Back at Samantha's house, with her still being under the covers and in a deep, deep sleep, heading out through the gap in her curtains and towards the back garden, to where Jack's barking was coming from earlier. Arriving around at the back of the garden and looking towards Jack's kennel, there's no sign of Jack whatsoever, only a lead that is dangling from the entrance door to the kennel.

Parked outside on the side of the Waterson's family home is a red post van, where looking at the side door to the house that the van is parked a few feet away from, which leads into the kitchen, the door opens slowly with Pete walking out at a steady pace due to being in the middle of another romantic kiss with Barbara.

"That tea was gorgeous babe," Pete says as his lips are only a few millimeters away from Barbara's.

"It couldn'tve of been better than my kisses, huh?" Barbara says as she hands Pete his air tight lunch box and a two liter flask, which contains two plastic cups that are screwed on top of it.

"Not even close," Pete says as he gives Barbara another well deserved kiss, "Nothing could beat the kisses you give."

"Huh, hum," Barbara says as she points in the direction of the ground. Where looking towards the direction she is pointing at, it's plain to see she's pointing at her belly, due to her expectancy.

"Ah, you know what I mean!" Pete says.

"Well don't you worry, there'll be a lot more of those kisses when you get back, but this should keep you going for now," Barbara says as her lips gently touch Pete's once more.

"Mmmmm," Pete hums as he enjoys every second of it. "Well I better head my babes', I'll see you later," Pete says as he looks into Barbara's eyes, then down towards her belly. "And I'll see you in about just under three months you little rascal." He says as he points his forefinger towards Barbara's belly, pretending to be in a bad mood. "And I hope you don't leave your Poppa bear stranded to race off on his own."

"Aw, you're still cheesed off with Amy not being here for the usual mornin' race, aren't you?" Barbara says as she looks a Pete sympathetically.

"Yeah, it's what keeps me goin' through the day," Pete says in a depressing manner. Then he lowers his head down in line with Barbara's belly and points at it hastily and says, "So I hope you're taking this in, you hear me?"

"I dunno about that, oh, ow!" Barbara says as she quickly grabs hold of her belly, "The little rascals just kicked me, ow!"

Pete quickly lowers himself inline with Barbara's belly again and smiles as he gives the thumbs up to Barbara's belly, "At least someone's on my side." Pete says.

"Yeah, but after getting a bit of training from Amy, you'd stand no hope." Barbara says as she continues to hold her belly.

"Ah, we'll see, we'll see!" Pete says, knowing rightly she's probably correct.

"Yeah, and I'll see you later," Barbara says to Pete who has his back turned to her as he heads for the post van. Then turning around to face Barbara as he opens the van door, Pete looks at Barbara strangely and says, "Who're you talking to, me or my side kick?"

Though before Barbara has a chance to follow up with an answer as Pete gets into the van, quickly speeding around from the back of the house is Amy with her punctured tire all fixed.

"Well, d'you wanna race Dad?" Amy says as she speeds up in line with the post van all hyper, with a grin on her face that would cover the house.

Then quickly putting his lunch box and flask on the front passenger seat Pete jumps out of the van and runs up to Amy acting all silly as he gives her non-stop kisses and cuddles.

"And where on earth have you been hidin' my little angel?" Pete says, putting on another crazy voice.

"I was around the back of the house pumpin' my tires up." Amy says all quite pleased with herself that she's got the wheels rolling again.

"Ah, I knew you wouldn't have left your old postman pop stranded to race on his own." Pete says as he acts all silly with giving Amy another unaccountable amount of silly non-stop kisses.

While Pete continues to mess about with Amy, Barbara heads back into the house. Where walking up to the big American fridge freezer, she opens the fridge door and takes out a chocolate bar and a bottle of black current juice, which contains a suction lid. Then heading over to the dining table she takes hold of a banana from the fruit bowl and Amy's helmet that's beside it and makes her way out to Amy and Pete.

As Pete notices Barbara coming out he has a serious look on his face, as he looks at Amy and quietly says, "Now you remember what I said, you organize it and I'll continue when I get home, and we'll give your Mom a little treat, huh?"

As Amy taps her forefinger on her nose and gives her Dad a wink, walking out of the house with a curious look on her face, Barbara looks at Pete and Amy, who are acting like butter wouldn't melt in their mouths.

"What're you two up to?" Barbara says knowing rightly they're up to mischief.

The two of them remain silent, then as Barbara puts the chocolate bar and banana into Amy's bicycle pouch and the bottle of black current juice on her bikes bottle holder, Pete opens the post vans door and looks over at Amy and taps his forefinger on his nose and gives her a wink while Barbara isn't watching, then as he gets into the post van Barbara makes sure the bicycle helmet is on Amy's head properly, where with Amy knowing that she's come to her Mum's satisfaction due to having the helmet over her head, she gets all excited and lines herself up to the front passenger door to the post van, where Pete winds down his window and looks at Amy with his dastardly eyes. Walking in between the post van and bike and turning herself around to face the two of them, Barbara takes out from both of her maternity trouser pockets two white plastic bags and holds them up in the air as she gets ready to flag the race on.

"Now you wanna race?" Pete says with a very devious high pitch voice as he looks into Amy's eyes.

Amy replies with a scary face as Pete quickly continues with his high pitch voice, "Well, let's race."

Pete starts to rev the engine as Barbara shakes the plastic bags in the air, then putting on a loud voice due to trying to shout over the noise that Pete is making, Barbara shouts, "NOW ARE YOU READY?" Pete and Amy reply with a nod.

"WELL ON YOUR MARKS, GET SET, GO." Barbara shouts as she leans herself forward and waves the bags down in front of her, having Pete and Amy speed off.

With Pete being in the lead and Amy trying her hardest to catch up, Barbara shouts down to Amy, "Now you make sure you're back for lunch at one o'clock Amy, okay?"

"OKAY MOM, I LOVE YOU." Amy shouts as she tries her hardest to gain speed.

"I love you too baby," Barbara says as she looks at Amy with a loving smile, "I love you too baby," Barbara repeats as she rubs her belly.

At the bottom of their driveway Pete gets out of the post van and dances around like a lunatic shouting, "AND THE WINNER IS PETE WATERSON." Where as Amy cycles up to him he gives her a big kiss and cuddle. "Better luck next time, huh?" Pete says.

"Yeah, better luck next time." Amy says as she cycles on a little bit more, "Because the winner is Amy Waterson."

"Huh?" Pete says with a curious look. "Whatta you mean?"

"If you take a look at your van it isn't quite over the finish line, which means I still hold the title with six wins in a row." Amy says as she gets off her bike and gives her Dad another kiss and cuddles him in a sympathetic manner, "Better luck next time, hay Pop?" Then Amy starts dancing around and shouting. "AND THE WINNER FOR THE SIXTH TIME

RUNNING IS AMY WATERSON, THREE CHEERS FOR AMY." Up at the house Barbara's cheering away.

As her Dad gets back into his post van, Amy starts singing in his direction as he starts the engine again.

"I am the champion my Pop, I am, and I'll keep on winning and never stop." Pete sticks his nose up in her direction for a few seconds, then smiles at her.

"It was a well deserved win I have to admit, but I will gain the number one title yet, ha, ha, ha." Pete says putting on a voice of an old time sea captain.

Amy smiles at him as he drives off slowly, where Amy shouts, "I LOVE YOU."

"I LOVE YOU TOO YOU LITTLE STINKER," Pete shouts back as his hand waves out the window. Then as the post van picks up speed, Pete eventually disappears out of sight.

Still standing at the side door to the house Barbara watches Amy cycle off, where shaking her head as she smiles she turns around and heads back on into the house holding her belly and says, "It looks like it's just you and me my little angel."

3.

Sniffing like crazy at the grass on the side of a single filed country road, Jack is sniffing away at the leaves as he makes a mark on his new territory. Then wandering off and sniffing like there's no tomorrow, it's like he's searching for a pot of gold or his one true love, though suddenly his quick pace starts to slow down very rapidly as his nose starts sniffing over a hundred miles per hour.

Sniffing towards a little ditch that's on the side of the country road, he suddenly stops, as lying near enough at the top of the ditch on the left hand side of the road that's right next to the woods, a person who's face and left arm can't be seen due to being covered with big thick grass and weeds is wearing worn-out dirty rugged clothing that looks like it's never been cleaned, where to top it all, the Stranger's body looks completely unresponsive. Even looking at the right hand side of the Stranger it looks like they've either been lying there for a week or hasn't been washed. Though with the old time worn-out army bag they've got, roughly a 1950's design, the Stranger's right hand still has a firm grip on it.

Slowly approaching the Stranger on all fours, Jack takes a sniff around both the Stranger and the bag. Then suddenly he starts barking like crazy and runs off. Even the noise of Jacks loud barks doesn't cause the Stranger to move an inch, as the Strangers figure remains as still as can be. It's hard to tell if there is any life at all.

4.

    High in the sky of the big Boston City where the morning traffic below is at its hectic standstill with non stop car horns going off, it seems like the members of the public who are walking on the foot path are getting to their destinations quicker than those behind the wheel.

    Slowing down and peeking through one city buildings window, it seems that some people have already made it to work on time, as sitting at her desk ready to do what seems to be a live news report, a lady with long black hair and glimmering bright brown eyes, that have had a professional mascara treatment done to them, has been covered with foundation and a bit of blusher on her cheeks, though it's plain to see she would still be able to show her good looks without all the makeup on.

    Noticing a rectangular badge that has a blue border going around it that is pinned on her top shirt pocket, the name on the badge reads, Tracey Lewis, who looking up at her face where she has such a lovely smile, the camera mans assistant does the count down with his fingers, where as his hand disappears Tracey's lips start moving as she starts off with the news.

    Heading towards another city building four blocks away, upon arrival there is one particular window that catches the eye due to the angle it's been left open at, where moving over to the window and heading into the apartment it leads into, whilst getting in through the little gap to the curtains that are still closed over, the only bit of light that is brightening up the room is the television, that has been left on silent.

    In front of the television is a sturdy circular wooden table that has an empty two liter bottle of vodka with a dry glass beside it, an uneaten bowl of chips, all kinds of bills, some containing the red colored titles, 'Final Reminder', a cellular and an FBI badge that's attached to the left hand side of a folding flap.

    At the right hand side of the flap which contains the photo and FBI details, the name that is printed out underneath the photo of a smiling face is Steve Hughes, but over at the settee to which Steve is lying on in an awkward position, with one leg as high as it can reach on the head rest part of the settee, it is plain to see with him being fully dressed and the bags he has under his eyes that he's suffering from a hefty hangover.

As his foot loses grip and slides off the headpiece to the settee, he suddenly jumps and opens his eyes in a slow moving hangover mode and looks in the direction of where the light is coming from, which is the television, where Tracey Lewis is still doing a live news report.

With Steve's television being on silent, he stretches over to the glass table and tries to grab hold of the remote control, but instead he manages to take hold of his cellular and says, "Oh, I'll give her a call."

As he presses a few buttons to his cellular the name, 'Tracey' appears, where still looking completely messed up from his hangover and being on cloud nine, he presses the call button. With the cellular not even having had a chance to ring he quickly lets go of it, where as it falls to the floor he quickly runs down the hallway disappearing out of sight, where the sound of vomiting is heard kicking off.

Though looking back towards the television, Tracey has a worried look on her face as her right hand disappears out of sight under the table like she's trying to reach for something. Then quickly looking in the same direction from where her hand vanished to, she pulls into view her cellular and presses the hang up button. Where quickly carrying on with the news she puts on a brave face with a worrying smile.

- -

In the news room, being seen from behind, a tall chubby man stands beside the camera crew who are watching Tracey continue with the news after having made an apology to the public viewers. Where as she carries on with the news report the tall chubby man looks in the direction of the camera crew and says, "When this is over, tell her she's fired!"

Back at Steve's apartment the cellular is still on the floor, though lying on the settee in a more comfortable position, Steve is fast asleep.

5.

The time above the entrance door is 09:22, where the big rectangular sign above the time reads, '**HUNTERS COLLEGE**', and looking towards the steps and brick wall which contain a banister that leads up to the college, there's three male students. One, being the only African American in sight, is sitting on the wall that the banister is attached to, reading away at his math book, as the other two, who are sitting on the two bottom steps that lead up to the college, are completely depressed looking.

Though coming around the corner and walking up towards the steps acting all cool is Alan Woods, who looking in Ryan's direction and noticing he still has his head in his math book, Alan puts on a voice like he's a television host and says, "Now ladies and gentlemen, if you look to my left you'll see the one and only Ryan Watson." Continuing to act silly, Alan points towards Chris and Paul like they're part of the audience and says as he looks at Ryan, "Now Ryan, would you like to tell the audience how far you are with studying for you final exams?"

"Alan, run and fuck!" Ryan plain and simply says as he shakes his head and focuses back into the math book.

"There you are ladies and gentlemen, Ryan's comment is, *Alan, run and fuck*." Alan says as he tries to impersonate Ryan's voice.

Standing up from the step together, Chris and Paul walk over to Alan. Where taking hold of Alan in a muscular manner, Chris places Alan on the wall and says, "Take a seat, can't you see the man's studyin'?"

"He's always got his head in the books, and he's sure as hell not taking the advice from the teachers anymore." Alan says.

"Yeah, like what?" Ryan questionably asks.

"Uh, give yourself a days rest before your final exam." Alan says impersonating the voice of a teacher.

"Yeah, but your problem my main man is that you've been restin' all fuckin' year." Ryan says, then suddenly Alan's cellular starts to ring.

"And don't even think on putting the blame on that little bro of yours, if anything he's the only one that has any faith on you gettin' anywhere." Ryan says as Alan takes hold of his cellular.

Putting his hand up to Ryan's face in a 'talk to the hand' kind of manner, Alan answers his cell phone.

- -

Earlier on in the morning, back at Alan's house, Alan stands up from the breakfast table, where hardly giving him a chance to stand up, his young brother runs over to him and throws his arms around Alan.

"This is for good luck on your final exams."

"That's good to hear Simon. So if I fail I can blame you then, huh?" Alan says as he strokes Simon's head.

"You'll not fail." A voice is heard saying coming from the hall. Then all of the sudden the noise of a hairdryer is heard going off.

Placing his hand on Simon's shoulder busy raising his eyes up and down as his head points in the direction that the noise of the hairdryer is coming from, it's as if he's trying to say that's a noise they could do without.

"Well bro, the lucks on your side anyway." Alan says.

"Whatta you mean?" Simon says looking at Alan weirdly.

"Put it this way, if I was ten years of age again and on my summer holidays before my big bro and getting left in the house with that good looking lady out there, I'd sure call it luck!" Alan says.

"Ha, ha, ah, who knows, one day you'll be big and strong like me and receive the luxury gifts and days off that I get." Simon says.

"Yeah, who knows bro?" Alan says as he walks towards the noise of the hairdryer, which is heard getting turned off.

As Alan reaches the hallway his Mum has her back turned to him as she bends over to put her hairdryer away in a little draw beneath the table that the telephone is sitting on top of.

"Well do I get a good luck kiss before I have to face these final exams of mine?" Alan says as he looks in the direction of his Mum, where as she stands up and turns around she reveals the one and only, Charlotte Woods.

With her face hardly having aged at all and her hair style near enough looking the exact same in both color and style, Charlotte still has her good looks, and from the looks she is getting from Alan and Simon, a lot of respect.

Giving Alan a kiss, Charlotte says, "Think before you put that pen to paper and you won't go wrong. As rushing it will cause the mistakes, okay?"

"Gotcha Mom," Alan says as he turns around to the front door.

"All you can do is try your best my babe." Charlotte says.

"No, you nearly got that right Mom. You're supposed to say. ALAN IS BEST, ALAN IS BEST, ALAN IS BEST, ALAN IS BEST." Simon says with his voice increasing in volume each time. Then joining in as Alan opens the door, Charlotte and Simon shout together, "ALAN IS BEST, ALAN IS BEST, ALAN IS BEST."

Alan nearly blushing, smiles at them both and gives them a 'piece out' hand signal and heads off closing the door behind him.

- -

Back at Hunters College, Alan hangs up his cell phone and puts it in his pocket, where after looking at his watch which reads 09:27, he carries on with the conversation he was having with Ryan and says, "Okay, so what's your plan for summer then, huh?

"Pulling some pussy?" Paul says with a grin on his face as if he's already there.

"I like your taste," Alan says as he looks at Paul and gives him the thumbs up, "But Ryan prefers the books," Alan says finishing his sentence.

"Uh, as in porn mags?" Paul questions silently as if he's gone to heaven just thinking about it.

"Uh, no!" Alan says.

But not even giving Alan a chance to carry on with his quick cocky questions and remarks, Ryan says, "If you'd like to know dudes, I've got plans."

"Yeah, like what?" Alan says in disbelief.

"Campin' out." Ryan says.

Then Paul, Alan and Chris turn their heads and start whistling as they put on the impression that they're not with Ryan.

"What?" Ryan says wondering what they're all playing at.

"You mean you'd rather be in the woods with a bunch of no hopes than in the town with the guys partying?" Chris says as he takes another puff of his cigarette.

"Well you go and fuck a streetlamp and come back with a bright idea." Ryan says all unimpressed.

"I rest my case." Alan says acting all cool.

"Rest all you fuckin' want, cuz that's what I'll be doing on my own, note, I say on my own while I'm away having a relaxing time." Then Ryan looks at his watch which reads 09:29. "Oh, did I mention time? I hope you've revised." Ryan says as he gets himself up from sitting on the wall and heads up the steps to the entrance door with Paul, Alan and Chris in their stupid silent manner, busy impersonating him as they walk up the stairs behind him.

6.

Steve still out for the count on the settee is starting to look a little bit more like he is in his FBI photo that's sitting on the table, though with him still being in a deep sleep, the smile from the photo is the only thing that he's missing more or less.

- -

Fading into Steve's dreams, the date on an FBI report sheet that's getting filled in by a member of staff is the 11th of May 2009, and walking through the entrance door with a grin on his face is Steve.

Looking at him curiously like he's in a world of his own, Jake says, "Steve if you smile anymore you're face'll cover the room." Then having a quick laugh Jake carries on with his sentence and says, "What's with the glowing sensation?"

"Aw," Steve happily sighs as he takes a deep breath and smiles as he sits down.

"And that language is? Come on, gimme somethin' I can work on here." Jake says as he looks at Steve in a weird manner.

"Hah, hah, hah, I took her out last night." Steve says as he looks at Jake and slightly tilts his head, to which a cheeky smile starts to appear.

"Yeah, now we're gettin' somewhere." Jake says busy sitting on the edge of his seat waving his hands around for more gossip. "And, and?" Jake says.

"I asked her." Steve says.

"Asked her?" Jake says still none the wiser.

"Yeah." Steve says, nodding away.

"Uh, I'm still clueless man." Jake says.

"Ha, she said yes." Steve says like he's not even on the same planet.

"Huh?" Jake says still none the wiser what Steve's waffling on about. Then suddenly Jake says, "No," like he's just clicked on to what Steve's fantasizing over.

"Yeah," Steve replies.

"You asked her to marry you?" Jake says.

"And she said yeah." Steve replies.

"Congratulations man. Get up off that butt. We've got some partying to do." Jake says as he pulls Steve up from the chair, dragging him out of the room with his arm over his shoulder. "The drink's on me." Pete says.

"Yeah," Steve says managing to agree whilst still in his little fantasy land.

In the cellar, to where the laundry room is, Angelina with her back to the steps is busy at the ironing and pulling a good few dance moves in the process as she folds up the clothes.

Up the stairs from the cellar the entrance door is open wide to the walls, probably to lighten the cellar up a bit, as the light in the cellar isn't exactly the strongest.

Grabbing hold of another piece of clothing and dancing away, following up with a twirl and finishing in front of the ironing board, Angelina, with her cleverly controlled voice starts singing: -

You are the heart, the soul, the dream of my little life,
You're the love I've always wished for,
The love I've never had.
You're the heart, the soul the dream of my little life.

Now am I going senile?
Am I going nuts?

Am I going crazy?
Or is this really us?

Do you feel what I feel?
Do you see it too?
It's right there in front of us,
It's bound to pull through.

You know my hearts going crazy?
Each time I see you,
I need you to hold me,
And make this love true.
As you're the heart, the soul, the dream of my little life.

As she continues ironing, dancing and humming away to her lyrics, the entrance door to the cellar has been closed over ever so slightly, darkening the cellar ever so minor, but concentrating on her every move with the ironing, dancing and humming, it hasn't obstructed Angelina in any shape or form.

From the top step to the cellar, the way Angelina's getting on you'd swear ironing was her main hobby, but also situated at the top step two damp muddy footprints are lingering.

Slowly heading down the soiled steps, with Angelina's humming being heard in the background, the dirtiness of each step is decreasing bit by bit, where slipping through a gap to the lowest banister, which is roughly inline with Angelina's shoulder, Angelina's bare feet are dancing away on a rug, to which her feet are spotless.

"What are we gonna do, what are we gonna do, what are we gonna do, to make our life's complete?" Angelina sings. Though as she turns around standing right in front of her is the Stranger.

"Aaaaaaaaaaaagggghhhhh," Angelina screams, but being seen from the top step to the cellar, the screaming quickly stops as the Stranger's quiet stabbing act takes affect. Where plummeting into the ironing board that topples over, the iron lands on the lower part of Angelina's left arm.

With the cellar door open, slowly heading towards it is Steve and Jake. Yet coming to a stop Jake lets Steve walk the rest of the way on his own.

Arriving at the bottom step and noticing the dry blood on the floor and walls, Steve turns slowly towards the direction of the body bag, to where the ironing board is now leaning up against the wall behind it.

Slowly crouching down to the body bag, Steve gradually unzips it and has a look on his face that is literally praying for it not to be Angelina, though unzipping it and opening it, strait in front of him is Angelina's cold and still battered face.

"NO, NO, NO, NO, NO," Steve shouts as he turns around and puts his fist through the banister. Quickly running down the stairs Jake tries to give Steve a bit of loving support, but Steve arrogantly brushes him off by pushing him away.

"WHY, WHY ANGELINA, HUH," Steve cries out as he forcefully kicks the boiler and creates a big dent in it as Jake quickly zips up the body bag.

"Why Angelina, why, why fuckin' Angelina?" Steve says not being able to keep his tears from appearing anymore.

Giving the signal to the evidence handlers to remove Angelina's corpse, Jake walks up to Steve and puts his arms around him, where Steve looking like he's going to need all the support he can get, takes the support that's at hand.

On the tombstone it reads:-

Angelina Summons

3 March 1979 ---> 14 May 2009
Angelina is the most loving
Angel of Angels
She will always be in the hearts
Of her family and friends
Forever and never be forgotten

Coming back a bit from the tombstone, the coffin not having been lowered yet is surrounded by a lot of family and friends who all have tears flowing out, some more uncontrollably than others, where Steve is one of them. Suddenly with the coffin starting to lower, Steve stands watching it as the tears roll down his face as he holds in his hand, that the engagement ring is on, a rose. Lowering himself down to the squatting position he takes hold of a piece of the burial muck and walks up to the coffin as it lowers. Placing the rose into the burial muck he has in his hand, the tears roll down his eyes as he says, "I love you, and always will," where as the coffin lowers down slowly he places the rose on top of the coffin and blows Angelina one last kiss, like he's still got contact with her soul. Then as he stands up and walks back and gets comforted by Angelina's relations, taking a look at his hand the engagement ring was on, there is no sign of it anymore.

On the settee quickly pouncing up from a nightmare, Steve, with his gun in his hand and poring with sweat in a frozen mode as if he's listening for any form of attack before he makes a move, suddenly catches on where he is, where not being one bit impressed and looking like he wants to hit for the drink, he slides his gun back into the rear of his pants with one hand whilst his other hand lifts his shirt up to cover the gun from being seen, where as he lowers the shirt down to hide the gun from being seen, big loud bangs start coming from the front door unexpectedly, having Steve grab his gun again faster than lightening.

Shaking his head like he doesn't even know what's going on, or what he's even playing at, Steve slides the gun away again and heads disjointedly towards the front door.

"Hello." Steve says in a low tiring pitched voice as he opens the door, unaware as to whom he's even opening the door to.

Then all of the sudden he's woke up with a massive slap across the face.

"THANKS TO YOU I'VE LOST THE ONE AND ONLY MEANINGFUL JOB THAT MEANT ANYTHING TO ME, NOW YOU STAY OUTTA MY WAY AND I'LL STAY OUTTA YOURS, YOU HEAR ME?" Tracey shouts. Then turning around and marching down the stairs, she storms past Jake as he makes his way up towards Steve's apartment.

"Morning Tracey." Jake politely says.

"Yeah, right." Tracey says and she continues to charge down the stairs.

With the front door being open and Steve no longer in sight, Jake heads on into the dark dull apartment finding the living room looking like a tip.

"Uh, don't tell me the Vodka bottle was, uh, leaking?" Jake says.

"Ah screw you," Steve says.

"And look at the place man. I'm tellin' you I can't keep coverin' for you like this, as they are absolutely chewin' the balls off me back at the office as to where the fuck you are." Jake says in a hasty manner.

"Ah, who care's." Steve says all slouched on the settee.

"Uh, Tracey, I don't think she gives a pile of crap anymore, as seen by her little exit a few minutes ago. And with Angelina man, it's near enough two years. What the fuck are you playin' at?"

"Ah, leave her outta this." Steve groans.

"Well drinking yourself oblivious ain't gonna help bring her back Steve. Plus it ain't gonna help us find the fucker who killed her any easier, is it?" Jake says. Then carrying on with his sentence due to Steve not replying, Jake says, "And just outta curiosity, does Tracey even know anythin' about this?"

"She doesn' need to know anythin' about it." Steve replies.

"Well you keepin' it tucked in ain't helpin' much is it?" Jake says.

"I'll tell her in my own good time." Steve says getting all worked up.

"And you'll find when that time comes it'll be far too late. Ah, but fuck it, I'm outta here man, and if you ain't bucked up by the end of the week, I'll be looking for a new partner in crime." Jake says. Then heading for the front door, Steve just wallows in his own self pity as the door is heard closing over.

- -

Outside Steve's apartment building, Tracey walks towards the news van depressingly slow as she kicks any small object on the floor along the way.

Arriving at the driver's window which is wound down, Tracey says, "Robert, I think I'll walk on back to my place from here."

"Tracey….," is the only word Robert gets to say as Tracey butts in.

"I know it's nine miles, but it'll gimme a little time to think." Tracey says.

"Tracey….,"

"I know I was looking for a holiday, but I didn't expect to take it this early. I just don't know what I'm gonna do next." Tracey says lowering her head in shame.

"Well…," Robert says, but interjected from talking again, Tracey butts in.

"Ah, you never know I might make out to be an underground rat. Yeah, that's right I could join those turtle dudes, huh?" Tracey says as if it's a realistic idea.

Taking hold of the scented dog that's dangling from the rear view mirror, Robert starts to wave it back and forth in front of Tracey's face as if he's trying to hypnotize her, where staring her in the face Robert speaks slowly and says, "You are not fired anymore. You still have a job."

"What?" Tracey replies with a look of disbelief on her face.

Finally noticing he's got her attention, Robert pretends to hypnotize her and says, "We're the closest to the hospital for a joint separation of twins. You're back on the band wagon. So at the click of my fingers you will get into the front passenger seat for to be brought to that location." Robert says clicking his thumb and forefinger together.

Near enough looking like she has been hypnotized, Tracey suddenly starts jumping for joy as she dances her way around to the passenger door shouting, "YES, YES, YES, YES, YES." Then getting into the passenger side of the news van, Tracey says, "And you know what, he deserved that slap anyway, there was no hypnotherapy required for that. Now pump up the vibes, I feel like partying."

Over at the building to Steve's apartment, Jake looks in the direction of where the music is coming from and notices it's from the news van that's busy driving off. Where smiling Jake says, "It's amazing what one little phone call can do." Then putting his cellular in his shirt pocket that contains a zip, he zips it up, turns towards the opposite direction to where the news van is heading and walks off.

At the news room, Tracey's boss looks around in a curious manner, as if he's being watched as he heads to his office slowly, where closing the door behind him a sign on the door is seen reading, 'Stay out no matter what.'

Taking a key out of his desk draw he walks up to a big picture on the wall, which opens like a door, where hiding behind it is a gigantic safe.

As he slowly opens the safe, all that can be seen inside it is ladies outfits, make up, shoes, jewelry, fake tits, lingerie, hair accessories, wigs and hand bags. He is more or less sorted out to be the Full Monty. Though suddenly making him jump, the speaker on his table goes off with a voice saying, "Your twelve o'clock appointment for a news reporter is here sir." Where heading over to the speaker, he presses a button and says, "Send them in in ten." Where heading back to his locker he quickly locks all up, then as he heads towards his table acting all professional his door suddenly opens, which he looks quite surprised over, as it looks like his secretarial assistant thought he meant ten seconds, not the ten minutes that his facial expression was calculating out for expectancy.

7.

The time above the entrance door to Hunters College is 12:35, where exiting out of college with a grin on his face that would cover the college twice over is Ryan, who just stops at the top step, lifts his head up into the air, closes his eyes and takes a deep breath. Then with the relieving air being blown out of his system, he looks down the stairs to see three depressive looking figures sitting at the bottom step, busy facing the ground.

"Ah, you know it was that easy I could do it all over again," Ryan says as he starts to walk down the stairs.

"I like that all over again bit," Paul says in an unhappy manner as he covers his face with his cap in shame.

"Yeah, me too," Alan and Chris say together, like they're a pair of little and large twins knowing rightly what each other are going to say next.

"So while I'm on **a killer of a camp** that you'd sell your own soul for, I take it you guys'll be studyin' for next year, or partying?" Ryan questioningly asks as he walks around to the front of them to see each face individually.

"Studyin'," Alan says as he expresses his answer in a depressing manner.

"Yeah," Paul and Chris say together.

Then continuing to answer Ryan's question with the pitch of his voice increasing a couple of levels, Alan says, "**And partying**."

"*Yeah*," Paul and Chris say together at the exact same time again.

Then with an unsure look on his face, Ryan wonders what they're all playing at, until they come out with a planned sentence and say, "Cuz *we're* headin' on your so called killer of a camp too!"

With Ryan completely gob smacked Alan takes the advantage while it's going and says, "Well, shall we go and get ready?"

Getting up from their sitting positions they take hold of Ryan, who isn't one hundred percent with it, then dander off.

Being seen from behind as they all walk away Chris says, "I'll bring the sleeping sacks and tents."

"I'll get the drink supply from Barry." Alan says.

"I'll get the fake ID's." Paul says.

"Fake ID's?" Chris questions.

"Fake ID's?" Alan near enough says at the same time as Chris.

"For night clubin'!" Paul says looking at them as if they haven't got a bit of common sense.

"Good thinkin'," Chris says as he smokes away. Then looking at Alan and blowing the smoke in his face he carries on with his sentence, "Cuz some of us might need one."

Then Chris looks at Paul again and says, "Why couldn't we have had this kind of thinkin' cap on when it was exam time?"

"Cuz you're all a pile of dimwitted pricks." Ryan says eventually coming back to reality.

"Well whatta you know, it talks. So whatta you bringing on this campin' spree?" Alan says as he pats Ryan on the back.

"I'll get my Pop's van and pick you up around two." Ryan says.

"Well pick me up first," Alan quickly says.

"No, pick me up first," Paul says.

Then flicking his finished fag but for six, Chris puts on a deep muscular voice as he gets Alan and Paul in a head lock and says, "He's pickin' me up first."

"Okay, pick me up second." Alan struggles to say as he gets choked.

"Ah, w, w, whatever," Paul replies with his squeaky voice, though managing to take hold of his water bottle and quickly squirting Chris in the face, Chris is forced to let go of them both. Where squirting Alan and Ryan as well, Paul runs like mad as they all chase after him as he sprints for six.

8.

With her bike leaning up against the public picnic table that's next to a lake, Amy's bottle that's still full, is sitting on top of it. Though next to the public picnic table is a row of trees and bushes, where unfamiliar noises seem to be coming from.

Being seen from behind as she removes her helmet, her lovely long black hair drops down and comes in line with her elbows, where walking towards the lake and picking up a few stones in the process, Amy starts to try and do a bit of skimming in the water, but isn't to good at it.

Throwing what seems to be her last stone due to rubbing her hands together, Amy turns around, takes a chocolate bar out of her pocket and peels the rapping paper off in seconds, where whilst starting to chew away at it she walks towards the table her bike is leaning up against.

Arriving at the table and taking hold of her bottle, Amy removes the lid, though as she attempts to take a drink, diving out of the bush and onto the table, then running like crazy is Jack, who has caused Amy to spill her drink all over her and drop her chocolate bar.

"Damn dog!" Amy says as she looks in the direction that Jack is running off in. Then trying to wipe the juice off of her and place the bottle in the bikes holder, her whole entire top is drenched with parts of chocolate having melted and smudged into it as well.

Not happy in the slightest Amy attempts to get on her bike, where noticing it's a bit uneven, as she gets off, straight in front of her is another flat tire.

"Ah, no way, not again!" Amy says. Then looking up into the sky Amy says, "Why me, huh?"

Struggling to push her bike due to the bumps, Amy's walking depressingly slow and losing her temper rapidly. Though looking behind Amy in the distance, another person is seen cycling towards her.

As the person gets closer, Amy notices who it is, where as they come in line with Amy, Amy says, "Oh, hi Rachel."

"Gee's you look like you've been walkin' for days." Rachel says noticing Amy's all drained out looking, "Is there somethin' on that I don't know about?"

Expressing her feelings Amy says, "Ah, it's this bike of mine it's bin nothin' but a pain in the ass. That's twice this day it's had a puncture already, I need a new bike altogether, this ones had it."

"Yeah, as there's not exactly much more entertainment to do around the countryside, huh?" Rachel says. Then looking up to the trees Rachel says, "Unless you wanna be a monkey?" Amy nods to Rachel's comment and Rachel says, "Here I've a suggestion."

"What?" Amy says weirdly as she follows up with a quick answer, "We climb the highest tree or become the first human with wings?"

"Ha, ha, ha, ha, ha." Rachel laughs. Then being a bit more serious Rachel says, "How about I head on back to my place and set up the play station three, where you can check out all the new games I've got, huh?"

"Yeah, why not?" Amy says impressed with Rachel's idea. "Sure it'll take me about an hour to get home anyway. And then after my Mom stuffing me like crazy with food, sure you know what Mom's are like." Amy says still looking happy with Rachel's plans.

"Yeah," Rachel says busy nodding away. Then suddenly Rachel's eyes enlighten up as she looks at Amy. "I've even got something better in mind."

"What?" Amy says.

"How about askin' your Mom if you can stay at mine for a night, it'll be excellent. We could have midnight snacks, play games non-stop and sleep in for as long as we want and eventually get a cooked breakfast." Rachel says like she's already there.

Looking a little bit unsure Amy says hesitantly, "Well?"

Then quickly trying to boost Amy around with the idea, Rachel says, "Anythin' would beet pushin' that thing around?"

"Ah, what the heck count me in," Amy says holding her head up high. Though suddenly lowering her head a little bit Amy says, "But I'm not promising anythin' now, as like I said, you know what parents are like!"

"Well I'll head on back to mine and get the play station set up and see what kind of delights I can get a hold of," Rachel says. Then putting on a strange voice Rachel says, *"And wait your arrival."*

"See you later," Amy says as Rachel starts cycling off, then following on with her sentence Amy shouts, "Hopefully." Where Rachel turns around to look at Amy and gives her the crossed finger signal.

As Amy continues walking and Rachel gets further away, she notices a peculiar dirty looking object in a ditch on the side of the road that Rachel had her back to as she gave Amy the crossed finger signal.

"Rachel, Rachel," Amy shouts as she tries to wave Rachel to come back, but Rachel turns around and waves goodbye, then continues to cycle off in the distance. Where knowing that she's on her own, Amy's pace of walking starts to rapidly slow down as she gets closer to the large dirty object.

9.

Standing outside the entrance door to Ravenswood nightclub and getting a bit impatient, Alan gives the bell another ring, where with doing so the door opens within a second.

"Barry, I thought you were never gonna open up man. I mean what way's that to treat your number one cuz, huh?" Alan says.

"I wish I never had," Barry says as he's seen holding a two liter bottle of Vodka that looks like it's been half drunk. "Is it you and your guy's plans to screw this day up for me or somethin'?" Barry says in an unhappy manner.

"What're you on about?" Alan says.

Then opening the door slightly wider, Barry shows Alan what he's on about as he points in the direction of a half naked lady lying on top of one of the clubs large tables with her breast in plain view. Where closing the door over slightly, Barry takes a swig from the Vodka bottle and says, "Now what're you after?"

"A bit've drink for the campin' spree that me and guys've got planned." Alan says in an innocent yet desperate groveling manner.

"I dunno, first fake ID's and now this," Barry says as he takes another swig from the Vodka bottle, "Here, take this and sling your hook, I'm busy." Barry says as he hands Alan the Vodka bottle and slams the nightclubs entrance door.

"I don't think you need screwed cuz, as you're screwed enough as it is already." Alan says as he walks off. Then suddenly taking a closer look to the Vodka bottle, Alan notices that the color is bright yellow with little white pieces floating in it. Then quickly realizing what Barry and his lady were up to, Alan throws it into the public dumpster that's right in front of him and says, "Sick shits." Then walking off as he shakes the hand that was carrying the bottle, Alan pulls some car keys out of his pocket with his other hand and walks around a corner out of sight.

With Alan disappearing out of sight, a scruffy old dude walks out from a dark alley that leads up towards the dumpster. Where taking a quick look around him and noticing nobodies watching, he quickly puts his hand down the dumpster and retrieves the Vodka bottle that Alan disposed of. Then noticing that it's half full he unscrews the lid and heads on into the dark alley, where after a few seconds of silence, slurping noises are suddenly heard, then they suddenly stop.

"It's a bit flat, hasn't got much of a twang to it, but it tastes a bit better than the last Vodka bottle I got outta that dumpster. You wanna taste?"

"Yeah, throw it this way," a deep horsy voice says.

A big rectangular sign that's been placed above both the window and door to the shop reads, "Roy's Key Cutting". Where heading in through the entrance door Paul acts very peculiar with looking around the place as he heads in the direction of the counter, to which the owner keeping a sharp eye on him says, "Can I help you?"

Walking up to the counter trying to act all cool, Paul says, "Roy I take it?"

"That's me, who's asking?"

"Uh, a friend of mine was telling me you do fake ID's." Paul quietly says whilst looking over his shoulder at the same time.

"Well sorry to disappoint you dude, but whoever it was seems to have directed you to the wrong place."

"Are you serious?" Paul says.

"I'm afraid so," Roy says acting all cool, "Sorry for your wasted journey."

"Well thanks a fuckin' lot Barry," Paul says as he turns around to walk off towards the entrance door.

"You mean Barry from....,"

"Ravenswood fuckin' nightclub," Paul says butting in as if he's down grading it.

"Well why didn't you say man?" Roy says.

"What?" Paul says wondering what Roy's playing at.

"I thought you were some undercover cop or somethin'. Come with me." Roy says as he heads into his back store room, being followed by Paul.

As Paul enters the store room behind Roy, busy wondering what he's playing at, he glances around the store that is covered in photos, news papers and doesn't have the brightest of lighting in the room either, more than likely due to the photo's needing developed.

"I take it you've got the photo for your ID with you?" Roy says.

"To be precise I've got four," Paul says.

"Why'de the fuck do you need so many? Have you committed that many crimes or somethin'?" Roy says.

"Nah, nah, it's nothing like that, it's just me and the guys headin' on a campin' spree, where we would like a bitta service in the nightclubs where the pussies are gonna hopefully be hangin' out at." Paul says as he takes a quick peek above him like he's talking to the lord. Then taking the photos out of his pocket he hands them to Roy.

"Ah, I get the drift, sure come on back in about half-hour, I'll have them ready by then I'm sure." Roy says.

"And how much is this gonna cost?" Paul says with a look like he doesn't want to know.

"Ah nothin', sure if you're a friend of Barry's have it on the house." Roy says.

Impressed with what he's heard Paul says, "Thanks a lot man." Then heading out of the store Paul looks back at Roy and says, "See you later."

As Paul walks out of the key shop, sitting in his car with the engine running is Alan with his window wound down.

"Yo Alan, any luck on gettin' the drink supply from Barry?" Paul says as he walks down the stairs and pats Alan on the shoulder.

"Yeah, all bad luck." Alan says not in the best of humors.

"Don't tell me he's still riding that chick?" Paul says

"He sure is. It must be the old age slowing him down. Well what about you, any luck on the ID's?" Alan says.

"Yeah, they'll be ready in about thirty minutes, and as for the price I'm payin' for you guys, they're thirty bucks a piece." Paul says.

"What, thirty fuckin' dollars? Get in the car. Shit thirty fuckin' dollars. Let's go and get somethin' to eat before I black out man." Alan says as he wipes the hand that was carrying the Vodka bottle on Paul's back as he sits in the front passenger seat.

"Now you're speaking my language." Paul says, none the wiser what's getting wiped on him.

- -

In at the back store to Roy's key shop, Roy is sitting on a stool smoking a cigar which is creating an unaccountable amount of smoke around the place while he sits down reading away at the newspaper.

Though back towards the table that the photos of Paul, Alan, Ryan and Chris have been set on, they have been placed on a pile of newspapers. Where looking at part of a title to the newspaper that their photos have been set on top of, which is covering the remainder of the title, the only part of the title in view reads, "**Killed**."

10.

Inside the house from the front door there's not a single sinner in sight and the hallway is as quiet as can be, as the only noise that can be heard are the tics coming from the glass clock that is sitting on the table in the hall, which is beside the front door, though the table which is just a little square shape no bigger than a bedside table has a rectangular shaped chair, which looks quite comfortable to sit on, attached to it.

Also beside the clock on the table there's a very big hi-tech computerized phone that must have the abilities to send faxes as well, as looking at the bottom part of the phone there's quite a bit of paper in view. Though noticing at the bottom part of the phone on the other side altogether, there's an envelope sticking out from underneath it, with the letters, 'SAM' in view, but that just seems to be part of a word, as with the rest of the envelope that's hiding under the phone a back slash symbol can be vaguely seen beside the letter "M" on the envelope too.

Suddenly hearing a thumping noise, it's hard to tell as to where it's coming from, but down the left of the hallway and taking a peek up the big long steep stairs, there's no sign of anyone or anything yet. Though down the right hand side of the hallway and heading into the kitchen, which leads on into the living room, there doesn't seem to be any clues as to where the mysterious thumping noises are coming from either. Then suddenly the thumping noises start to interact again and the direction of the noise seems to be coming from the top of the stairs, where looking towards the top step a nightgown comes into view, with more of it unveiling very slowly and eventually revealing Samantha's presence, where it's plain to see she's still half asleep as she slowly makes her way to the bottom of the stairs.

Arriving at the bottom step, Samantha doesn't even pay a blind bit of notice to the envelope underneath the telephone. Then heading towards the direction of the kitchen with her eyes barely half open, she loses sense of direction and bangs into the wall.

Finally arriving in the kitchen, Samantha opens up one of the top kitchen cupboards as she gives her forehead a rub, then she grabs herself a cereal bar and heads on into the living room whilst attempting to unwrap the cereal bar with her eyes nearly closing over again.

Taking a seat on the settee as she chews away at her cereal bar, Samantha takes hold of the remote control for the television and presses the power button, where while the television is slowly revealing a picture, Samantha sets the control on the table beside her, setting it next to the phone.

Pressing a button to the recliner and literally bouncing into the lying position, Samantha looks as comfortable as can be, though as she tries to reach for the remote control again whilst chewing away at her breakfast bar, she quickly pauses, as the television has captured her full attention.

TELEVISION NEWS

It has now been over a week since Naomi Lain was last seen. As on the night that Naomi came back from a school disco that was organized, she was dropped off at her driveway which is approximately 100 feet from her house. Where having mysteriously gone missing, the only clues the police have come across are on certain cut outs of photos and pieces of newspapers that were found at the scene. If you know anything or may have seen anything out of the ordinary please phone 1-800-9 ….,

Having hold of the control Samantha turns the television off not looking overly impressed in the slightest.

"Sick!" Samantha says as she pushes the cereal bar back into its wrapper then sets it on the table like she's lost her appetite.

Taking hold of the cordless phone on the table Samantha shuffles herself about on the recliner chair to try and get more comfortable, quickly followed by dialing a few numbers on the phone where she waits for a few seconds.

"Guess who?" Samantha suddenly says, where nodding her head back and forth she looks towards the television and says, "So you've still not asked him?" Then remaining silent for a few seconds as she taps the arm rest she says, "I dunno, I'm gonna get myself a man tonight even if it kills me. In fact gather the others together and come on down early, I'll make sure you all get a few drinks on the house before the main man walks in."

Busy listening for a few seconds Samantha starts pressing the recliner button to put her back up into the sitting position and says, "So I'll see you there then, huh? Good luck for now."

Finishing her phone call Samantha sets it back onto its holder, then grabbing the remainder of her cereal bar she gets up and heads on into the kitchen.

11.

Roughly five meters away from the dark clothed figure on the floor, Amy's speed of walking is near enough that slow, it looks like she's more or less stopped. Even looking at her arms also, they are starting to shake quite abruptly.

"Hello, can you hear me?" Amy says nervously. Where getting no answer she steps back a step.

"Are you okay?" Amy says with the sound of her voice making out on how scared she is whilst getting all worked up. Where stepping back another step Amy nearly loses her footing altogether due to the punctured tire causing her to go off course, but regaining her balance and keeping it well under control, Amy steps back another step like she's wanting to retreat from her horrific find, but shockingly she sets her bike on the floor as she looks at the unresponsive still figure and takes a step forward.

"What's happened?" Amy questions.

Still irresponsive Amy takes another step forward, but suddenly flying out of nowhere a flock of birds scare Amy that much she nearly dives for cover. Then quickly looking back at the still figure, to whose clothes are all worn-out and tatty, the body didn't flicker an inch with the bird noises.

"Do you want me to go and get some help?" Amy says being a little bit more at ease due to the still body being three feet in front of her and not having moved a single inch.

Slowly crouching down to the body to who's arms have been covered by the grass and weeds, and who's face can't be seen due to being squashed in the dry muck, only the back of their head that's covered in dirty black hair that looks like it hasn't been washed for a year can be seen as Amy crouches down and quickly taps their back.

"Do you want me to phone for an ambulance?" Amy says as her curiousness gets the better of her and the scarceness that was in her eyes has disappeared, which is quite noticeable due to her hands not shaking as much.

"I'll get help if you want." Amy says as she gets down to the squatting position with being only inches away from the body, then looking at Amy's face as she daringly rolls the body over, she says, "Can you hear me okay?" Then all of the sudden Amy's face disappears as the dirty black clothed Stranger's figure, being seen from behind blocks her from view, where Amy let's off an enormous loud scream that suddenly stops as continuous stabbing noises take over, with a troubled voice silently repeating the word, "No, no, no, no, no, no."

12.

Picking up her handbag from the kitchens work surface then walking to the front door, Samantha is gorgeously dressed up in a sexy cream dress that has a light brown design on it, while her hair has been very nicely platted up with a designer ribbon put in it. Also seen glittering from her neck as it dangles whilst she lowers her head to look into her handbag, a pure solid gold necklace with a diamond in the center part of it is seen, where as she takes a set of keys out of her handbag and raises her head up, the necklace looks like it's worth a million dollars as it caresses against her skin.

Taking a quick glimpse in the mirror to the left of her, which is hanging on the wall before you come in line with the couch and little table the phone is sitting on, Samantha lets out a glamorous smile then messes about as she also blows a kiss at her reflection.

"Tonight is the night lady!" Samantha says to herself. Then with her face suddenly dropping like something's gone wrong, Samantha dips into her handbag again and pulls out some lipstick.

With the reflection of her lips in the mirror turning into a kissing mode, Samantha puts her lipstick on and rubs her lips together mildly.

"I'd nearly take you home myself lady." Samantha says messing about and letting out a little bit of a laugh as she grins at her reflection.

"Shut up lady, you are home. Get outta here!"

Then picking up her handbag again and putting the lipstick away and grabbing hold of the keys once more, Samantha heads for the front door. Trying to get hold of the right key due to the amount of keys she has on her key ring, finally succeeding Samantha goes to slide the key into the door, until all of the sudden big loud scratches are heard coming from in the direction of the kitchen, causing Samantha to jump ever so slightly and loose grip of the keys.

Leaving the keys on the floor and setting her handbag down, Samantha turns around and heads in the direction of the kitchen.

Opening the lower kitchen drawer and taking out what looks to be a spare set of keys, Samantha slowly puts a key into the back door, where opening the door at a nice and steady pace Samantha looks out at the back garden. Taking a look to her left all is clear. Then looking towards the right all seems to be clear too. Then as Samantha takes a step back into the kitchen and starts to close the door, the kitchen door suddenly bounces open knocking Samantha onto the floor, where jumping on top of her and barking his head off is her boarder collie, Jack.

"Jack, Jack calm down you little mutt." Samantha says as she tries to get up from the kitchen floor, which thank the heavens is clean or her dress would be as grimy as can be.

"What is this, a bark your brains out or jump on Samantha season?" Samantha says as she stands up, where Jack is still trying to jump on her due to being all hyper.

Heading over to the cupboard underneath the sink, Samantha opens it up and takes hold of a doggy bone.

"Jack, look what I've got for you." Samantha says as she takes hold of a bone. Then holding it up in the air Samantha walks back out to the garden as Jack jumps up and down like crazy for the bone.

Arriving at Jack's kennel the lead that's been fixed onto his kennel mustn't have been tied properly enough to Jack's collar, as it looks completely undamaged as Samantha picks it up.

Still being all hyper, Samantha watches Jack jump like she's trying to calculate on when's the best time to drop the bone and take hold of his collar to tie him up again.

"Three, two, one and..., grab." Samantha says as she quickly takes hold of Jack's collar when he lands on the floor from his continuous jumping. Then dropping the bone in front of Jack's entrance, Samantha ties Jack up good and strong.

"Good boy," Samantha says lovingly as she gives Jack a stroke as he lies in front of his kennel chewing away at the bone.

Being happy with the outcome Samantha heads back on into the house locking the kitchen door behind her and putting the keys back into the kitchen draw.

Walking up the hallway towards the couch and telephone, where Samantha doesn't even recognize the letter that's been placed under the telephone for her, she takes another glimpse into the mirror.

"Let's just hope you can tie up your date like that tonight," Samantha says as she points towards the kitchen.

"And he better be a good looking hunk if he thinks he's gonna get me lying down." Samantha says as she walks away from the mirror, though suddenly leaning back with only her face in view Samantha says, "Cuz if he ain't I'll be playin' dead for sure." Samantha says as she puts on a dastardly face.

Lifting up her handbag then the keys one after the other, Samantha unlocks the door and walks out of the house locking the door behind her.

Wandering away from the front door and heading towards the single filed country road that's just off the property, from the back of the house where Jack is, Jack starts barking his head off like crazy. Where it sounds more like a protective angry bark he's letting out.

"Ah, there's just no pleasing some." Samantha says as she waves her hand back at the house whilst not even facing it as she walks off. Then closing the gate behind her and walking off out of sight, as Samantha disappears in behind the trees to the woodlands that cover her house, Jack continues horrendously with his non-stop barking.

Heading around to the back of Samantha's house, Jack looks in towards the trees to the woods and continues to bark his head off like crazy, though looking in the same direction that Jack is staring at, the Stranger can be seen moving unsteadily in the distance in the same direction that

Samantha is heading, though there seems to be a large bright object being carried on their shoulders.

13.

"Well shall we go and get the fake ID's? As they look like they're gonna be the only hope on us gettin' any alcohol." Alan says to Paul. Where Paul isn't paying one bit of attention due to his eyes being stuck on the waitress who's carrying a tray in one hand, which she's holding above her head as she walks up to a table to serve drinks to other customers.

Outside the café and glaring through the window at the waitress, Paul shouts, "WOULD YOU LIKE MY NAME, OR EVEN MY ADDRESS?"

"Paul, get in the car." Alan says completely ashamed to be in the presence of Paul. Then as Paul opens the front passenger door to get into the car, he quickly runs up to the window, looks at the waitress through the glass and shouts, "I LOVE YOU." Where whilst doing so he blows some steam on the window from the warmth of his breath, where with not being able to see the waitress due to having made the window all cloudy, he starts to draw a picture of a love heart over the steamy widow.

Finishing his artistic attempt on drawing, he tilts his head to the right of the love heart and glares through the window and blows the waitress a kiss, then walks over to Alan's car and jumps into the car closing the door behind him.

"Paul you're fuckin' nuts, you know that?" Alan says as he starts to drive off. Though Paul isn't paying one bit of attention as to what Alan's saying, as Paul is in his own fantasy land.

"I wonder what she's like for dessert?" Paul says with a facial expression like he's trying to make a mental image of her in a dessert bowl.

"Don't you mean you wonder what she serves for dessert?" Alan says trying to correct Paul.

"No, *I wonder what she's like for dessert.*" Paul says nearly starting to drool over his thoughts like he's already got the dessert spoon in his hand.

Arriving back at the key shop Alan looks at Paul and says, "I take it you're back to normality now, huh?"

"Whatta you mean, I'm as normal as can be." Paul says to Alan weirdly.

"Yeah, my ass you're as normal as can be," Alan says.

"Well be it your ass or not, how does this sound, I'd like thirty bucks now please." Paul says straight out as if he's getting one up on Alan.

"What?" Alan says as he gives Paul a hefty look. "You want thirty dollars off me?" Paul doesn't reply and Alan continues, "Let's have a little bit of a recollection over who owes who money. Uh, last week who paid who into the nightclub? Who bought who the drink? Um, three days ago, who rang who over being stranded for cash and not having enough bucks to get their little smelly hole back home? Uh, who drove for three hours to that little pool club to where some prick lost all their money due to gambling it in New York? Oh, and not forgetting, who bought who the food on the journey also? Would you like me to go on?" Alan says not one bit impressed.

"Uh, you can if you wish, but in the long run the ID is still thirty dollars dude." Paul says not having a care in the world over what Alan's done for him.

"Here fuckerbrains," Alan says, "Here, here's thirty dollars, hope you choke on every one of them."

"Thank you," Paul says as he takes the money off Alan with not a care in the world or one single sign of guilt showing on his face as he pretends to choke over the notes that's been handed to him.

In at Roy's key shop, Paul walks on in where he see's Roy standing behind the counter.

"Well Roy," Paul says in a manner like he's known him for years.

"You're just in time man, they're just this second finished," Roy says as Paul arrives up to the counter. "But you'll have to be very careful with them though as the plastic cover the photos have been illuminated in are still a bit warm and might stand a chance on smudging the photos a little bit. I mean take a look at this old dudes face." Roy says busy showing Paul another ID to where a persons face has been completely smudged.

"Will do man." Paul says.

Heading into the back room, Roy picks up the original photos that are placed on top of an old news paper, dating back nearly 18 years. Where looking at the news paper as the ID's are lifted, the title on the news paper reads, "Husband, Wife & Son Killed."

Coming back into the shop from the back room, Roy hands Paul the photos and ID's, where with Paul noticing Roy and Alan isn't watching him, he quickly looks at Alan's ID, places his forefinger over Alan's face forcefully and presses into it, then he quickly slides the ID's into his shirt pocket.

"Uh, how much were you sayin' this was gonna cost again?" Paul says inquisitively.

"Ah, like I say, if you're a friend of Barry's have it on the house." Roy says.

"Are you serious now?" Paul says.

"I'd run incase I change my mind man." Roy says.

"Well it was nice doing business with you." Paul quickly says as he literally runs for the exit door.

"Ha, ha, ha, anytime dude, just pop on in," Roy says, "Enjoy your camping spree."

"Will do, and thanks again man." Paul says heading out of the key shop, where Roy just waves.

A little bit to the left and across the road from the key shop is a big hospital, where standing on the right hand side of the entrance door is the paparazzi and news reporters who are busy doing live news reports.

"…, with such good news over the successful separation of the conjoint twins Brian and Orlando today, I'd like to hand you back to our news room for the latest news up dates." Tracey says.

"And cut." Robert says, "That's a rap."

With the smile on Tracey's face dulling down a bit, she looks down towards the busy road where Paul is seen heading in the direction of Alan's car. Where noticing he's acting quite peculiar, she also notices Alan smiling away and rubbing his hands together as Paul gets into the car.

Removing her microphone that's attached to the top part of her dress, she gives her head a quick shake and takes hold of her cellular from her handbag.

"Well, any missed calls from you know who?" Robert says as he watches Tracey taking a quick glimpse at it.

"No, thank God. But I was more concerned that the cellular was on silent for both calls and messages." Tracey says starting to look a little bit hacked off.

"Was he actually conscious when you left him?" Robert says.

"Personally I couldn't give a shit." Tracey replies as her facial expression looks like she's picturing him in a boxing ring so she can throw another swing at him.

"So you haven't heard about the news then I take it?" Robert says whilst looking through his camera equipment.

"What? That he's vanished and been sucked up into outer space by devious man eating aliens?" Tracey says wishfully.

"No it's due to the phone call you got from him earlier," Robert says.

"Ah, no, don't tell me, I'm jobless, I'm jobless right?" Tracey says as she starts to get into a fighting mood.

"No, no, it's nowhere near anything like that," Robert says trying to give Tracey a bit of relief and reassurance.

"Well, what is it?" Tracey says nearly driving herself to despair.

"Thanks to him," Robert says lifting his head up a bit, "We all, as in everyone in our company, you know like news reporters and news groups, literally everyone ...,"

"Come on out with it!" Tracey says butting into Robert's sentence.

"..., we all got a nice big pay rise." Robert says finishing his sentence.

"What? Quit screwing with my mind," Tracey says not believing a single word said.

"No, I'm serious. Apparently some cell phone company made a yearly ten million dollar deal with the boss man." Robert says reassuringly.

"Bull. I don't believe you, you're talkin' the biggest pile of bullshit," Tracey says like she's near enough ready to black out.

"With you havin' taken the cellular outta your pocket while in the middle of doin' a live news report, this cell phone company was that impressed with it, they've made a deal with the boss man to have their cell phones advertised before and after every single news report we do, as in the whole company." Robert says.

Tracey just shakes her head in disbelief and remains silent.

14.

Walking through her front door and wiping her feet on the mat, Rachel heads on up the stairs busy being her nosey little self as she peeks on into all of the bedrooms, with hers being the last one. Where on the door before she enters the room a designed poster reads, 'No Men Allowed: Queen Rachel's Orders,' where below those words there's a photo of Rachel and Amy all dressed up with their angry cheeky faces.

As the door opens, looking around the room it is very tidy and well kept, though the posters and pictures on the wall are a representation of a lot of girl power.

Opening the bottom draw to her bedrooms large bookcase, she takes out the play station three and starts setting it up to her television that's placed on a make up table that's opposite her bed.

With having the play station connected to the television, then successfully having it tuned into one of the TV's channels, Rachel suddenly hears a noise coming from down the stairs. Where quickly getting up she runs to the top of the stairs and shouts down, "Mom, is it okay if Amy stays for the night?"

"Well sure I've a beauty appointment with Barbara at seven thirty, so we'll see what Barbara thinks," Rachel's Mum says.

Then as Rachel put's on a silent moaning impression, impersonating her Mum's moaning with her hand as if its her mothers lips, her Mum is at the bottom of the stairs watching her.

"And what's that supposed to mean?" Jean says making Rachel jump.

"Uh, nothin'," Rachel says knowing rightly she's been caught in on the act.

"Yeah, right, you're on thin ice." Rachel's Mum says, busy staring at Rachel. "Now come on down the stairs for lunch."

Heading down the stairs and impersonating her Mum again with more silent moaning impressions, her Mum quickly steps back and looks up the stairs at Rachel, catching her in the act for the second time.

Knowing rightly she's been caught out, Rachel comes to a halt, but quickly turns around as her Mum starts charging up the stairs in a joking manner and shouts, "Why wait till I get you, you little....,"

15.

At the location that Amy was last seen, there's no sign of her anywhere, no sign of her bike, and no sign of the Stranger that was lying in the ditch.

Though heading into the woods and dodging a few trees, Amy's bike has been thrown up against a tree on the left, where the front tire is parallel to the ground busy holding it up as the rear part of the bike leans up against the tree.

To the right from where the bike is, pieces of photos and newspapers have been torn up into little shreds, lying everywhere, where there's also big thick pieces of adhesive tape scattered around as well, with some pieces marked with blood. Though there is no sign of Amy or the scruffy looking Stranger anywhere.

16.

Sitting in the office alone, Steve is busy looking through some crime scene folders and doesn't look happy in the slightest. But down at his cellular on the table the only name that's in view is, 'Tracey', which Steve is just staring at, then distracting him, Jake walks into the room.

"Well are you up for it?" Jake says to Steve. Then Jake points at the television that's on silent, to which Tracey appears busy representing the joint separation of the twin's conditions.

"Cuz she only got keepin' that job through the skin of her teeth. Apparently she was in the right place at the right time. Plus, if you manage to get out of the boss mans room alive, cuz I think he's gonna chew you up, spit you out and dance all over you, we'll have to settle that twenty bucks bet we had goin' a while back." Jake says.

Getting up from his chair Steve walks to the door where Jake is standing, where patting Jake on the back Steve says, "Wish me luck partner."

"Kick some balls bro." Jake says.

"The last time you said that dude it was my balls gettin' kicked man. You recollect." Steve says.

"Come on, you're never gonna let me live that down are you?" Jake says as Steve heads out of the office closing the door behind him, busy getting stared at from all the other work colleagues.

17.

With the afternoons sky being as bright and clear as a whistle, on the road a clear white van, which looks quite smart due to the borders of it having been painted black, it's entering into a busy housing estate, where the houses are of a large size and very spacious from each other.

On the driver's side of the van, to which the window's rolled down, Ryan has a grin on his face and is singing along to the music that's playing on the radio station, near enough carrying out the dance moves in the process too. Though starting to slow down with the grin on his face turning into an unimpressed look, he notices Alan's car is parked outside Chris's house already.

"I dunno, if these guys are screwin' with me I'm gonna kick their fuckin' butts from here to the pissin' camp site," Ryan says as he parks the van down Chris's driveway behind Alan's car.

Suddenly Chris's front door opens as Ryan is just about to start up the engine and drive off, due to thinking the jokes on him and that the guys have pulled a prank, though stepping out of the front door and waving him on in is Chris's fiancée, Alison Neilley. So removing the keys from the van, Ryan opens the drivers van door and heads towards Alison.

"I take it these guys are screwin' around and that the jokes on me, right?" Ryan says.

"Well you *could* say that," Alison says as she pats Ryan on the back as he enters the house. Though arriving on into the living room Alison points at Alan, Paul and Chris as they act like a bunch of babies trying to sort themselves out.

"I'm telling you Ryan they have been so disorganized since they've got here, they still can't decide what they wanna take." Alison says as she strokes a piece of her long black hair away from her eyes.

"And what happened to the….," Ryan impersonates Chris's voice, "Uh, you mean you'd rather be in the woods with a bunch of no hopes than in the town with the guys partying?" Then going back to his normal voice Ryan says, "From the looks of it I'm taking a bunch of no hopes."

"Ah, get bent!" Chris says as he strokes the penknife he's holding.

"I rest my case," Ryan says as he does a spitting image of Alan over what he said before the exams.

"Ah, screw you." Alan says as he shines a torch right into Ryan's face.

"And look at the babies, they're still not ready." Ryan says.

Paul, Alan and Chris stick up their middle fingers at Ryan and give him the evil looks. But nearly making them jump out of their skin Alison shouts, "COME ON, COME ON. GET UP OFF THOSE FAT ASSES AND GET THAT GEAR IN THE VAN." Then she smiles at Ryan and puts on her gentle voice and says, "Tea Ryan?"

"Yeah, uh, thanks a lot." Ryan says in a manner that he doesn't want to mess with her. Where as Alison heads off to the kitchen, Alan, Paul and Chris give Ryan hasty hit men looks as they take hold of their camping gear and start walking out of the room also.

"How'd you like it Ryan?" Alison shouts from the kitchen.

"Black, two sugars and damn hot." Ryan says starting to sound like he's another man altogether.

"Is it not supposed to be you are what you eat, not what you drink?" Chris says as he takes a little peek back into Ryan.

"Yeah, I suppose you've gotta a point." Ryan says where Chris nods happily and walks out of sight again. Though continuing with his sentence Ryan says, "As you look and smell like a heap of shit man, I'd hate to see what you've been eatin'." Where startling Ryan from behind, Alison comes up with a black cup of tea and hands it to him, where Ryan has a look on his face that he's just about to get a boxing over the comment he made about Chris.

"I've got to admit, you've gotta a point Ryan. He could improve with his cooking." Alison surprisingly says.

"But I don't cook." Chris is heard shouting from down the hallway.

"Precisely!" Alison says.

As Ryan takes a sip of his tea he says to Alison, "How on earth do you manage to get your hair layered like that? Does it not take you forever?"

"Nah, it only took a few seconds, plus I don't like having my long hair dangling down when I'm sorting things out in the kitchen anyway," Alison says as she offers Ryan a biscuit from the selection of assorted biscuits she has on a plate.

"Thanks." Ryan says taking hold of a digestive biscuit, but as he's just about to slip it into his mouth Paul swipes it from him and puts it back on the plate, then on the other side of Ryan, Alan takes hold of the cup of tea and says, "I'll take that," where he sets the tea on the table.

"What the fuck are you pricks playin' at, excuse my French?" Ryan says as he looks towards Alison.

"No worries, I'm quite shit at French too." Alison says.

"Right it's time to go." Paul says busy escorting Ryan towards the living room door, with assistance from Alan.

"Hay he hasn't even finished his tea." Alison says as Chris walks up to her.

"Sorry but we got our orders from the boss man," Alan says as he points towards Chris.

"Help I'm getting attacked by aliens." Ryan whimpers as he pretends to fight for his freedom.

"We'll be out in the van big man. Take your time." Alan says as he walks to the hallway still pretending to drag Ryan out with Paul.

Walking up to the fire place, Chris takes hold of his wallet and a wad of cash sitting beside it and fires it in his pocket. Then as he turns around Alison's already standing right in front of him and says, "Oh, do you have to go?" Where Chris taking hold of her hands as he kisses her on the forehead says, "Yeah, they look like they're gonna be needin' someone to do the baby sitting for them," where not even getting a chance to say another word, Alison puts her arms around him, slips her tongue into his mouth and starts to kiss him big time.

Yet glaring through the living room window from outside, Paul, Alan and Ryan are staring in with their depressed, deprived and gloomy faces.

"I'm gonna miss this with you bein' away." Alison says.

"Well it doesn't look like you're gonna be the only one that'll be missin' it," Chris says as he notices they're being glared at.

"I'd like to think so!" Alison says as if Chris isn't going to miss a bit of love.

"No, it's the miserable faces perverting through the window I'm talkin' about." Chris says. Where turning around Alison laughs and starts to blow three kisses in the direction of Paul, Alan and Ryan, where all three of them pretend to grab hold of the kiss that's been sent to them, which they all place on their hearts then start to act stupid with continuously blowing each other kisses.

"I better get going babe," Chris says as he gives Alison another romantic kiss.

"Huh, it's a pity Ryan's cuppa tea went to waste." Alison says as she notices the scalding cup on the table letting off steam.

"You should know nothin' goes to waist in this house," Chris says as he takes hold of the cup of tea and drinks it down in one gulp.

With the tea completely finished the only thing that remains at the bottom of the cup is the slimy remainders of biscuit pieces that slither's back into the cup as Chris sets it back on the table. But looking at Chris's face as he stands up tall, his eyes are as watery as can be, where with him doing just one blink the tear starts to roll down his face.

"See, even I don't wanna go," Chris says pointing at the tear.

"I know, I know," Alison says as she gives Chris another sexy kiss.

Where still glaring through the living room window from outside, Ryan, Paul and Alan are pretending to put on the water works as they cuddle back and forth to each other as well.

Walking behind Chris to the door and giving him one last kiss, Alison says, "Hurry back now." Where as Chris gets into the van and Ryan starts the engine, they all blow Alison kisses non stop, and Alison busy laughing blows a kiss directly to Chris.

"That was to me man," Alan says as they start to drive off.

"Just you dream on you little prick." Chris says, where as he looks back at Alison his lips read, 'I love you'.

18.

Sitting in an unmarked car with their windows wound down, busy having a bight to eat, Jake and Steve keep peeking across the road towards a large selection of shops that are in the centre of Boston Cities High Street.

"So how'd your little talk go with the boss man?" Jake says as he takes another chunk of his well dressed colorful donut.

"Instead of being in one of his dancing moods and dancing all over me with his mumbo jumbo, he's sure managed to kick the beat off." Steve says as he squints his eyes like he's going through some form of pain.

"Whatta you mean?" Jake says.

"As my ears are still pumpin' due to Master Loud-Mouth's shoutin' off over the usual shit. At least I think it was the usual shit he was filling my head with anyway, as my ears popped half way through and started kickin' off with a beat." Steve says.

"You must have an infection of some kind," Jake says.

"What?" Steve says.

"I say you must have an infection."

"What?" Steve says messing about as if he can't hear him.

"Ah, fuck you, you prick." Jake says catching on that Steve's messing with him.

"Gotcha." Steve says as he takes a slurp of his drink, but Jake pushes the drink higher, where with Steve not being ready for it some of the drink ends up in his face and on his clothes.

"Gotcha back," Jake says, "You've gotta be quicker than that man."

After a few seconds with Steve giving himself a clean over Jake says, "It's good to see you're back dude."

"Ah, you knew I'd be back eventually," Steve says.

"And thank the heavens." Jake says.

"Why's that?" Steve says.

"Cuz the boss man was gonna get rid of you, on a permanent basis, a couple of times and try hooking me up with the wrong arms of the law." Jake says.

"Let me guess, B.O., the wrong arms of the law." Steve says taking hold of his nose.

"Yeah, you got it in one, Mr. Brothers, the heap of shit you couldn't stay in the same room with for more than two seconds." Jake says.

"How the heck has he managed to remain in this job? I'm surprised the tracker dogs haven't chewed up his smelly whole." Steve says.

"He's a nephew to the boss man," Jake says.

"Ah, that explains a lot." Steve says.

"And speakin' of the boss man, you remember us stickin' that twenty dollar bet on Tracey's boss man, over bein' a bit of a fruit with dressin' up in ladies wear?" Jake says.

"Uh, vaguely." Steve says.

"Well let me remind you. Remember when I told you he's a trans and you said he was just gettin' some lingerie for his other half, and there was twenty bucks ridin' on it?" Jake says.

"Ah, now I remember." Steve says.

"Well look who's off into the 'Sex-ray Shop' across the road." Jake says, "I bet the bender will walk out with two bags worth."

"They are hardly gonna be for him man," Steve says.

"Here, let me let you into a little secret. You see with Tracey nearly gettin' fired earlier?" Jake says.

"Yeah, due to me screwin' up on my end and callin' her while she was live on air." Steve says, still unimpressed with himself.

"Ah, but you know how she got her job back?" Jake says.

"How?" Steve says.

"Cuz I gave him a little call earlier, due to gettin' his number off Tracey a while back, where when he got a little talkin' to he got strait onto the phone to Tracey in regards to her being the closest to that news report we seen earlier about the joint separation of the twins, where she got her job back there and then." Jake says.

"I still think you're dreamin' man, it's for his old lady friend he's gettin' the shit for." Steve says.

"Let's see his reaction when he comes out." Jake says.

A few minutes pass and Jake says, "Keep your eyes peeled on the door Steve."

"I can't wait to see that twenty bucks of yours." Steve says.

A couple more minutes pass and Jake and Steve are finishing off their donuts and drinking away at their drinks, then suddenly a blond lady walks out of the door wearing a lovely designed top and bottoms, a bit of facial make up and a couple of bags in her hands, though looking down at her feet, Jake notices she's wearing manly shoes.

"Right are you ready to check this out?" Jake says as he opens up his cellular and presses a few buttons. Suddenly the long blonde female across the road comes to a halt and takes out a cell phone from their pocket.

"This is the police, stop what you're doing, drop your bags slowly and turn around slowly unveiling yourself, though if you make any wrong moves we'll be forced to take action." Jake says as he looks across the busy road with Steve as they both remain seated in the car.

Then turning around in front of a numerous amount of people from the publics busy high street, who are wondering what the blonde is up to. As the blonde turns around and loses balance, their blond wig falls off revealing a manly face.

"It's me, the manager to BIDN news," he shouts as he looks around for where the police warning is coming from, "I'm not a criminal." He shouts as he attempts to remove some make up.

"Hand it over," Jake says as he waves his own twenty dollars in front of Steve, so handing Jake twenty dollars, the two of them drive off as Jake hangs his cellular up.

"What do you want me to hand over?" Tracey's boss shouts as every Tom, Dick and Harry look at him strangely.

"Hello, hello…," Tracey's boss shouts down his cellular not having the foggiest what to do.

19.

With the exasperating noise of music that's playing, backed up by the pitiful attempt to sing along with it, Ryan's van looks like it's about to erupt with the way it's bouncing up and down as the wheels go around.

Trying his utmost hardest to concentrate on the road, Ryan's not able to alter the volume to the music, as it's coming from the radio that Paul is holding in the back of the van.

"Do you wanna stop and get somethin' for the trip?" Ryan says as he tries to talk over the music.

"WHAT?" Chris shouts, unable to hear what Ryan's going on about.

"I SAY, DO YOU WANNA STOP HERE?" Ryan shouts.

"I CAN'T HEAR YOU." Chris shouts.

Not even attempting to waist another bit of breath on them, Ryan takes the next right off the freeway, where arriving in front of a large petrol station, shop, café, chemist and gambling arcade, that's all combined together in one big building, Paul turns the volume to the music down and says, "Whatta you at?"

"Well I was trying to ask you noisy little pricks on whether you wanted to stop off and get somethin' for the camping spree," Ryan says as the van completely stops with him turning off the engine.

"So I take it we're stopping?" Paul says.

"Well, duh!" Alan says to Paul sarcastically.

"And if you're not back in half an hour I'm gone." Ryan says as he gets out of the van.

"Well here, you might need these," Paul says as he dips into his pocket.

"What?" Chris says as he gets out of the van.

"The fake ID's," Paul says being the last one to get out of the van. Then closing the door behind him he starts handing out the fake ID's.

"Oh, I forgot all about the ID's that were gettin' made on the account of our little baby bear Alan!" Chris says being the first one to receive his ID, where as soon as it's slid into his pocket, he dips into his other pocket for his box of cigarettes, quickly setting a light to one of them.

"Yeah," Paul says as he hands Ryan and Alan theirs at the same time.

"And what the fuck happened to mine?" Alan says looking at his angrily.

"Whatsa matta?" Chris says.

"Look at it," Alan says as he hands it to Chris in disgust.

Starting to laugh his head off like crazy, Chris hands the ID to Ryan, to who also starts laughing uncontrollably too.

"Doesn't it make him look so manly?" Ryan says still laughing.

Taking the piss out of Alan as they walk off, Chris and Paul say together, "He's the man, he's the man."

Not impressed one bit Alan looks at the three of them walk off in front of him with Paul being in the middle.

"What a fuckin' con artist. If I were you guys I'd keep the thirty bucks he's intending on taking off you, in your pockets." Alan says.

Then the atmosphere turns silent with the laughing coming to a halt, where walking in between Ryan and Chris, Paul says, "What? Thirty dollars an ID ain't bad."

"Yeah, well you can give me back my fuckin' thirty bucks, as this is a pile of shit." Alan says as he comes in line with Chris and Ryan, with Paul still walking off on his own. Though Chris, Ryan and Alan just stand still and look at Paul harshly. Though not waiting around, Paul continues to walk off busy checking over his shoulder every five seconds.

20.

To the rear of Mixtures, where there's two gigantic metal dumpsters behind it that are approximately four foot high, behind the dumpsters there's a brick wall, which is the height of the dumpsters and the width of Mixtures itself.

Behind the dumpsters and beyond the wall, it's completely covered with wood land surroundings as far as the eye can see.

Suddenly hearing a noise coming from the fire exit door to Mixtures as the door opens slowly, as it gradually opens bit by bit, Samantha eventually appears, busy struggling to drag a large heavy black bag from the fire exit towards the dumpster.

Eventually managing to get the bag up to the dumpster, Samantha stands up strait and gives her back a big stretch, with the relief wrote all over her facial expression. Then psyching herself up, Samantha goes for glory and opens the lid to the dumpster whilst trying to lift the rubbish bag up at the same time.

"Mmm-mmm!" Samantha whimpers as she tries her utmost hardest to pick up the bag, though failing to tip the bag into the dumpster as she near enough reaches the top, Samantha just lets it fall to the floor whilst quickly moving her foot away from being crushed.

"Ah, I'll leave it to the big guy." Samantha says as she closes the lid to the dumpster and heads back on into Mixtures, closing the fire exit door behind her.

Arriving back into Mixtures, Samantha takes a look around the bars lounge with a depressing look on her face.

"I've gotta get a new job." Samantha says. Where looking around the bar the place looks like it's just been hit by a tornado, as it's an absolute pigsty.

Glimpsing up at a little poster that's on the wall it reads in big black block capitals, "**EARLY ARRIVALS RECEIVE AN AWARD**," Samantha just shakes her head which lowers in a shameful manner.

    Back at the rear of Mixtures to where the dumpster is, the lid to the dumpster that Samantha had closed, is open again, where drifting back a bit from looking at the dumpster the scruffy looking Stranger just stands there like a statue glaring on into it.

    Taking a look into the dumpster, the figure of a body which is rapped up in big thick adhesive tape has been placed on top of the rubbish, where the only part of the body that can be seen due to it not having been covered properly is the dead eyes. Also looking at the chest part to the taped up figure, a little cut out of what looks like a photo can be seen.

    Drifting back from the dumpster a bit, the Stranger is no longer in sight. Though looking up towards the woods a dark figure is seen fading away in the distance.

    Coming from the same direction as to where the Stranger is slowly disappearing out of sight, dog barks start going off like crazy from the same direction. Though all of the sudden they change into whimpers, then suddenly stop.

    Looking back towards the body in the dumpster, the cut out of a photo that is placed in between a part of the adhesive tape that the bodies been rapped up in, only shows the lower part of somebody's legs, which is completely impossible to make out as to who it is.

    Breaking the silence all of the sudden, standing on the lid to the dumpster, Jack notices the rapped up body inside it and starts barking his head off like mad, where he continuously has his two front paws bouncing up and down on the lid as if he's trying to push what's scaring him away. Though with his non-stop barking and his front paws bouncing up and down, the lid to the dumpster closes itself over due to the force he's putting on it, where landing nice and steady on the ground Jack turns around to the dumpster again and starts barking his head off like mad.

Inside Mixtures which is starting to look a lot tidier, Samantha finishes filling another bag of rubbish, totaling the amount of rubbish bags up to a bunch of five hefty filled bags that are packed to the brims.

"Who the heck's mutt is that makin' all that noise?" Samantha says as she takes hold of one of the rubbish bags which she's able to lift as she heads for the fire exit door.

Opening the fire exit door and lifting up the rubbish bag that she set down for a second, Samantha looks towards the dumpster and notices it's her own little mutt, Jack.

"Jack what're you playin' at, huh? I think the next time I tie you up I'll make sure your ropes tied up in quadruple knots for both your collar and your kennel." Samantha says.

Throwing the rubbish bag on the floor beside the bag that Samantha could hardly lift, Samantha takes hold of Jack and brings him towards the fire exit door, where with the remainder of the lead that's attached to Jack's collar, Samantha ties it up through the metal hole coming from the door stopper to the fire exit door.

Heading in and out of Mixtures a few times, Samantha throws the remainder of the rubbish bags on the floor next to the other heavy bags that she couldn't lift, more or less looking like she's doing it for revenge on her work colleague.

Walking out of Mixtures again, instead of carrying more rubbish Samantha has a bowl of water in her hand that she sets down beside Jack.

"Now you be a good boy and I **might** come back for you later, okay?" Samantha says giving her orders as she strokes Jack's head gently.

Inside Mixtures with Samantha having the place looking like it's brand new, as Samantha walks in from the back entrance and arrives behind the bar the front door to Mixtures opens, where walking in is an old man in his mid sixties who is dressed up in near enough winter clothing.

"Are you expecting weather we're not Norman?" Samantha says as she stares him up and down.

"Nah, it's just the age." Norman says, "And it's a true fact, the blood gets colder as one gets older."

"If you had've been here a couple of hours earlier I'm sure I would've had plenty of work for you to keep you warm, as this place was like somethin' the devils swallowed and spat out." Samantha says.

"Yeah, the poker was on last night and went on all night." Norman says.

"So that explains as to why I walked into this Barbaric pit hole." Samantha says, "Well what about yourself, were you in on the poker?" Samantha says making Norman feel uncomfortable.

"Yeah, though I got my butt kicked within the first three rounds." Norman says.

"Ah, well." Samantha says coming around to her polite mannered usual self. "Better luck next time, huh?" Samantha says as she takes hold of a couple of different sized glasses.

"Yeah, better luck next time, huh?" Norman says looking a little bit more relaxed.

"So what can I get you?" Samantha says.

"Well I'll take a new knee bone, an arthritis cure and anythin' you can give to make the vision a bit better." Norman says messing around.

"Ah," Samantha says putting her thinking cap on. "So you want alcohol, alcohol and lots more alcohol?" Samantha says as she starts to laugh.

"Yeah, you can kick me off with a nice hot whiskey first, huh?" Norman asks as he takes his wallet out of his pocket and opens it up with a pile of notes coming into view.

"I thought you said you got your butt kicked on the first three rounds?" Samantha questions.

"I did…," Norman says busy looking all innocent, "…, on the drink, but I won eight hundred dollars of poker bucks if that's what you were on about?" Norman says.

"You're fly," Samantha says as she hands Norman his hot whiskey, which is being supported by an empty cool glass underneath it.

"Bottoms up," Samantha says as she sets the glass in front of Norman.

"What would I do without you? Here, get yourself a drink too." Norman says.

"Don't be silly put your money back, have the first one on the house. After all it was me who cleaned this place up like crazy. I have to get my revenge on the boss man some how." Samantha says.

"Well I'll be gettin' you a drink before you leave this place tonight for sure, even if it means me gettin' behind that bar and servin' you myself." Norman says.

"Oh, you're bad, what are you?" Samantha says.

Suddenly Samantha's friends start walking in.

"But until the boss man enters on in the drinks for Norman, Cheryl, Alicia and Lucie are on the house." Samantha announces out loud.

Running up to the bar they quickly call out their orders, though as they do a car parks up outside.

"You may throw them down you quick if you're after another one," Samantha says as she quickly hands everyone a drink, "As there's the boss man just arrived," Samantha says pointing to a photo of a her boss who has a trophy in his hand, where the title on the poster reads, 'Lee Granger – Bar of the Year'.

With throwing the drink down them as Samantha quickly pours out a second round, as Samantha lays the drinks in front of them Lee walks in through the door, where they all look at him innocently.

"And look who's finally arrived?" Samantha rudely says.

"I am impressed Samantha," Lee says as he looks around on how tidy the place is.

"Yeah, but I notice you come when the jobs done." Samantha insinuates. "It was like a bomb hit the place. What the heck went on last night?"

"When you left at one in the morning, they were still playing cards running on until seven, and I was just out for the count on doin' anythin'." Lee says.

"Oh, so you thought you'd leave all the dirty work for me, ah, I get the picture!" Samantha says.

"Well you can finish early tonight if you want," Lee says.

"Ah, I need the money anyway. Plus I'm still looking for Mr. Right tonight." Samantha says all disheartened.

"How about a pay rise then?" Lee says.

"Keep talkin'," Samantha says quickly perking on a smile.

"How's four dollars sound?" Lee asks.

"What, an extra measly four dollars for a whole nights work? Ouch, last of the big spenders." Samantha disrespectfully says.

"No, I was thinkin' of four dollars extra per hour on top of your usual hourly wage." Lee states.

"As in my hourly wage being increased by an extra four dollars per hour?" Samantha states in a clarifying manner.

"Yeah, I couldn'tve put it better." Lee says.

"Nice, nice. The next drinks on the house." Samantha says making everyone's eyes rise, though Lee's isn't overly impressed whatsoever.

"Yeah, right," Lee says, "After the amount've money Norm walked out with last night. I think you'll find he'll be the main dude buyin' all the drink tonight." With Lee's reactions, everyone suddenly starts to slow down with their drinking procedures.

"I dunno, after all the times Norman's helped you out, and this is the way you repay him. I mean helpin' me clean this place over earlier and bein' our main customer and all, who's even helped you behind the bar when you were snowed under." Samantha says busy forcing the guilt on Lee.

"What, when he was behind the bar last time he drank more drink than he handed out." Lee sharply says.

"Ah, but after helpin' me clean this place up in the state it was in."

Samantha says as her friends and Norman are busy looking back and forth from Samantha to Lee to see who's going to win the argument.

"Well you're only gettin' one round on the house, then after that it's pay your own way or you'll all drink me dry," Lee states.

"Hmmm, drink dry!" Samantha says busy fantasizing over getting drunk.

"You've still got it in you," Norman says as he pats Samantha's hand like he's laying on five.

All of the sudden, taking everyone's mind off the arguing, loud barks start going off from outside.

"What's that?" Lee says.

"Uh, to my knowledge they are dog barks," Norman sarcastically says.

"I know that, but what's it doin' here?" Lee says.

"Uh, barkin'," Norman says cockily.

As Lee looks at Norman like he wants to box the lights out of him Samantha says, "It's Jack, he's tied up outside, he got off the lead back home and ended up barking his head off outside earlier, so I tied him up out back."

"Well he better not scare off the customers, as the way you dudes are goin' I'll need all the profits I can get." Lee says.

"Don't worry we'll go easy on you." Samantha says, "Won't we everyone?" Samantha says as everyone puts on an innocent sympathetic face.

"Well I'll be out back dealing with stocks and orders." Lee says.

As he walks out of sight, Samantha quickly hands everyone a third drink and says, "Here's to revenge!"

21.

With the cafeteria picking up business and the car park to the freeways lay-by only having a few spaces left, with cars coming and going, Ryan, sitting at a table to the cafeteria on his own is all depressed as he gazes out the window, as over towards the amusement and gambling arcade, where the time on the wall reads 17:15 hours, below the clock is a coin dispenser, where with a few gambling machines to the left of it, Paul, Alan and Chris are gambling their hearts out.

Getting up from his chair and walking towards the compulsive gamblers, as Ryan looks over the little banister, he can see how the three of them have their eyes so fixated on the different shapes, colors and pictures busy spinning around at high speeds, and he says, "Guys the stop off was supposed to be thirty minutes, not three fuckin' hours. Are we movin' or what?"

"Yes, yes, yes, **yes, yes, yes, YES, YES, YES!**" Paul crazily shouts.

"What's up with you you prick, he only asked a question?" Chris says to Paul.

"I've won!" Paul replies in disbelief.

"What did you get?" Alan says as he eventually manages to remove his eyes from the machine he's playing.

"*Five mothering fucking thousand dollars,*" Paul says as he presses the collect button. "And I was down to my last buck as well. Thank fuck I got that thirty bucks off of you earlier." Paul says as he looks at Alan, then at the money as it flies out of the machine.

"You know what this means?" Paul says as the money pounces out of the machine, "**PARTY.**" Paul shouts whilst he rubs his hands together.

22.

Busy getting dinner organized in the kitchen and chopping away at the food, Barbara hears the front door open.

"And where have you been?" Barbara says as she quickly dries her hands with the tea towel.

"Uh, work," Pete says peeking into the kitchen.

"Oh, I thought you were Amy, I was ready to give her a right chewin'. I still am too, as she hasn't been home since she raced off with you this mornin'." Barbara says.

"Jeepers, that's not like our little angel, huh?" Pete says looking slightly worried.

"Well for her sake she better have a good explanation for it." Barbara says.

"Sure I'll go and take a little spin around and see if I can find her anywhere." Pete says.

"But dinners gonna be ready soon." Barbara says.

"Sure I'll warm it up when I get back." Pete says as he points towards the microwave, where continuing with his sentence he says, "After all we did get this for a reason I'm near sure, huh, huh?" Then Pete starts acting silly as if he's a comedian trying to make a joke out of it.

"You'll probably find she's just got carried away with her friends and didn't recognize the time." Barbara says. Though looking into her eyes it's plain to see there's a definite sign of worry that is starting to unfold slowly.

"Well there's no harm in lookin' then is there?" Pete says to Barbara as he gives her a kiss on the lips, then giving her belly a gentle rub he bends down and gives it a kiss as well and says, "I love you's."

Barbara looking down at Pete, who's face is still in line with her belly replies back to him using sign language, where she points at her eye and belly at the same time, points towards her heart, then points at Pete, with finally showing her two fingers combined together, meaning, 'We love you too'.

"I'll find her and bring her home." Pete says as he looks into Barbara's eyes.

Then as Pete heads off closing the door behind him Barbara looks down towards her belly and says, "I hope so."

23.

Packing up the accessories from doing their news reports outside the hospital, the paparazzi are packing up like lightening. One van in particular has a person jump in it like crazy shouting, "Go, go, go. There's just been a brutal murder and bank robbery down at…," the news reporter slams the sliding door over before the rest of his sentence even finishes as the van speeds off like crazy, with the rest of the paparazzi packing up and following the news van like wildfire .

"Come on are you not up for this one?" Robert says whilst getting all hyper and packing his equipment away quicker. Then suddenly Tracey's cellular rings, to which she takes a quick look at it to see whose name is in view.

"Ah! Who the hell could this be?" Tracey says before she answers the phone due to not recognizing the number on her cellular.

"Hello," Tracey says as she presses the call button uncomfortably. Then the look on her face suddenly glows in disbelief, she remains silent for a few seconds.

"Uh, okay!" Tracey says in the process of slowly hanging up her cellular.

"Who was that?" Robert asks.

"It was the boss man," Tracey says still looking like she's on cloud nine.

"Don't tell me, you're fired again?" Robert says.

"No. Nowhere near! It's quite the opposite. He's said with my news report at the hospital being so good I can have two weeks full paid vacation." Tracey says.

"Shit that man must be sniffing with the decisions he's been makin' this day." Robert says. "And whattabout the shooting and bank robbery that's goin' on at the moment?"

"He's already got someone else coverin' those tracks." Tracey says,

"He told me to just get on with enjoying my holiday which starts from tomorrow."

"Holey crap, I think the man's lost the plot altogether." Robert says.

"I know, as he's given you two weeks paid vacation too, starting from tomorrow as well." Tracey says as she looks at Robert.

"Well come on then hurry up, let's get packin'." Robert says.

"But we're not needed for anythin'." Tracey says.

"No, it's incase he changes his mind." Robert says.

Taking another look at her cellular, Tracey looks quit tempted to make a call to Steve, but hesitantly she puts her cellular back in her handbag.

- -

Walking into his apartment, to which the room is still darkened from the curtains still being closed, Steve closes the front door behind him and heads towards the living room, where with taking one look into the complete abomination, Steve turns the light off and walks in the direction of his bedroom, to which the door remains half open after he heads on in.

24.

With the night starting to darken in the secluded woodlands, strange as it may seem there is a lovely smell coming from somewhere.

Following the direction of the smell and seeing a fire flaming away up ahead, arriving at the fire there's still Alan, Paul and Ryan attempting to put up tents while Chris is Barbecuing away.

"Grubs up guys," Chris says as he smokes away at a cigarette and dishes out the burgers, sausages and bacon onto some disposable plates. But whilst dishing out food on one of the plates he drops a sausage on the floor, quickly picks it up, where with none of the guys watching him screw about, he quickly puts it back on the plate.

As he walks up to the Barbecue with Paul and Ryan, Alan says, "Ah, it's not a bad place we've found here guys, huh?"

"Wow, a measly fuckin' forty minutes drive from home, big deal," Ryan says unimpressed. "I may as well of camped in my Pop's backyard."

"Look on the bright side, with the amount've money I've got and that place Mixtures we passed earlier on only being a stone throw away from here, we won't be short've drink now, huh?" Paul says.

"Well come on never mind the money for now, get tuckin' into all my hard work before it starts goin' cold," Chris says as the hefty weight of his foot stumps down on the remainder of his cigarette while he chews on a piece of burger.

Grabbing hold of his food first, Alan says, "Well has anyone got any shit scary stories to tell while we eat?"

Watching Alan munch away on his sausage, Chris says, "Yeah, you see that sausage you're chewin' on, that was the one that fell on the floor and I accidently stood on it!"

Alan's mouth stops chewing as the guys look at him and laugh.

"Now you think that's scary, place your big buts in front of the fire and I'll tell you some real shit scary stories that are true." Chris says.

Walking towards the direction of the flames Alan spits the remainder of the sausage he has in his mouth onto the fire.

"Was that not cooked to your perfection dude?" Chris says as he watches Alan disperse of the sausage.

25.

"Well this is me here," Tracey says as herself and Robert drive down a very private secluded driveway, where thirty yards up ahead is Tracey's Grandma's house which is completely pitch black.

"It's a nice little cottage house," Robert says as the lights from the news van beam on it, "But it looks like no ones home."

"No, that's cuz my Grandma past away two years back," Tracey says.

"Jeepers, I'm sorry to hear that," Robert says as they park up in front of the house.

"Oh, you shouldn't be," Tracey says, "I know it's a sin to say but with the non-stop pain she was goin' through, I think the little angel was better off being up with my grandpa now, as the agonizing pain she suffered was unreal. But one thing about her, even though you could see the pain she was goin' through in her eyes, is that she always managed to smile without a fail, and with having lost her ability to talk she always managed to get the words out, 'I love you', without a fail." Tracey says.

"She sure sounds like she was a mighty lady to be with." Robert says.

"Yeah, it's a pity I couldn'tve got spendin' more time with her." Tracey says as she lowers her head a little.

"Well I'm sure she's in good hands now and proud to be lookin' down on how you're gettin' on with your life, huh?" Robert says trying to perk Tracey up a bit, but suddenly looking a bit agitated himself Robert looks towards Tracey for a few seconds as if he's trying to think on what way to word his next sentence.

"Just outta curiosity," Robert says as Tracey takes hold of her cellular from her hand bag and just glares at it, "Did you ever hear, or did Steve ever tell you about the story on what happened to his last partner?"

"As in partner in crime?" Tracey questions.

"No, no, uh, as in lady friend, who at that time was his wife to be." Robert says, still uneasy on going any further with supplying her with anymore information.

"No why what happened, did she dump him or somethin'?" Tracey asks.

"Now I want you to swear if he ever asks on where you got this information from that it wasn't my small talk that told you, alright?" Robert says busy waiting for her to hold her right hand up to God, or something to that affect.

"What?" Tracey says more or less looking for an answer. Then noticing that Roberts keeping his silence and near enough giving her the evil eye, Tracey takes the hint and says, "Okay, I won't, you've got my word." Then she just glares at him.

"Well it was roughly a year before the two of you started goin' with each other that he was lined up for the wedding bells to start kicking off." Robert says.

"And what was her name?" Tracey asks looking more jealous than curious.

"Angelina Summons." Robert says where he literally stops talking altogether.

"And, and?" Tracey agitatedly says.

"She was found on the floor stabbed to death in the cellar next to the ironing board." Robert says in disbelief.

"Holey fuckin' shit," Tracey says looking like she's completely gob smacked.

"Now I want you to swear to me you'll not tell him I told you about this, huh, please?" Robert uncomfortably says, not looking one bit happy that it was him that broke the news.

"No, no, I'll keep it under raps," Tracey says, "Shit no wonder he's hit the drink big time."

As the van remains silent for a few seconds, Tracey says, "God only knows why he's never told me about this before."

"Who knows, there was probably never a right time to tell you, but like I say you didn't hear it from me, I wanna stay around for a little bit longer." Robert worryingly says.

"You've got my word." Tracey says as she pats Robert on the shoulder, "And thanks."

"No problem," Robert says still looking worried due to working himself up.

"Now," Tracey says, "To calm those nerves down, do you wanna cuppa?"

"Personally I wouldn't say no, as I've had jack shit in me all day." Robert says.

"I hope you take it black, as there'll be no shoppin' done till t'morrow," Tracey says as she gets her belongings and opens the passenger door to the van.

"I take mine anyway, be it food or drink, I've got to admit I've never been a fussy individual." Robert says as he turns the lights to the van off making everywhere completely pitch black. Though quickly locking and unlocking the van automatically, by pressing the button that's attached to the vans keys, it has the lights inside the van going on and off, enabling Tracey to get to the front door of the house and find the keyhole a bit easier.

Inside the house Tracey turns the hall light on that isn't overly bright and says, "Jeepers do you smell that?"

"Uh, no, I don't have a sense of smell." Robert says.

"That's probably why you drink and eat anythin' put in front of you, huh." Tracey says.

"More than likely." Robert says.

"Well personally it stinks like shit. Do you fancy headin' on down to Mixtures for a few drinks?" Tracey says.

"I take it that's a local bar?"

"Yeah, it's roughly two hundred meters from here." Tracey says.

"Why not, I've gotta get somethin' in me before I head back or I'm gonna black out." Robert says.

"Sure give your wife a call and let her know that you're stayin' here for the night, and tell her the good news over the two weeks paid leave, where she can get pricin' some holidays on the internet tonight till you get back tomorrow." Tracey says.

"You woman," Robert says as he heads towards the front door with Tracey whilst taking his cellular out of his pocket, "You sure know how to get the bucks spent before hand."

"It's a profession we all have." Tracey says.

"I'm sure." Robert says as he follows Tracey out the front door.

"Do you wanna leave some outside lights on?" Robert says before he closes the door.

"Yeah, may as well, at least that way we'll find the house on the way back." Tracey says. "Well are you gonna give your wife a call."

"I would love to, but there's no reception here." Robert says as he closes the front door behind him that can only be opened with the key, as there's no door handle to it on the outside.

"Let me check mine." Tracey says as she reaches into her handbag and takes out her cellular, "No, it looks like mines dead around this area too."

"Ah, I'm sure that Mixtures'll have a pay phone." Robert says.

"Hopefully, or your wife'll report you missin'." Tracey says.

Inside the house in the hall as Tracey and Robert's voices can barely be heard, the place is as quiet as can be, but out of the blue a mild squeak starts coming from the hallways cupboard door, then all of the sudden the door literally smashes open with a big bang. Where dropping down flat on the hallway floor is an old dead dusty body lying awkwardly, with their face flat on the floor. With the shape of the hair and figure of the body it looks like it belonged to a female, as it's not the easiest to tell due to the filth of the clothing and darkness of the hallway, due to the light being on the outside of the house.

The cupboard is more than likely where the smell is coming from too.

Suddenly blackening a good part of the lifeless figure altogether, over towards the kitchen door stands a pitch black figure, disguised by the darkness, holding a bag in their left hand.

26.

Walking back into his house, to which some of the lights have been turned on due to the red sky disappearing out of sight, Pete heads into the living room where Barbara, Rachel and Jean are.

"Well, any calls while I was gone?" Pete says.

"No, and I take it you had no luck either, huh?" Barbara says.

"No, I couldn't see her for love nor hate, plus the lack of light ain't helpin' much either." Pete says.

"Well Rachel was tellin' me she bumped into Amy around two o'clock this afternoon when she was out for a cycle, and that Amy was walkin' her bike home due to havin' another puncture." Barbara says.

"Have you any idea as to where about's that was?" Pete questions.

"It's roughly two or three miles from here, but it's up on the hills just after that lake, oh, I can't think of the name to it off the top of my head." Rachel says as she takes hold of her forehead that shakes side to side like she's trying to bang her thoughts together to find the answer.

"Lake Wellington?" Questions Pete.

"Yeah, I think that's the name for it." Rachel says.

"Yeah, that's roughly three miles from here for sure, but either way you'd think she'd be back by now. I think I'll call the cops, as this isn't like our little angel at all," Pete says. Then picking up the phone he starts dialing a few numbers.

"I'd like the police please," Pete says.

"I've got the number for Lee if he wants to give him a call to keep a look out for Amy, as his bars not for from that direction." Jean says to Barbara quietly due to Pete being on the phone, "He's the manager to that Mixtures bar. We can always ask him to keep an eye out for her."

Hanging up the phone from making his call to the police Barbara looks over at Pete, "Here, Pete," she says wanting to hand him the number that's displayed on Jean's cellular, "Do you wanna give Lee a call from Mixtures to ask him to keep an eye out for Amy?"

"Yeah, he's a good man I'm sure he wouldn't mind keepin' his curtains open and keep a look out for our little angel." Pete says as he sets the cellular on the kitchens work top and starts dialing away at the number.

27.

"Hay Samantha, open up them curtains again," Lee says as Samantha is in the process of closing the last curtain.

"Uh, you're just after asking me to close them, now you want me to open them? You can't go losin' your marbles on me at this time of night, as it's gonna get a lot busier when 'The Crews' come in to play their music, as they sure draw the crowds into this place." Samantha says.

"No, this isn't a joking matter Sam." Lee says acting all serious, "As I'm just after comin' off the phone with Pete."

"As in Pete Waterson the postman?" Norman questions.

"Yeah," Lee says, where noticing on how everyone's gone all quiet to listen in as to what the news is, he continues, "As he's asked me to keep a look out for his daughter Amy, who hasn't been seen since this mornin' from when she went off on a cycle. Though apparently she, uh, bumped into her friend Rachel down this direction earlier on and was walkin' her bike home due to havin' a puncture."

"Shit, let's just hope she's alright," Samantha says.

"I've got to admit I didn't see her on my way down this direction." Norman says.

"I take it the cops have been called too?" Lucie says.

"Yeah, they have, they were phoned before he started phonin' around." Lee says.

"That's good," Norman says as he finishes his drink, lights up a cigarette and takes hold of his curled up twenty dollar bills, "Sure get another round in for everyone there, and let's hope they find the little angel alright."

"Hopefully Rachel hasn't been told about this, as her and Amy are literally joined by the hips," Alicia says.

"Yeah, that's right. Rachel's your little cousin ain't she?" Cheryl says.

"Yeah, and herself and Amy are always together as they get on like a house on fire." Alicia says.

"A bit like you lot, huh?" Samantha says as she opens the last curtain.

"You got that right," Lucie says, "And don't forget you're one of us lady." She says pointing at Samantha.

Samantha runs over to the girls shouting, "Group hug," and watching them cuddling each other and lifting his eye lids up and down Norman says, "And how do you get into this group?"

"You're welcome anytime Norman," Samantha says as a little gap is opened for him, where darting out of his chair and filling the gap, he's a quick runner for his age.

"Oh, I could get used to this," Norman says as he throws his arms around Samantha and Alicia.

"And as for you, you've got some makin' up to do to get into here," Samantha says as she looks at Lee.

"Hmmm, more for me," Norman happily says whilst getting all the cuddles he can.

"Don't worry I'll turn the outside lights on so we can keep a look out for Amy." Lee sarcastically says as if it's Samantha's job.

Turning the lights on and heading outside the front door, Lee suddenly hears some kind of noise coming from the direction of the trees to the woods that are across the road.

"Amy. Is that you out there?" Lee says with his loud voice.

With no answer Lee walks down the couple of small steps that lead up to Mixtures entrance and heads over to the other side of the road and stands at the edge of the woods as he tries to look in between the trees.

"Amy. Amy." Lee hollows as he stands waiting for a reply for a few seconds.

Standing outside the entrance door to Mixtures, Samantha, Norman, Alicia, Lucie and Cheryl look over towards Lee to see what he's come across, but as he turns around and heads back towards Mixtures, looking left to right for any cars coming of course, Samantha says in a questionable manner, "Well?"

"Nah, I just heard a bitta noise and thought it might've been Amy trapped or somethin'." Lee says.

"Ah, you'd hear any Gods amount've different noises if you stood there for a few minutes." Norman says, "You've probably heard a rabbit or mouse runnin' around."

"Yeah, probably." Lee says as they all head back on into Mixtures with the door closing behind them.

Back towards the direction that Lee was standing at and looking at the big thick barks to the trees, the Stranger is seen appearing out from behind one of the trees and walking deeper into the woods and disappearing out of sight quickly due to the darkness of their mucky clothes.

Up at Mixtures with everyone back inside, Lee is seen looking through the window, where with the Stranger being out of sight Lee shakes his head and rolls his eyes as his eyebrows lifts in disbelief, probably due to him thinking the noise he heard could have been Amy.

28.

"And that's what happened!" Chris says as he blows a puff of smoke into Paul, Ryan and Alan's faces, then flicks what remainders he has left into the fire.

Staring at Chris with worried looks on their faces, Paul, Ryan and Alan stare at him in a shocked worrying manner. Then making them jump out of their skin Alan's cellular lets off a mighty loud ringtone.

"Aw, look at it, Mommy bears ringin' up to make sure her little baby's alright," Chris sarcastically says.

"Aw." Ryan says sympathizing.

Walking over to the tent and speaking quietly Alan says, "I wish you were here too bro, but with what we've got lined up, you ain't at that right age just yet."

"Huh, and like you are?" Simon says whilst sitting on the end of his bed looking quite down in the dumps. "Oh well, send us a text and keep me posted on how it's goin', as I miss annoyin' you." Simon says, knowing rightly he's getting nowhere fast.

"I'm sure you do," Alan says, where as he looks at Paul, Ryan and Chris he can see they're taking the piss out of him as they pretend to cry.

"Well bro I better head on here, as some dudes are starting to cry with being left on their own." Alan says.

"Oh, okay," Simon says.

"Keep your chin up, you'll be able to come sometime." Alan says.

"Well just you make sure you send me a postcard if you're sober enough," Simon says as he stands up from sitting on the bed and heads out of the bedroom.

"See you soon man." Alan says as he walks up to the guys and hangs up his cellular.

"Who was that bro?" Chris says smoking another cigarette already.

"Ah, it was Simon." Alan says.

"Aw, is he missin' his big brother already?" Ryan sympathetically says.

"Yeah," Alan says, "He misses annoyin' me the little shit."

"Now shall we head to this bar or what?" Paul says as he unveils a box of durex, "Cuz I'm hungry for some pussy," he says with his tongue hanging out of his head.

Quickly startling Paul a cat starts rubbing up against his leg whilst purring at the same time.

"Check it out guys he's pulling some pussy already, talk about a quick service around this place, but personally I think that's gonna be the only pussy you'll be pullin' tonight." Chris says. Then suddenly Alan's cellular bleeps again.

"As for this dude, there's just no partin' the brotherly love," Ryan says whilst pointing at Alan.

Sympathizing, Chris says, "You just can't separate them."

"I think I'll be leavin' this here," Alan says as he walks back over towards the tent and reads the message, which reads: - 'Please take me with you, Mom's driving me up d creek.' Then Alan types a message back which reads: - 'Who knows you might get lucky yet bro?'

Placing his cellular on the sleeping sack Alan zips up the tent then heads towards the guys, though as he's only five feet away from the tent his cellular starts bleeping again.

"Thank God I got rid of that thing." Alan says as they walk off.

"Yeah, cuz this is wasting precious pussy time." Paul says busy flapping the durex box in front of Alan's face as he arrives in line with them.

29.

Walking through the door to Mixtures, Tracey and Robert get glared at up and down.

"Gee's Louise," Norman says, "Or should I say Lewis, Tracey, Tracey Lewis the news reporter."

"That's me," Tracey says as she looks at everyone whilst walking up to the bar with Robert.

"What brings you to this neck of the woods?" Norman says.

"It's nothin' to do with Amy I hope," Alicia says.

"No, no, I'm just down here on holiday for a couple of weeks, and stayin' at my Grandma's house that's a stone throw away from here." Tracey says.

"That's right your grandma was Leona Lewis wasn't she?" Norman says.

"Yeah," Tracey says.

"God rest her soul, she was a little angel to this area here. As with all the baking she did to raise money for all the different charities with the church, the children in need was always at the top of her list." Norman says.

"Well, what would you like to drink?" Lee says as he asks Tracey first, while Samantha behind him looks down in the dumps.

"I'll have a vodka and white rum thanks." Tracey says.

"And you sir?" Lee says to Robert.

"Now there's a word I don't hear to often, *sir*." Robert says all impressed. "I'll have a beer good man."

"Need I ask who the boss in your relationship is?" Samantha says.

"No, we're not a couple," Tracey says.

"No, I'm a happily married man," Robert says

"Oops, my fault," Samantha says looking a little bit perked up due to not being the only loaner.

"No, Robert's my cameraman for the news, and he's kindly gimme a lift up to my Grandma's house for my two week holiday." Tracey says.

"So I take it we'll be seeing more of you here during those two weeks then, huh?" Lee says, busy looking for more business.

"Possibly, possibly," Tracey says taking a sip of her drink.

"So I take it you haven't heard about Amy yet then, huh?" Alicia says.

"No, why is there somethin' up?" Tracey says.

"Yeah, apparently she was last seen near here at around one or two by my cousin Rachel," Alicia says.

"Does she live local?" Tracey asks.

"About two and a half to three miles, give or take," Lee says.

"I take it the cops and all have been informed?" Tracey says.

"Yeah, all the locals have been informed about it too," Lee says.

"That's why the curtains have been left open as well, so we can keep a look out for her." Samantha says.

"Fingers crossed she's found." Tracey says.

"Is there a phone about here by any chance?" Robert asks as he looks at his cellular that still has no reception.

"Yeah, it's just over there," Lee says as he points in the direction of a little box that you can't even see the entrance to.

"I'll be back in a minute," Robert says to Tracey, "Just gonna give the Mrs. a call and let her know what's happenin'."

"No worries." Tracey says taking another sip of her drink. Then looking at Samantha's miserable face Tracey just blurts out, "So what's up with you tonight? Your boyfriend dumped you or somethin'?"

"What boyfriend," Samantha says strait up, "Let's just say it's been a long time. And plus there's hardly any half decent looking males around here anyway, no offence Lee," Samantha says as she looks at Lee, "And like we agreed Norman, if I don't get swept off my feet in the next month, we're running away together." Samantha says.

"Don't worry I'm countin' the weeks, days, hours, minutes and seconds." Norman happily replies.

All of the sudden from the rear of Mixtures, Jack starts barking his head off like crazy, as there's noise coming from inside the woods, where after a few seconds Alan, Ryan, Paul and Chris pop out from behind the big thick tree trunks and make their way to the wall behind the dumpsters.

As Ryan, Chris and Paul jump from the wall to the floor, being a show off, Alan gets on top of the dumpster that's the closest to Mixtures fire exit, whereas he leaps off the lid to the dumpster he pressurizes it into opening. Though as he lands on the floor they're all distracted from looking inside the dumpster, as Jack starts barking his head off like crazy again. It's as if he's about to start attacking them, but not waiting around for it to happen, they all scarper off out of sight as quickly as they can.

Inside Mixtures and in the middle of a conversation, Tracey says, "You'll find it'll happen when you least expect it."

"Ah, we'll see." Samantha says. Then looking towards the entrance door to Mixtures, walking through the door first is the little baby faced Alan, followed by Paul, Ryan and Chris.

"Hay, check it out Samantha," Cheryl says.

"Tonight could be your lucky night," Norman says busy egging on Samantha to raise her head up and see what's just walked through the door.

Lifting her head up slowly Samantha suddenly looks at Alan, to whom she can't keep her eyes off. It's as if he's completely on his on and Ryan, Paul and Chris are invisible altogether.

"And you would like, uh….," Samantha says not even being able to finish her question.

"Poke somethin' up her butt, she's fadin', she's fadin' man," Norman whispers to Lee.

Butting in between Alan and Samantha's glary eyes Paul says, "We'll take a bottle of your best champagne!" Then he places a fifty dollar bill on the counter between the two of them, which still doesn't distract them from glaring at each other like crazy.

"Champagne? Uh!" Chris says as he takes a seat at a table with Ryan.

"What the heck is this someone's weddin' bells or somethin'." Ryan says.

"We'll be over here slave boy," Paul says tapping Alan on the shoulder and pointing in the direction of Chris and Ryan as he walks off.

"Slave boy, huh?" Samantha says as she glares into Alan's eyes as if she could think of a few jobs for him to do, which must be good enough, as she starts to release a little smile that she's completely unaware of, where Alan returns a shady happy grin back as if they're reaching for the same star.

"Now if he's at the age to drink, I'd love to know what on earth he's been taking to stay lookin' so young," Norman says to Lee as Alicia, Lucie and Cheryl are busy eyeing up Ryan, Paul and Chris.

"Is that mutt of yours gonna shut up or what?" Lee says as he walks up to Samantha, who isn't even paying the slightest bit of attention as to what she's supposed to be doing.

"But he hasn't even said a word," Samantha says constantly staring at Alan.

"I'm on about that little mutt of yours, as in dog, uh, d, o, g, that's outside and constantly barkin' its head off." Lee says tapping Samantha on the shoulder.

Snapping out of her dream world, Samantha is handed a tray from Lee containing four glasses and a bottle of champagne in a bucket of ice.

"Here you go." Samantha happily says to Alan.

"But before *you* head off with that, I'd like to see some form of ID please," Lee says to Alan.

"Oh, there y'are," Alan says as he hands his splurged photographic ID to Lee.

"And you expect me to believe this is you, uh, Mr. Walters?" Lee questions as he continues reading the details of the ID, which look like they are sticking in his head due to the disbelief.

Though Alan's not even paying attention as to what he's being asked as he's suctioned himself back into glaring at Samantha's gorgeous looking face, which is completely dimple and freckle free, where her lovely long thick black hair has been very well platted, which is obviously due to working behind the bar no doubt.

"And your date of birth is?" Lee says to Alan who's still oblivious as to Lee's even being there. But with Samantha giving Alan a quick groaning noise, then continuously edging her head towards Lee's direction for Alan to pay attention to, Alan suddenly snaps out of his trance and says, "Uh, what's that again?"

"Your date of birth please Mr. Walters?" Lee says.

"Ah, the 8th of June, 1979," Alan says.

"I'm definitely gonna be lookin' for that beautician's number that he goes to," Norman says to Tracey.

Coming through the entrance door to Mixtures while Lee looks like he's in doubt on letting Alan remain on the premises, heavy equipment is getting carried in by 'The Crews', who are starting to set up their equipment for a musical night ahead.

"Well I hope there's gonna be no jip from you guys tonight, as this is a very well respected establishment, and I'd like to keep it that way." Lee quickly says as he hands Alan back his identification and heads over to 'The Crews'.

Taking hold of the tray, with the change from Paul's fifty dollars sliding around on it, Alan says to Samantha, "Sorry for startin' your dog off with the barking earlier, as me and the guys came in through the back."

"Don't worry about it." Samantha says, "Have a nice night, I'll get the dog seen to."

Still staring at Alan as he walks off to his table, Alicia, Lucie and Cheryl are trying to egg on Samantha to do something about getting Alan instead of letting him slip away.

"Samantha, remember when I said this place is a nice quiet establishment and that I'd like to keep it that way?"

"You did?" Samantha says wondering what Lee's going on about.

"Yes," Lee says catching on she wasn't paying the slightest bit of attention to him, "Get something done about your mutt and shut him up, pleeeee-ase."

Walking back over to Tracey from his telephone call, Tracey has her eyes peeled on the television as a picture of Naomi Layne appears, where coming back into the bar from giving Jack some water, Tracey says to Samantha, "You wouldn't mind turnin' the volume up a little bit there would you Samantha?"

"Shit, when you think about it this place is startin' to get creepy, I mean there's Naomi who lives five miles away from here and has been missing for ten days, and Amy today," Norman says. Though looking over at Alicia she is not overly impressed with his thoughts, to which he obviously hasn't taken into account as he still has his eyes glued on the box.

Over at Alan's table Samantha continues to stare at him, where Alan's just as bad, as he also can't keep his eyes off of her either.

"Hello, are you there?" Chris says busy clicking his fingers together in front of Alan's face. Then coughing his head off due to Chris blowing cigarette smoke in his face, Chris says, "What's up with you man?"

"Other than your fuckin' smoke?" Alan says as he looks back at Samantha, "Nothing." He says drifting back into his own little fantasy land.

"I think you're turning delirious if you think it's you she's after man. Did you not see her eyes when I handed her the fifty bucks?" Paul says as if it's him Samantha's staring at.

"He's not gonna snap outta this one guys," Chris says as he clicks his fingers in front of Alan's face to which he doesn't even blink at.

"Right here, let's put a bit of excitement into it," Paul says as he takes the box of durex out of his pocket and sets it in the centre of the table they're sitting at. "I'll even risk the loss of my PJ's if you end up getting her before me before this night comes to a closure."

"Okay," Alan says like he's in his own little fantasy land.

As the band starts doing their surround sound techniques, the bar is starting to pick up with more visitors, but still being able to be heard outside and making a few of the customers uncomfortable, Jack is barking his head off like crazy.

"Samantha, deal with that mutt of yours before I give it a drink it'll remember." Lee says busy holding a bottle of gin in his hand.

Heading to the rear door from the little hallway that leads out from the bar, Samantha opens the door and steps outside.

"Whatta you barkin' at Jack, huh?" Samantha says to Jack who's busy staring at the lid to the dumpster and barking his head off.

"Is it only this that's bothering you?" Samantha says as she walks over to the dumpster and takes hold of the handle. Though as her hand makes contact with the lid, Jack starts barking even more angrily which distracts Samantha from seeing what's inside it as the lid closes over.

"There, now it's closed, are you happy now?" Samantha says as she gives Jack a pat, where Jack also jumps up and starts giving her crazy licks.

"Down boy, down. I think I'll be lookin' for my own kind of male species to be lickin' my face tonight, and maybe more." Samantha says, where Jack lets off a little whimper and places his head under Samantha's arm pit as if he's hiding his face in shame.

"Hay less of the jealousy you," Samantha says, "Just think he might even have a pet of his own to keep you amused, huh?" Jack suddenly starts barking.

"Ah, ah, ah, less of the barkin' now you hear me?" Samantha says as she walks back towards the rear entrance, "Or we'll both end up with nothin'."

Arriving behind the bar again Lee says to Samantha, "Well is that him sorted?"

"Should be, I think he was barking over the lid to the dumpster being open." Samantha says. Which Alan vaguely overhears.

Holding the glass in her hand and looking in the direction of Alan, Tracey says, "I'm near sure I've seen that baby faced looking dude somewhere before, but I just can't put my finger on it."

"Ah, who knows, but whatever's in the air tonight true love is about to prosper the way them two have been glaring at each other." Robert says.

Then all of the sudden Jack starts letting off a mighty howling noise followed by a non-stop bark, where 'The Crews' band with their mikes say, "It looks like we've got a howling fan out there for us already this night," where everyone lets out a laugh.

"No seriously Samantha, you've gotta get him home as I don't think I could take another minute of that, my head is pumpin'." Lee says.

"And how are you gonna cope, huh?" Samantha says.

"Norman you recall that favor you owe me?" Lee says.

"Ah!" Norman sighs.

"Free drink all night." Lee says.

"You remember what happened the last time?" Norman says.

"But come on that's in the past." Lee says.

"Yeah. But we're now in the present and I'm thinkin' of your unforeseeable future!" Norman says.

"I'll take my chances, no come on man, you owe me big time. Or would you like me to spill a few stories of what I've had to put up with before." Lee says.

"Okay, okay, you win." Norman groans as he gets off his stool beside Robert.

"No, no, come on we wanna hear the stories," Lucie says.

"Put it this way, one's similar as to where I'm going now," Norman says, "Behind bars."

"You know Norman, you're the man." Samantha says as she gives Norman a kiss on the cheek.

"And where's mine?" Lee says.

"Mmmmm?" Samantha hesitates, but she then gives him a quick kiss on the cheek. "You're lucky you got that one and only just."

"Now please, get that little mutt of yours outta here," Lee says.

Heading over to Alan's table, Alicia, Lucie and Cheryl egg Samantha on by saying, "Go girl, go."

"Are you comin'?" Samantha says as she stands at Alan, Paul, Chris's and Ryan's table. Where leaping to his feet Paul says, "I'd love to." Though putting her hand on Paul's shoulder and effortlessly pushing him back onto his chair Samantha says, "Sorry, not you." Then pointing at Alan she says, "You." Where noticing he's completely flabbergasted she makes sure Alan is listening, and in a sexy manner says, "Are you comin'?"

Jumping to his feet like a robot, Alan grabs hold of the pocket of durex, slips it into his pocket and says, "Okay." Then as the two of them head to leave through the front door Lee says, "Samantha aren't you forgettin' somethin'."

Then as she walks back to the bar Norman hands her an expensive bottle of wine bought from his poker winnings and says to Alan, "It looks like the best man won."

"Jeepers, you did say you'd get me a drink before the nights out Norman, but come on talk about servin' in style," Samantha says a she gives Norman another kiss on the cheek.

"Hope you's have a nice night." Norman says.

"Will do," Samantha says heading for the front door with Alan again.

"Uh, Samantha!" Lee says.

"GO GIRL, GO GIRL, GO GIRL, GO GIRL," Alicia, Lucie and Cheryl shout, busy interrupting Lee to carry on with his sentence.

Walking past Paul, Ryan and Chris, they start whistling at the two of them as they open the entrance door and Alan says, "Don't wait up guys."

Suddenly ringing the bell at the bar as if it's time for last orders, Lee manages to get Samantha's full attention as she has the front entrance door fully open.

"Samantha?" Lee says.

"What are you closing up already or somethin'?" Samantha says.

"No!" Lee says.

"Well you only ring that bell for closin' time or if you're offerin' everyone a drink on the house to my recollection." Samantha says.

"Yeah, but…,"

"She has a good point there," Cheryl says.

"Yeah," Alicia agrees.

"Yeah, but I was only tryin' to get her attention and make sure you don't forget your mutt out back." Lee says.

"I know. I was goin' to walk around the back for him." Samantha says putting her fingers up in a one nil kind of manner.

"Why you little….,"

"And that's revenge for earlier on me havin' to clean up the pigsty from the night before." Samantha says. Where as she closes the door and disappears out of sight she can be heard shouting, "ONE NIL, ONE NIL, ONE NIL, ONE NIL."

Where from outside Mixtures everyone is heard ordering in on their free drinks Samantha's got for them.

30.

At Paul, Alan, Ryan and Chris's campsite, it's completely silent, where the tents are as still as can be due to the night's hot humidity, but looking over at Alan's tent, it's been unzipped, where heading into the tent the Stranger can be seen from behind kneeling down on Alan's sleeping sack busy holding Alan's cellular in their hand. Though as the Stranger's dirty thumb presses a button, a message suddenly appears reading: -

MESSAGE
Mom's annoying me, can I please come?

Then looking at the Stranger's thumb it moves very slowly and manages to type out the letters, **Y, E, S**.

- -

In Simon's bedroom where he's sitting in front of his computer playing away at his games, his cellular suddenly beeps a crazy tune. Where picking it up and pressing a few buttons he starts to jump up and down with joy and he runs out of his bedroom, to which the sound of his feet are heard bouncing down the stairs.
Arriving into the living room he is all hyper as he looks at his Mum.
"Mom, Mom!"
"What on earth's rattled your cage man?" Charlotte says.
"It's Alan. I've just got a text from him." Simon says.
"And?" Questions Charlotte.
"He says I can go campin' with him and the guys. Can I, can I Mom?" Simon grovels.
"Uh, you'll find there ain't a hope in hell you'll be leavin' at this

time of night. Plus you don't even know where he is for that matter do you?" Charlotte says.

"I'll text him back and find out, huh, huh, can I, can I go please?" Simon says.

"We'll just see whereabouts he is first before we even think of sendin' you anywhere. So don't get your hopes up Si." Charlotte says.

- -

Back at the woods and inside Alan's tent there's no sign of the Stranger anymore, though drifting through the woods and eventually arriving at a country road which consists of a T-junction, the Stranger is seen from behind standing at the edge of the woods. Suddenly a basic cellular tone, which also lightens the Stranger's hand up as it beeps, is coming from Alan's cellular. Where loosening the grip they have to the cellular, the Stranger opens up their hand slowly and opens up the cellular, where the message that appears strait away reads: -

MESSAGE
Mom says I can join, but not till tomorrow,
Where shall I get the bus to?

Across the road to the T-junction a sign reads, "Village Everette Road," where looking back at the cellular the dirty thumb has managed to type out, "**Village Everette Road**." Where pressing another button the cellular suddenly sends the message.

A bit up the road from where the Stranger is standing the sound of some people talking is getting louder, to which the Stranger being seen from behind again is walking back into the woods.

"Hay, do you see that light up there?" Alan asks Samantha as he points towards the direction of the woods. Where with Samantha trying to see what he's pointing at, the light has already disappeared.

"What light?" Samantha says.

"There was a light there a few seconds ago." Alan says.

"Do you usually go this senile on your first night with a date?" Samantha says.

"Yeah, but you should see me on the second night." Alan says.

"Mmmmm? Have I got the right man Jack?" Samantha questions. Then Jack starts barking his head off in a happy manner, then licks Alan on the hand.

Holding his head like he's got a headache, Lee looks at Norman as he shakes his head.

"What's up with you?" Norman asks.

"I can't get the noise of that mutt outta my head!" Lee says.

"Ah, who knows you could've caught the tinnitus." Norman says.

"What the heck is that?" Lee questions.

"It's where you hear particular noises constantly goin' off in your ears twenty four seven." Norman says.

"As in an ear infection?" Lee asks?

"More or less, but this one you can't get rid of." Norman says.

"Oooh, the next time I see that mutt I'm gonna blow its brains out." Lee says as he gives his head a quick shake and carries on with serving the customers.

"Well is your house much further from here?" Alan says.

"Ah, there's only about ten more minutes left." Samantha says.

"What? Ten minutes walk?" Alan says as he puts on a silly voice. Then messing around like he's unable to walk another step, he drops to his knees and says whilst putting on his silly voice again, "I dunno if I can make it." Then dropping onto his back like he's pretending to be dead, Jack starts to whimper whilst continuously licking his face.

"Oh well, it's a pity he's as dead as a door nail Jack, cuz I've got somethin' really damn hot lined up for him this night." Samantha says as she walks on past Alan.

But suddenly bouncing to his feet like he's been muscularly reincarnated, Alan puts on a higher pitched voice and says, "Oh, me feel a lot better. I just hope we do not disturb the neighbors."

"You'd be lucky. My closest neighbor is from where we're just after coming from." Samantha says. Where pointing back from where they're just after having walked from, Samantha says, "Mixtures."

"That's some heck of a walk if you're stuck for a bitta sugar, huh?" Alan says.

"I take it it's not like your place then, huh?" Samantha says. "Mind you where are you from anyway?" Samantha says continuing with her questions.

"Ah, I've been livin' in the big city in Boston for about thirteen years now." Alan says.

"Oooh, so I got myself a sexy city man?" Samantha says as she glares into Alan's eyes. Suddenly Jack quickly starts barking like he's answering for Alan.

31.

Smoking like usual, Chris blows some smoke out of his mouth and looks at Paul who has a face like a wet weekend.

"Paul dry your eyes man, Alan won fair and square. Now come on lighten up, we're here to enjoy ourselves." Chris says.

"Okay, pass me a butt to smoke then." Paul says.

"But you don't smoke." Ryan says.

"Maybe, but my magic puffs might have some horny chicks appear before me," Paul depressingly says.

"Gimme that thing," Ryan says as he snatches the cigarette out of Paul's hand.

"Ah, but without babes man, I dunno." Paul says.

"I take it your magnetic bearings were left back home?" Ryan says as he slips the cigarette back into Chris's packet.

"Who fuckin' knows?" Paul says. Then standing up and heading towards the bar slowly, he looks back at Ryan and Chris, "But I'm tellin' you, if I don't get some half decent lookin' pussy after this next round've drink, I'll be headin' back to the campsite and makin' out with the one and only pussy that was touchin' me up earlier."

"Who knows the poor little dudes probably keepin' his sleepin' sack warm for a little one on one?" Chris says to Ryan as Paul turns away from them and heads up to the bar slowly dodging in and out of the crowd that's appeared.

Arriving up at the bar with the pumping of the vibes from 'The Crews' kicking off as they sing away, Paul is busy looking around the crowd to see if he can see any sexy ladies.

"What'll it be man?" Lee says to Paul. But not even catching on he's being spoken to, Paul is busy watching Norman serve Alicia, Lucie and Cheryl.

"And what can I get you lovely ladies?" Norman says in a romantic manner, like he's looking for more kisses and cuddles.

"We'll have three vodka's and diet cokes," Alicia says to Norman politely as she dips into her handbag. Though having her back turned to Paul; Lucie and Cheryl notice Paul is looking in their direction and points for Alicia to turn around and take a peek. Where as Alicia turns around Paul's eyes lighten up like he's just struck another jackpot. "That'll be six dollars thirty Alicia." Norman says as he places the glasses and bottles in front of them.

"Hay man," Lee says to Paul still trying to get his attention, but still not paying any heat, Paul takes another fifty dollars out of his pocket and walks towards Alicia, Lucie and Cheryl's direction.

"Here, let me get that for you, huh? It's the least I could do with your friend having been high-jacked by my main man earlier on." Paul says whilst physically putting another fifty dollars in Norman's hand. Where with Lee having gone on to serve another customer he's not particularly impressed with what he's seeing.

"Do you's fancy comin' on down to join me and the guys so we can fill each other in on your friend Samantha and Mr. Lucky-Fuck?" Paul says as his eyes rise up and down.

Looking at Cheryl and Lucy, Alicia gets the nod.

"Yeah, why not," Alicia says to Paul as they head towards the table.

"By the way my names Paul," Paul says as they all head towards the table. Arriving at the table with Ryan's eyes rising up a bit like he's impressed over Paul's success, as Paul arrives at the table he says, "This is Chris who's built like a brick house and smokes like a chimney, more than likely due to him getting married soon enough. It shows you what pressure it causes. And this is our brainy little shit Ryan, who even studies in his sleep." Paul says.

As Chris gets a few seats together for the ladies, Paul starts to head back up to the bar, "Excuse me for a few seconds." Paul says.

Arriving back up at the bar, Norman walks up to Paul again, "Are you lookin' for another round already?" Norman says.

"No, no," Paul says, "But I'll make a deal with you, if you keep the change and get yourself and your partner a few drinks, could you keep them drinks coming when I give you the thumbs up," Paul says.

"Will do," Norman says as Paul hands him four fifty dollar notes, though as Paul attempts to walk away with the money not having completely changed hands, Norman takes a tight grip of Paul's wrist and pulls him back, "Providing you guys don't give them any shit, as I hold many titles from the boxing ring, deal?" Norman says in a muscular manner.

"Deal man," Paul says as he heads back to his table all happy as the crowd behind him starts to pile up around the bar.

Over at Tracey and Robert's side of the bar, Tracey watches Paul head back to his table and suddenly gives her glass a slight bang on the tabletop surrounding the bar and says, "That's where I've seen him and his little baby faced friend before."

"Where?" Robert questions.

"Down at the hospital when we were doing that news report on the Siamese twins." Tracey says nodding her head towards Paul's table, "The baby faced dude that disappeared with Samantha earlier was the one who was heading in and out of that key shop that was across the road from us." Tracey says as if it's took the weight off her shoulders.

Over towards the till Norman takes hold of a spare glass and puts the four fifty dollar bills in it. Then opening the till he places six dollars thirty from his and Lee's tips into the till to pay for Alicia, Lucie and Cheryl's drinks, then as he places the remainder of the tip money into another spare glass Lee walks up to the till with twenty bucks in his hand.

"I'm not too sure about those guys." Lee says.

"Ah, lighten up, look what he's give us." Norman says pointing towards the glasses on either side of the till.

"Yeah, and God knows where he's got that from," Lee says as he takes hold of some change and closes the till, then hands the change to a customer as he heads to take another order whilst the music puts a good few people into the mood for dancing.

32.

With it being pitch black, all that can be seen are two dark figures walking towards a large two story house with a small wiggly figure walking beside them, though arriving closer to the house a tracker light quickly turns itself on revealing Alan, Samantha and Jack.

"Well, here we are." Samantha says as she takes her keys out of her pocket.

"It's sure as hell some size," Alan says as he looks around in amazement.

"Mmmmm, that's what I like to hear," Samantha says as she looks Alan up and down, "That it's a nice size to keep ones amused for the night."

"Ow, and I thought I was bad," Alan says as he enters on into the house after Samantha and Jack.

"Do you fancy one of my homemade cocktails?" Samantha says as she walks towards the kitchen holding Jack by the collar as Alan closes the front door behind him.

"Yeah, I'd love one, thanks," Alan says as he looks around the hall in amazement over the size of the place.

"Sure head on through to the lounge and I'll bring it on in when I get Jack sorted out back." Samantha says.

"And the lounge is?" Alan says as he prolongs the last word in his sentence busy looking for an answer.

"If you wish I can always give you a guided tour once I get this little Jack of all trades sorted out." Samantha says.

"Yeah, why not." Alan says.

"I'm just prayin' the little shit doesn't get away this time," Samantha says.

"If you've got some more rope to tie him up with, I can show you how to make a choke rope if you want." Alan says.

"Really?" Samantha says.

"Yeah, guide the way." Alan says.

"It'd be a blessing to get the little prince to stay in the one area for a change, as today alone he's broke himself free twice." Samantha says.

"Well look on the bright side, he got you off work early enough, huh?" Alan says smiling.

"Hay, you've gotta good point there, I think he deserves a couple of treats, huh?" Samantha says as she opens the kitchen cupboard and takes hold of a few doggy treats, handing them to Alan.

Out in the garden Alan shows Samantha how easy it is to make a double sided choke rope, where with Alan giving Jack his treats, Samantha puts the rope around Jack's neck, where taking hold of Alan's hand as she escorts him back into the house, Jack tries to run after them, but quickly being brought to a halt the rope tightens around Jack's neck.

As Alan and Samantha enter on into the kitchen again Jack makes his way back to his treats, but looking towards the kitchen door that closes over, Alan and Samantha's figures can be seen through the blared window getting closer to each other with their mouths eventually connecting.

Inside the kitchen with the two of them still romantically kissing, they eventually stop, where with Samantha busy smiling away she strokes Alan's cheek with her left hand and says, "Well, would you like the guided tour of the house now?"

"On one condition," Alan says as he acts all serious.

"And what's that?" Samantha questions.

"Come with me," Alan says as he takes hold of Samantha's hand and walks her towards the front door.

"So come on then, what is it?" Samantha says as they arrive at the front door.

"Before we continue I'd like to clarify this ain't some note from your ten foot hunk of a hulk that'll be home in ten minutes." Alan says as he points at the note he's noticed underneath the telephone.

"Who knows?" Samantha says as she gives Alan a devious look whilst picking up the note. Where looking on the outside of the letter, the letters 'SAM' come into complete view revealing 'SAMANTHA', where opening up the letter and finding money inside the envelope, Samantha's eyes start to lighten up as she reads on with the letter.

"I hope your guys aren't expecting you back in a hurry," Samantha says whilst Alan patiently waits for an answer as Samantha puts the note and the money back into the envelope and sets it back next to the telephone.

"Why's that?" Alan asks.

"It's a note from my Mom and Pop tellin' me they're gonna be gone for the whole weekend, leavin' the house all to my poor little self." Samantha says as she takes hold of Alan's hand again.

"So where would you like to see first?" Samantha says walking around Alan and leading him towards the steps, "The bedroom?" She says finishing her sentence.

"Lead the way." Alan smoothly says.

33.

At Steve's darkened apartment, which is as quiet as can be due to no television having been left on. Over towards his room to which the door has been left half open, he is seen lying there under the covers in a deep, deep sleep.

"Angelina," Steve helplessly says as he turns to lie on his front whilst slipping his hands under his pillow and moving agitatedly.

"I love you." Steve says vigorously. Where looking at the body figure under his bedcovers, it seems to have stopped the heroic movements and come to a relaxing still motion.

Though suddenly making him jump out from under his covers and pull his gun out from under his pillow, Steve quickly looks around the room for any unlawful target, though catching on that he's not under attack he gets suddenly startled from the noisy banging coming from his front door.

Slipping his pants on over his plain black boxers and putting his catchy designed slippers on his feet whilst placing his gun to the rear of his pants, to which the handheld part of the gun is left out for safety purposes, Steve doesn't bother putting a top on over his vest and just heads for the front door which still sounds like it's getting hammered on from the outside.

Opening the door and pointing to his cheek like he's looking for a slap across the face, Steve says, "Have you come back to gimme another slappin'?"

"Personally dude, if you were gettin' anythin' from me it would be a kick in the balls or a boxin, slappin's for pussies." Jake says as he bombards past Steve. "I take it I woke you up?" Jake asks.

"What give you that idea, huh? Maybe the early night I mentioned about taking earlier on, to which was succeeded without the need of alcohol." Steve says.

"Whatta you after a medal or somethin'?" Jake says. Where Steve isn't overly impressed with Jake's lack of encouragement.

"Nah, just kiddin', good goin', but seriously I've got a lot more important shit for you to take heat of here now." Jake says as he unravels a pile of documents out of a very large envelope.

"What've you come across now?" Steve asks as he turns the living room light on.

"I think it's the main mother fucker you're after, who only seems to come out around this time of year." Jake says as he sets the photos and documents on Steve's dining table.

"Why, what've you come across?" Steve says.

"You remember that little girl Naomi Layne that went missin' near eleven days ago?" Jake says.

"Yeah." Steve says.

"At the end of the road to her house to where the ripped up pieces of old news paper and cut outs of certain photos were found. The labs finally managed to put together a complete photo."

"Of who?" Steve asks.

"Jamie-Lee Walters." Jake says.

"As in the dude whose land rover went flyin' off the mountain 18 years back killin' him and his son??" Steve says.

"That's him." Jake says as he puts the photos and documents back into the envelope.

"So what leads have we got other than a photo?" Steve questions.

"Well call it a hunch. I know there may be near enough an eleven day gap in it, but I think it's too much of a coincidence they're only four miles difference between each other." Jake says.

"I take it you're on about Amy Waterson who was reported missin' earlier?" Steve says.

"Yeah." Jake says.

"If it is, I just hope we catch the little bastard soon before another episode of the yearly killin' spree kicks off, cuz it's been near eighteen years runnin' and we still haven't caught the murderous mother …..," in Steve's eyes it's plain to see he wanted to finish the sentence with 'Mother Fucker', but controlling his anger he managed to do what many still can't. Stop.

"So, are you comin' for the spin?" Jake says.

"Two tics," Steve says turning around and heading towards his bedroom, where as he turns around Jake notices that Steve's gun is in view of his rear.

"One of these days bro you're gonna blow yourself another whole wide open man." Jake says.

Only in his bedroom for two seconds, Steve walks out all ready and set, "Well are you comin' or what? What's the hold up?" Steve says walking towards the front door.

"It's good to see you back to your old self man." Jake says as he follows Steve out of the apartment.

34.

"So Whatta you guys think of the music so far?" Shouts the lead singer as the music comes to a finish. Where between the entire crowd that's arrived at Mixtures, which is quite large, the people on the dance floor do most of the cheering to show their respect.

"And that's what I like to hear," the lead singer says, "Now don't be leavin' just yet, as we're only taking a fifteen minute break and we'll be back to pump up the vibes with all different kinds of songs to kick off the beat this night."

With everybody giving them another round of applause, Lee walks up to the end of the bar.

"Hay guys whatta you drinkin', it's on the house," Lee says as he looks towards The Crews as they make their way towards the bar.

"Hay, Lee," Tracey says.

"Yeah."

"You wouldn't mind turnin' the news up before you start porin' the drinks like a good man." Tracey says.

"Yeah, no hassle," Lee says, but with having loads of drinks to pour he hasn't got time to look at it.

NEWS REPORT
With just having received some news about the missing girl Naomi Layne, the only clues the police have come across at this present moment in time is in regards to a photo that they've managed to put together, which is that of a Jamie-Lee Walters that is thought to have been killed approximately 18 years ago when his land rover

143

plummeted over the edge of a mountain when it collided with a lorry, causing the land rover to explode upon landing from the 215 meter drop. If you have any reason to believe as to why or what this picture has to do with Naomi Layne's killing, please phone the police as soon as possible on 1 – 80….,

Handing The Crews their drinks, which is four beers, Lee says, "They're on the house, and is it possible to get you guys booked for the same time next month?"

"Yeah, no problem, though the month after that we're taking no bookings, as we're off on a holiday for a few weeks."

"And just to clarify, it was two hundred bucks for the night, yeah?" Lee says.

"Sure is boss, fifty bucks a piece."

"What the heck I'll get you sorted with that now." Lee says as he heads over to the cash register, "It'll save you waiting around later when you're gettin' yourselves all packed up."

Noticing the dumpsters full that's near Norman as he's busy serving away at a customer, while Lee counts the money for the band, Norman walks up to the till.

"Norman you don't mind emptying that dumpster when you've gotta chance, huh?" Lee says.

"Ah, you're just makin' me work for the money aren't you?" Norman questions.

"Who said you're gettin' paid." Lee says, "I think with the amount've mess that was left here last night, you've got off lightly. As after all you wouldn't want me to tell Samantha who it was that made all the mess, huh, as in pretending to be a drunken skunk not knowin' what he's doin', makin' a mess of the place and encouragin' ones to go all in, when you knew rightly what you were playin' at." Lee says.

"Okay, okay, I'm going." Norman says.

"Good man." Lee says.

Over at Paul, Ryan and Chris's table, to which Alicia, Lucie and Cheryl are still keeping them company, Ryan says, "Who only knows what time we'll be seein' Mr. Lucky Fuck tonight."

"Oh, so who's Mr. Lucky Fuck then, huh?" Alicia says.

"A ...., ah ...," Chris quickly kicks Paul under the table, due to noticing he was about to say 'Alan'.

"Jo." Chris says butting in.

"And from the love in their eyes when they were leavin' this place I think he's actually forgot he's on this campin' spree of ours." Ryan says as Paul's busy rubbing his leg.

"Yeah, we'll be lucky to see him at all." Chris says.

"So you're all on a campin' spree then, huh?" Lucie asks.

"Yeah, that way we're not at home when the examination results come through the door." Paul says, still busy rubbing his leg.

"Oh, so you guys are on the same boat as us then I take it?" Cheryl asks.

"I don't think so," Paul says.

"Why's that?" Alicia says.

"Cuz ours would be goin'...," Paul says as he looks at Ryan and Chris who can read him like a book and know rightly what he's going to say, where joining in to help him finish his sentence the all say, "Glug, glug, glug, glug, glug, glug, glug, glug." Then they all laugh.

With three cups of coffee in her hand Jean walks into the living room and over to Barbara, who's being accompanied on the three-seat settee with Pete, who's comforting her with his arm around her. Where over at the two-seater settee, Rachel is covered by a light blanket and is fast asleep.

"There you go there's a cuppa coffee for you both." Jean says as she takes a seat on the other side of Barbara, due to Barbara sitting in the middle of the settee.

"It's gettin' awfully late. You'd think they would've called us by now," Barbara says busy working herself up.

"It's a pity your Matthew's away on a business trip or he could've give us a hand to look around for her." Pete says.

"Yeah, tell me about it, he's away for a week." Jean says.

"Never mind what he's doin', *it's Amy, it's Amy we need to get findin'*." Barbara says working herself up and starting to cry.

"Oh, I'm sorry Barbara," Jean says setting her coffee on the table and taking hold of Barbara's coffee that's being held in a very unsteady manner, where as Jean sets it on the table Barbara tries to pull herself together as she wipes her tears that are rolling down her face and says to Jean, "So am I."

As Pete stands up and heads towards the telephone, he sets his coffee next to the telephone holder that's on the work surface and starts dialing a few numbers, where in the process Jean gives Barbara a cuddle due to her tears starting to become uncontrollable.

"Hello, can you put me through to police," Pete says waiting for a few seconds, "Yeah, I'd like to know if there's any news about my daughter Amy Waterson." Pete says quite agitatedly. "Well it would be nice to get the odd call to be notified on what's bein' done." Listening to the other end of the phone for a few seconds Pete says, "Well I'd be grateful if that could be carried out, many thanks." Pete says trying to control his frustration as he finishes from the phone.

"So what's happenin'?" Jean says.

"Apparently they've got some guys driving around to see if they can find her," Pete says, "But I think I'll take another spin myself. You don't mind stayin' with Barbara do you?"

"No, not at all, I'll stay for as long as you want." Jean says.

"Thanks Jean," are the only words Barbara manages to get out.

"Think nothin' of it Barbara, that's what friends are for." Jean says.

"See you soon," Pete says as he kisses Barbara's forehead. Then looking at Jean, he quietly and emotionally says, "Thanks." Where Jean just holds up her hand and waves Pete on and shakes her head as if she's giving her own sign language that it's okay.

Walking out of the living room Pete takes a look at Rachel whose innocent face is fast asleep, where as he reaches the front door and opens it, it's plain to see that the worries are starting to hit him due to leaving the house all shook-up.

- -

With a complete bundle of rubbish all bagged up, Norman opens the rear door to Mixtures and looks in the direction of the dumpsters, where he just shakes his head in disgust due to noticing the amount of garbage bags that have been left sitting in front of it by Samantha.

"I dunno, have they ever heard on what a dumpsters actually for?" Norman says as he walks up to the dumpster and sets the bag he's carrying on the floor and heads to the rubbish bag that's the closest to the dumpster. Though looking down at the bag as he opens the lid to the dumpster, attempting to lift it up with the one hand he quickly notices that it's impossible. So grabbing the rubbish bag with both hands, Norman eventually manages to rest it on the top part of the dumpster with the lid half open, where opening the lid to the dumpster that bit wider as he attempts to push the rubbish in, before he pushes the bag in he notices something peculiar, where trying to make out what it is, he suddenly notices the dead eyes looking at him and glimpses at a bloodied hand that's sticking out of the big thick adhesive tape that the rest of the body is rapped up in.

Quickly standing back from the dumpster, Norman nearly trips over the other garbage bags that were left lying around, though with the rubbish Norman tried to place into the dumpster, more of less hanging half out of it, it suddenly falls to the floor slamming the dumpster closed, leaving Norman virtually standing still and going into a deep shock as he stares at the dumpster with incredulity all over his face that is getting paler by the second.

Walking back into Mixtures at a very slow pace, where The Crews are starting to get themselves set up again, Norman arrives back behind the bar and just stands still and stares.

"Are you gonna do some work man or what?" Lee asks Norman as he takes a quick glance in his direction, where Norman just turns his head slowly towards Lee's direction and stares at him.

"What's up Norman?" Lee asks as he looks at Norman weirdly, where Norman just remains quiet.

"Are you okay man?" Lee questions Norman again as he stops poring the drink he has in his hand, then walks towards Norman.

"Whatsa matta?" Lee says. Where as The Crews start singing, Lee does a loud whistle and gives them a slit throat signal to stop.

"Norman," Lee says as he walks back to Norman to feel his forehead.

On the other side of the bar everyone seems to have turned silent so they can see what's up with Norman.

"I think you need an ambulance man." Lee says as he takes hold of the phone.

"In …, in …, in …, the, dum …," Norman mutters as he struggles to get his words out right, whilst looking at Lee with his scary eyes.

"Whatta you say Norman?" Lee questions.

"I's, in, the, dump." Norman says, not even being able to get his words out properly.

"What is?" Lee asks.

"A, b ..., bo ..., body," Norman says with great difficulty.

"What?" Lee says in more of a disbelief that an actual question.

"In the dumpster." Norman repeats whilst heavily in shock.

Looking at some of the visitors they don't like the look of things and they start to leave quite quickly.

"Hay, I don't like the look of this guys'," Chris says.

"I think we better leave, somethin's up." Ryan says as he watches a lot of people heading for the exit.

"Well it was short and sweet," Paul says as he rises to his feet with Ryan and Chris, "Maybe some other time, huh?"

"Yeah, why not." Alicia says.

Walking towards the dumpster at a slow steady pace, as Lee opens the lid he can see the body all rapped up in big thick adhesive tape, with the eyes staring at him and the bloodied hand sticking out. Where dropping the lid to the dumpster and running back into the bar, he grabs hold of a gun that's buried at the back of the bottom shelf and takes a shot at Paul who is last to leave the place, but he misses with the bullet ricocheting through the window.

Keeping her head down as she sits in a crouched position on the floor beside Robert, Tracey says, "Head on back to my place and grab the cameras and I'll give the head man a call." Where handing the house keys to Robert, Tracey heads over to the pay phone out of view while Robert follows Lee out of Mixtures.

Outside Mixtures Lee heads in one direction while Robert quickly darts off in the other direction keeping his head low.

Driving down the road with a pile of cars flying past them, running on foot Robert sprints past their car.

"Was that who I thought it was?" Steve says. Where answering his question before Jake gets a chance to, Steve says, "Nah, it couldn'tve been."

Suddenly as the arrive at Mixtures, Lee takes a shot in the direction of the woods that Paul, Chris and Ryan are running in, where quickly getting out of their car and hiding behind their doors Jake and Steve pull out their guns.

"DROP THE WEAPON AND GET YOUR HANDS IN THE AIR NOW." Steve shouts.

"*But they're getting away!*" Lee cries out.

"I SAID DROP THE WEAPON," Steve shouts again, where looking a bit confused Lee gradually puts his weapon on the floor.

"NOW GET YOUR HANDS BACK UP IN THE AIR AND STEP AWAY FROM THE WEAPON." Steve shouts. "Keep me covered, I'll get the cuffs on him," Steve says to Jake, where slowly approaching Lee who still has his back turned and hands in the air, Steve literally lassoes the handcuffs around Lee's right hand first, whilst at the same time he grabs hold of Lee's left hand with quickly tightening both cuffs at once.

"Now would you like to explain to me on what you were shooting for?" Steve says as he quickly and professionally searches Lee from top to toe for anymore weapons. Though not even getting a chance to answer, the door to Mixtures is thrown open.

"Lee, Norman's losin' it in here. I think he needs an ambulance." Alicia says.

"Just make sure the place is safe before we all head on in." Steve says giving Jake the head signal, where on his way in Jake takes hold of Lee's gun.

After a few seconds with Steve waiting outside Mixtures, Robert's News van pulls over with Robert getting out of the van and quickly setting up the camera and speakers.

"What the fuck are you doin' here?" Steve says. But before Robert even has a chance to answer, Mixtures front door flies open.

"All's clear Steve," Jake says, though Steve just shakes his head at Robert as he enters and escorts Lee on into Mixtures.

"Now would you like to fill me in on what the shootin' was about," Steve says to Lee.

Though with being accompanied by Alicia; Norman, suddenly stares at Steve with his shocked facial expression.

"In …., in …., in …., the dum ….," Norman struggles to say, where Jake and Steve look at Norman weirdly.

"He found it when I asked him to put the rubbish in the dumpster," Lee says.

"Found what?" Steve asks.

"A body." Lee says.

"IN THE DUMPSTER, IN THE DUMPSTER, IN THE DUMPSTER, IN THE DUMPSTER, IN THE DUMPSTER," Norman continuously shouts hysterically.

"Now I'm trusting you man," Steve says as he lets go of Lee who is still handcuffed, "But if you screw around my partner will do what he feels is necessary." Then looking at Jake who is trying to reassure Norman, Steve says, "I'm gonna check out this dumpster, you wanna call an ambulance for him?"

"Will do," Jake says. "I think I'll get calling for back up and the evidence crew too."

Still not having seen Tracey in Mixtures due to her being out of sight at the pay phone that has its own little hideaway, Steve makes his way to the back of the bar keeping himself covered.

Arriving at the dumpster, Steve opens the lid slowly and can see a small body figure completely rapped up with big thick adhesive tape, where the only part of the bloodied adhesive tape he can see any form of body to is the still eyes that are looking through the little wholes that have not been properly covered, along with the bloodied hand that's sticking out.

Whilst closing his eyes Steve slowly brings the lid to the dumpster down as he shakes his head in disgust, though opening his eyes before the lid comes to a full closure Steve looks in the direction of the dumpster and suddenly notices a slight cut out of a photo that's sticking out of a piece of the adhesive tape he can still see. Where taking an evidence handling bag out of his pocket and turning it inside out, Steve slides his hand into the bag. Then dipping his hand into the dumpster and taking hold of the cut out of the photo with the inside of the evidence handling bag, as he gets a grip of the photo he closes the dumpster over, then with the hand that closed the dumpster he takes hold of the outer part of the evidence handling bag and pulls it over the evidence, literally placing the evidence into the evidence bag without having to make any form of skin contact with it to increase his chances of forensic accounting.

Arriving back into Mixtures where Jake has Norman calmed down, Jake looks over at Steve who has the evidence bag held up for him to see.

"Jake, they're back." Steve says.

"I take it that's another one of the usual calling cards, huh?" Jake says noticing the evidence bag in Steve's hand.

"It looks like your hunch was right," Steve says.

"Could you tell who it was in the cut out?" Jake says.

"I think I'll leave that part to the big guys." Steve says as he puts the evidence away in his jacket pocket.

Suddenly entering on in through the front door to Mixtures, Robert looks around for Tracey.

"Tracey," Robert says trying to get her attention or even see where she is for that matter. Then popping her head up from around the corner to where the payphone has its little private hideaway, Tracey just looks at Steve.

"We're ready to roll Tracey," Robert says due to noticing where she is, as Steve just gazes at her in disbelief. Where standing up and coming out from the payphone with her handbag in her hand, she looks at Steve.

"We've gotta talk." Tracey says looking for some form of reply from Steve, who is near enough looking as bad as Norman from the shock.

"Now just ain't the time or the place," Steve says not even being able to look in Tracey's direction. Though as he looks towards Jake, it's like he's amazed she's even in Mixtures.

Not wanting to make things any tenser than they already are,

Tracey heads for the door to which Robert is holding open for her, where she just leaves the place with not even a single squeak coming out of her.

35.

Still driving on the pitch black country road that doesn't even have any cats eyes in the centre of the two lanes, Pete at a steady pace is trying to keep his eyes peeled on literally everything as well as the road as he looks around to see if he can see any sign of Amy. Then suddenly out of the corner of his eye with slowing the car down to a very slow speed, Pete can see a single filed country road to the right of him. Where reversing the car back a bit and keeping his eyes peeled out for any other vehicles that may be coming from the rear of him, you can tell rightly that his eyes are trying to look everywhere for Amy as the car lights shine on different objects.

Heading up the single filed country road with only covering roughly thirty meters, Pete brings the car to a halt, then opening his glove compartment he takes out a torch.

"If it wasn't for the flat tire I had the other night you wouldn't be here." Pete says as he looks at the torch whilst turning the post vans front lights out.

Then getting out of the post van, where the only light in sight is the post vans inside light, the light automatically turns itself off, where as it disappears making everywhere completely pitch black, it's not even possible to see Pete.

"**AH!**" Pete suddenly shouts painfully as a thumping sound is heard. Then with a few seconds of complete silence a painful whimper is heard. Then revealing the problem Pete manages to find the switch to the torch, where as he shines it on himself it's plain to see what the painful shout and whimper was due to, as he fell flat on the floor smacking his knee on a rock.

Managing to get himself up and shine his torch around, which is very bright, Pete starts walking up the single filed country road with a bit of a limp.

"AMY, AMY," Pete shouts, "It's your crazy Poppa bear, are you alright my little angel?" Pete says as he continues to shine his torch on the path and into the woods.

"AMY, AMY," Pete hollows again, "WHERE ARE YOU MY LITTLE PRINCESS? AMY." Pete shouts as he continues to walk.

From inside the woods the light to Pete's torch can be seen swaying between the trees and branches, though as it gets brighter with Pete getting closer, Amy's bike can be seen still leaning up against the tree. But looking at the torches light flickering in between the trees and branches, the brightness suddenly starts to dim down as Pete makes his way back towards the direction of the post van.

Getting back into the van Pete does a U-Turn on the single filed country road, where as he drives down to the T-Junction and checks as to whether the road is all clear, with there being no sign of any traffic at all, Pete takes a right and drives down the road to as far as the eye can see. Arriving at the end of the road and taking a right, as his car turns the corner with another road coming into view, all seems to be down hill, where approximately one mile ahead towards the bottom of the hill, all that can be seen are flashing lights.

"Hello, I'm Tracey Lewis from the BIDN News, who at this present moment in time is standing outside a country bar called Mixtures, to which only twenty five minutes ago a shooting occurred over a body that was found in a dumpster to the rear of the building. Where at this precise moment in time as you can see from behind me, the evidence handlers have just parked up outside Mixtures and will be carryin' out a full investigation, though the main thing that is of a major concern to the members of the public that are living around this location, is of the two young girls that have been reported missing, called Naomi Layne and Amy Waterson. As Naomi Layne, to who's family live approximately four miles from this current location, was reported missing nearly eleven days ago now and has been on the news on a daily basis to see if any of the members of the public have seen her anywhere in their vicinity. Though sadly there's been no major leads called through our help lines as of yet. Also, only recently, another girl called Amy Waterson was reported missing tonight, where her family live approximately three miles from this current location as well."

As the cops cordon off Mixtures Tracey finishes her news report as Pete arrives, where getting out of his car and walking towards Mixtures, Pete walks up to the cop that's finishing off with the cordoning.
"What's going on here?" Pete says hastily whilst looking as worried as can be.
"There was a bit of shootin' goin' on about half hour ago over some City thugs that were acting peculiar at the bar." The cop says.
Taking a sigh of relief, Pete turns around and walks off slowly in the direction of his car, until all of the sudden Alicia is heard screaming in the background as a body figure gets taken out from Mixtures front door.
"AH, TELL ME IT'S NOT AMY?" Alicia shouts. Where as fast as lightening Pete turns around to take a look at the small figure covered up in a body bag that's being carried on a stretcher by two men that are covered up in their evidence handling suits from top to bottom.
"**AMY, AMY!**" Pete screams as he leaps over the Police cordons. "**TELL ME IT'S NOT AMY.**" Pete cries out as he's held back by Jake and Steve, to who he continues to try and fight through.
"Now come on man, calm yourself down." Steve says as he tries to keep hold of Pete.
"**CALM DOWN? YOU EXPECT ME TO BE CALM WHEN THAT COULD BE MY LITTLE BABY ZIPPED UP IN _THAT_ THING?**" Pete shouts as he looks Steve strait in the eyes.
"We need you to calm down before we even think of lettin' you identify the body sir." Jake says. Where shaking himself free from being held back by Steve and Jake, Pete takes a step back, looks at the stretcher,

then arrogantly and forcefully rubs his hand from his forehead then through his hair whilst lowering his head at the same time in the form of confusion.

"I think I'll go and get us some fresh coffees," Barbara says whilst taking hold of the two untouched coffees on the table.

"Do you wanna hand?" Jean says as Barbara takes hold of Pete's untouched coffee from beside the telephone.

"No I'm okay, though thanks for staying with me anyway, it's very much appreciated." Barbara says.

"Think nothing of it." Jean says as Barbara arrives in the kitchen pressing the on switch to the kettle, which starts to boil very quickly due to the water being lukewarm from being boiled not so long ago.

"You're two sugars and milk aren't you Jean?" Barbara says.

"No, I'm sugar and milk free now, as I've been told I'm as sweet as can be due to losin' the weight," Jean says making Barbara smile a little bit.

Poring water into the cups as Barbara adds another sugar to her cup of coffee she says, "You wanna turn on the box and see if you can find anythin' decent to watch?"

"That's not always a guarantee, but I'll give it a try." Jean says as she takes hold of the TV control and presses the power button.

Lifting the two coffee's from the work surface, Barbara heads towards the living room with a slight smile on her face, though all of the sudden Tracey comes into view on the box with the microphone in her hand, where Mixtures can be seen behind her. Standing as still as can be Barbara just glares at the box due to noticing Pete being escorted by Jake and Steve to the stretcher.

BIDN NEWS WITH TRACEY LEWIS

As you can see at this present moment in time, with the body that was found in a dumpster at the rear of Mixtures roughly forty minutes ago, a father of one of the missing girls is being escorted by the FBI to see if he can identify the body.

All of the sudden Barbara lets go of the cups, where they smash all over the floor wakening Rachel.

"What was that Mom?" Rachel says as she quickly sits up. But her Mum doesn't answer due to running over to Barbara who still has her eyes glued to the box, where they are as watery as can be with the tears rolling down her face, though as Barbara still glares at the box Jean takes hold of her hand and cuddles her for a bit of comfort and support.

Looking at the television Jake has hold of Pete who is being held for safety reasons.

"Now are you sure you are ready for this?" Steve asks Pete, where with not being able to answer Pete just nods.

With the camera not being able to see the figures face in the stretcher, Pete's face starts turning a beetroot color, "Ah, no, no, no." Pete says quietly, where with the devastated look on his face he turns away from looking at the dead figure.

Powerlessly falling to her knee's and getting cut by the smashed cups on the floor, Barbara leans forward and continuously smacks her fists on the floor which are poring with blood something crazy.

"No, no, no, no, no." Barbara shouts.

"Barbara, Barbara." Jean says as she takes hold of Barbara's hands and gives her a cuddle, to which Barbara squeezes the life out of Jean as she closes her eyes tightly like she's trying to get rid of the nightmare that's happening to her.

Still looking at the news whilst Jean is trying to comfort Barbara from being so worked up over Pete's reactions on identifying the body, as Jean tries to talk to Barbara, Rachel continues to listen to the news.

"Well sir, was it possible to identify if this is your daughter?" Steve says quietly as he looks at Pete to who still has his back turned to him. Then as Pete turns around with tears rolling down his beetroot face, Jake puts his hand on Pete's shoulder for a bit of comforting and support as Pete shakes his head side to side.
"No, no, it wasn't Amy." Pete says looking more relieved even though the tears are still rolling down his face.

"Mom, Barbara, did you hear that?" Rachel says whilst Jean is still trying to talk to Barbara.
"What?" Jean says as Barbara lifts her head up slowly.
"It wasn't Amy. Pete's just said it wasn't Amy." Rachel says looking all relieved.
Not knowing whether to laugh or cry Barbara suddenly starts to get severe pains.
"Are you alright Barbara?" Jean says as Barbara starts to try and control her breathing. But suddenly Barbara blacks out.
"Barbara, Barbara, stay with me," Jean says as she tries to hold Barbara from falling on anymore glass.

"Rachel, quickly phone an ambulance." Jean says as she checks Barbara's pulse and breathing. Where seeing that she's still breathing and has a pulse, Jean puts Barbara in three quarter prone position, then quickly grabbing a pillow Jean places it under Barbara's belly to give the unborn and Barbara some support.

"Hello 911, we need an ambulance it's an emergency. Yes the address is….,"

Still remaining beside Barbara, Jean looks up at Rachel as she makes the telephone call and gives her the thumbs up on her excellent telephone skills, then sends her a loving motherly wink.

"Now sir, are you sure you're gonna be okay on drivin' home?" Steve says as he notices the state Pete is in, but all of the sudden with interrupting Pete, his cellular rings.

"Hello." Pete says, then continuing to talk on his cellular and starting to get all agitated Pete says, "Shit when did this happen? Is she okay?" Then with quickly hanging up his cellular he starts running towards his car.

"Hay, what's the matter?" Steve says as he runs after Pete.

"My wife Barbara, she's blacked out in the middle of trying to control her breathing, as we're expecting our second baby that's not due for another two months." Pete says.

"Well man, you're in no fit state to drive." Steve says as he closes Pete's driver's door. Then looking back over to Mixtures, Steve whistles and waves a cop over to them.

"I'll get this cop to give you a lift to the hospital so you can meet your wife there instead of driving. Then whenever we hear from your daughter we'll give you a call." Steve says as he takes out his note book.

"What's the number for your cellular?" Steve says to Pete.

"Here, I'm shit for numbers, you may give your cellular a call from mine, that way my number should show up on yours," Pete says busy handing his cellular to Steve.

"Well if you've got this turned off whilst in the hospital, I'll phone the hospital and keep you posted." Steve says reassuringly as his own cellular suddenly rings with Pete's number coming into view.

"Thanks, thanks a lot man." Pete says looking more at ease.

"Well you give your house a call and let them know that you'll meet them in the hospital while I let the cop know what's happenin'." Steve says as he hands Pete his cellular back.

"Thanks again man."

36.

Arriving back at their tents and puffing and panting like crazy, Paul and Chris lean forward a bit whilst they try and catch their breath. Then looking back to where they've came from there's no sign of Ryan.

"Shit, I didn't think we were runnin' that fast," Paul says to Chris.

"Somethin' must be up." Chris says.

"How'd you know that?" Paul questions.

"Uh, back flash, who's usually the Mr. Blink-of-an-eye when it comes around to the runnin' with us guys, huh?" Chris says.

"Well!" Paul says busy humming.

Then slowly making his way towards them with a limp is Ryan.

"What took you so long man?" Paul says.

"Yeah, we thought you would've been back first and had this place packed up for us," Chris says busy getting his cocky remark in before Ryan has a chance to answer Paul's question.

"I've been shot," Ryan says as he starts to get more breathless by the second.

"You what?" Paul says starting to work himself up.

"Where, where man?" Chris gasps.

"In the back of the leg," Ryan says as Chris takes hold of him to give him some lenient support.

"Whatta we gonna do, whatta we gonna do," Paul says as he starts to crack up whilst walking back and forth with his pace increasing by the second.

"Let's get you covered bro," Chris says as he helps him towards the tent.

Starting to shiver with scarceness, Paul stands still watching over his shoulder as if he's next on the shooting list.

"Paul, I could do with a bitta help here man," Chris says as he tries to get Ryan in the tent without injuring him anymore. "Come on," Chris says, busy trying to crack Paul out of working himself up. Then making his way towards the tent Paul continuously keeps turning around to look back towards the direction they came from.

Inside the tent which is Chris's and Ryan's, obviously due to the length of it for Chris's sake, Chris grabs hold of a long thin towel from his bag and starts to compress it against the area that Ryan's been shot, while Ryan lies on his back with his leg hoisted up in the air.

"Ow, shit." Ryan agonizingly cries out.

"Oh, shit, you okay bro?" Chris says whilst easing off on the wound.

"I'll live, now keep at it, as I don't wanna drain out man." Ryan says in a tiresome manner.

"How's that feel?" Chris says.

"Not much better, but it's stopped the blood from flowing out anyway," Ryan says.

"Do you think you'd be alright on taking hold of it?" Chris says.

"What? Have you not tightened that thing up yet?" Ryan desperately says.

"No, it just needs compressive force don't it? Or does it?" Chris questions.

"Gimme that thing." Ryan says.

As Ryan does his own bandaging himself, Chris looks at Paul who's all worked up.

"And how are you feelin' now, huh?" Chris says.

"What went on back there? And why was the mother fucker shootin' at us, huh?" Paul says in disbelief.

"Well I don't think you waving the fifty dollar bills around helped much," Ryan says.

"Ah, who knows what the fuck was goin' through the psycho's nut, but I don' think I'll be headin' back there in a hurry, huh?" Chris says.

"But the pussy was good," Paul whimpers.

"I'll drink to that I think," Ryan says as he reaches for his bag and takes a little hand size mettle bottle out of it, removes the lid and takes a little sip.

"Not a bad idea," Chris says as he also takes hold of the bottle and takes a quick sip.

"Yo Paul, get some of that down you, it'll help rest that mind of yours," Chris says as he holds the bottle in front of Paul for him to take hold of.

"Ooh, shit man, it's sure as hell taking my worries away. That's my good old pop for you. Nothin' can beet his good old home brews." Ryan says as he starts to look a little bit tipsy already.

"Here take your worries away man," Chris says to Paul.

"Ah what the heck," Paul says as he grabs hold of the mettle bottle and takes a little sip.

"Hmmm," Paul hums in delight, "Does your Pop take orders?"

37.

Walking into the living room from the direction of the kitchen and balancing the tray she's carrying in the one hand all professionally, as Samantha holds it high in the air with such an excellent balance, as she arrives in front of Alan she brings the tray down at a dramatic speed with Alan nearly falling off the edge of his seat.

"So whatta you think of that cushiony bed of mine then, huh?"" Samantha says.

"It's like a ship that's sinkin' once you get on them covers," Alan says busy lifting his eye lids up and down.

"At least in this case you know who you're sinkin' with."

As Samantha places the tray on the table in front of the settee and sits next to Alan, she waves the cocktail in front of his face then kisses him on the cheek.

"Well, whatta you think of that smell?" Samantha says as she smooches up to Alan.

"Honestly? You could wave shit in my face and I'd still not be able to tell you what it smells like." Alan says not looking impressed.

"Why's that, you just getting over a cold or fever or something?" Samantha questions.

"Nope, I've just never had a sense of smell." Alan says.

"Ah, you poor little man, you don't know what you're missing out on." Samantha says as she sniffs the cocktail herself.

"But I'm a good guy when it comes around to tasting things, I mean look at my taste in women," Alan says as he looks at Samantha's gorgeous figure up and down, "I just can't wait till I get my teeth into you." Alan says.

Then getting himself into a comfortable sitting position he takes hold of Samantha's glass and sets it on the table as he puts his arm above Samantha's shoulder, to use the headrest behind her for support, where as he sets the glass down, the same hand that lets go of the glass raps around

Samantha as they glare into each others eyes, where it's hard to tell whether it's a look of worry, nervousness, happiness or scarceness, as the air in the room could near enough be cut with a knife due to the extreme intenseness. Then suddenly the answer is revealed as Samantha and Alan's mouths collide as they continuously kiss in all forms possible, then starting to kiss each other on the cheeks and necks, Alan says. "I just had to get a taste of you first babe, cuz you'd beat anythin' or anyone, and after all I don' wanna start droolin' on my first night, huh?" Alan says.

"Well now you've gotta have a taste of this and tell me what you think." Samantha says as she takes hold of the cocktail, gives Alan a kiss on the lips then hands it over to him.

"Is it safe?" Alan says as he looks back and forth from Samantha to the cocktail.

"I wouldn't worry I'm quite good at the mouth to mouth resuscitation." Samantha says giving Alan a little bit of reassurance.

"Oh, so I'm in safe hands." Alan says as he looks at Samantha and lifts his eye lids up and down, "Well, here goes nothin'." Alan says as he starts to drink away at the cocktail.

"Well, whatta you think?" Samantha questions as Alan takes the glass away from his lips.

"Oooh, it's bad, but I like it," Alan says as he puts on a squinted facial expression.

Getting themselves together like they are two little sheep trying to keep themselves warm, as they look all nice and comfortable Samantha takes hold of the control and turns on the box.

Starting to bark his head off outside as the romantic music to a movie on the box starts to kick off, Alan takes hold of Samantha and kisses her hand, "It looks like someone else is looking for a bit've loving care out there, huh?" Alan says.

"Who knows, who knows?" Samantha says as the control falls to the floor. Attempting to take hold of the control Alan is literally on top of Samantha as he attempts to reach for it, then pausing and looking into

Samantha's eyes, Samantha says, "Do you believe in love at first sight?" Then starting to lick Alan's neck and go onto what looks like an unstoppable mouth watering kiss, Alan replies, "Hmmm, hmmm, hmmm," in his own form of language whilst kissing.

Suddenly falling to the floor and the lips not even having the ability to separate, the clothes start getting thrown around the living room, where looking towards the window where the barking noise is coming from, a glimpse of a dark figure suddenly disappears.

With half an hour having past by and Alan lying on the floor with only a pair of boxers on him, while Samantha's figure is caressed up beside his body with only a pair of knickers on her, the subtitles of the movie that was on the box start to appear, though are quickly interrupted by a news flash.

NEWS
Welcome to the BIDN's eleven O'clock news. With the incident that occurred outside a village bar, just on the outskirts of Boston City earlier on today, called Mixtures. We are just after getting a report that the body which was found in the dumpster to the rear of Mixtures, where with her family having been informed, to which we offer our sincere condolences to, it is of one of the young girls that have been reported missing within the past 12 days called, Naomi Layne.

"Mixtures?" Samantha says in disbelief as she takes hold of her top and puts it on.

NEWS (continued)
With shots having been fired at four
individuals who were acting very peculiar
whilst at Mixtures, the owner to Mixtures,
Lee Granger was held at gun point by the
FBI who was heading towards Mixtures at
the time of the incident.

Talking over the volume of the news, Alan says, "I've gotta go and make sure it ain't my guys that your boss was shootin' at." Then taking hold of Samantha's hands and looking into her eyes Alan says, "I'll give you a call, huh?" Then throwing the rest of his clothes on, Alan gives Samantha a big long kiss and says, "And yes, I do believe in love at first sight."

Then making Samantha look away from Alan and towards the box, a picture of Jamie-Lee on his own suddenly appears, followed by Jo and his Mum, Veronica Walters, where the picture of Jo looks near enough like a spitting image of Alan.

NEWS
Now for all the members of the public
who are living anywhere near the vicinity
of Mixtures, we are warning you all to stay
indoors until you are advised any further.

Obstructing Samantha from the box, her back door closes over with no sign of Alan anywhere, though all that can be heard are loud dog barks coming from Jack as Samantha just stands there looking at the back door from inside the living room.

Heading out towards the kitchen, shaking her head side to side in disbelief over what's just happened, and more to the point how quick it's all happened, Samantha locks the back door over. Where heading back into the living room, just before entering on into it Samantha looks up towards the front door and can see the envelope containing the money is no longer there. Shaking her head in disgust, anger and disappointment over what's happened, Samantha looks back into the living room and continues to watch the news as she slowly walks back on in.

NEWS
At this present moment in time it is a complete mystery as to why ripped up pieces of old photos and news papers keep being found at near enough all the similar crime scenes the cops and FBI have been coming across over the past 18 years. But for some reason the only photo out of all the pieces of evidence the cops and FBI have come across, that has actually been able to be pieced together, is that of Jamie-Lee Walters, as the picture of Jo and his Mom, Veronica Walters, were captured by the cops from old photos they managed to get hold of.

Samantha just stands in disbelief as the news shows a picture of Mixture's again, as Jack continuously barks outside like crazy.

NEWS
Now here's a report on the weather where you are ....,

Walking up to the living room window to see what Jack's barking at,

169

Samantha can see him continuously jumping and barking in an angry manner as he looks towards her. Though looking back at the ground to the living rooms entrance, standing there are the worn-out grubby shoes and dirty bloodied pants that slowly and quietly walk on into the living room, where only being seen from waste height and down, the Stranger is carrying the bloodied worn-out rucksack in their left hand, which has the handle of the knife and a rusty looking crowbar sticking out of it.

"What's the matter Jack?" Samantha says. Where starting to bark and growl a lot angrier, Samantha notices Jack is starting to take his eyes off her and slowly look to the left of Samantha, turning around slowly Samantha suddenly see's the dirty shoes and grubby clothed individual standing behind her.

"AAAAAAAAAAAAAAAH!" Samantha screams. Then suddenly she gets rapped over the head with a rusty heavy metal pole, where while she's down and continuously getting a deep grubby painful sound of a voice says, "Shut up, shut up, shut up."

With there being no more painful cries or angry shouts coming from Samantha anymore, the news comes back into hearing mode again.

NEWS
And now we'll join Tracey Lewis who is currently at Mixtures for any up-to-date news.

TRACEY
Thanks Anna. Now first of all I would like to offer my sheer condolences for the grieving family of Naomi Layne, and pray to the heavens above that whoever is behind this is brought to justice soon.

Suddenly the Stranger's dirty foot starts kicking Samantha continuously again as they're heard crying the words, "No, no, no, no, no, no," once more. Though looking at Samantha she's not moving in the slightest.

- -

At Mixtures the door is flung open with Lee appearing.

"That's him, that's the guy that was here earlier," Lee shouts as he looks back and forth at Tracey and Steve.

"Who?" Steve says.

"I heard you mention their surname on the news earlier." Lee says all flabbergasted.

"Walters?" Tracey questions.

"Yeah, that's it, the Walters dude," Lee says.

"Hay man we're talkin' eighteen years back with Jamie-Lee Walters, are you sure you've got yourself on the right track with this guessing game?" Steve says not believing a word Lee is saying.

"No, no, it's that, oh shit, what on earth is that frickin' name on the ID again?" Lee says all agitated. "It's J, J …., Jo …., Jo frickin' Walters. That's it, Jo Walters." Lee says all relieved on actually remembering.

"WHAT! JO WALTERS?" Tracey shouts over to Lee.

"Yeah, yeah, I mean I checked his ID, obviously he's a bit older now like, but that's him for sure and, uh, I asked him his date of birth, which was, uh, June the 8th, 1979." Lee says to Steve.

Over at Tracey as she looks into the camera she says, "Well as you can see it doesn't look like we're anywhere near finished on receiving extra news over today's occurrence, which will hopefully help crack down on finding the killer once and for all, I'm Tracey Lewis from the BIDN News, where I'll hand you back to the main news headlines." Tracey says.

As Robert brings the camera to a halt, Lee who's still standing beside Steve and Jake, suddenly loses the plot altogether.

"Shit, shit, shit, shit!" Lee says bouncing himself back and forth like crazy, "Samantha too, the murderous mother fucker's back at her place."

"Who's Samantha?" Jake says.

"SHE WORKS BEHIND THE BAR FOR ME." Lee shouts.

"Right, get your guys rounded up," Jake shouts to the cops. "What's Samantha's address?" Jake says to Lee.

38.

"Guys, guys," Alan says as he runs in the dark towards the tents, "What on earth was that that was happening on down at Mixtures?" Alan says as he opens the zip to the tent to get in, where lying there with his leg lifted up in the air with Paul and Chris on either side, is Ryan.

"God only knows man, but the anger was taken out on me." Ryan says as he points to his leg.

"Why, how'd you find out?" Chris asks.

"It was on the news about some young girl's body havin' been found in the dumpster." Alan says.

"No wonder that mutt was barkin' its head off none stop. He was obviously barkin' at the body that time he went crazy on us." Chris says.

"So that's why the mother fucker shot at us." Ryan says.

"He was shootin' at you guys?" Alan says.

"Who knows, it was more than likely the unfamiliar faces no doubt and you waving your fifty fuckin' dollar bills around. He probably thought we'd robbed a bank or somethin'." Chris says.

"Ow." Ryan whimpers.

"What's up with you?" Alan says.

"It was me that caught the bullet." Ryan says as he finds it hard to move an inch.

"Shit, you've been shot, where?" Alan says.

"In the back of the leg." Ryan says whilst pointing at it.

"It's been covered up though, but not brilliantly." Chris says.

"Well keep it high in the air you drip or you'll have no fuckin' blood left." Alan says. Where with getting Chris to give him a hand on raising Ryan's leg at a forty five degree angle, Alan says. "Sure I'll get the first aid cream I've got in my wash kit that my little bro insisted I took with me, or should I say demanded I took with me." Alan says as he turns around to leave the tent.

"I suppose the brains have to be somewhere in the family," Ryan says.

"Yeah, it's a pity there's none in here though." Alan's says. "Now put a bit of compression on where you're bleeding, I'll be back in a second."

"I'm sure I'll be here when you get back." Ryan says messing around.

Heading over to his tent, which he's sharing with Paul, Alan doesn't pay any attention to one part of the tents entrance already being open, so getting down on his hands and knees and entering on into the tent, Alan feels around on the ground and uses either side of the sleeping sack for his bearings. With crawling over his sleeping sack slowly, a crunching noise of what sounds like a plastic bag is suddenly heard, then as the noise quickly comes to a standstill a torch, which isn't the brightest, suddenly lightens up.

Shining the torch into his plastic bag, Alan opens the wash kit and takes out the first aid cream that Simon gave him. Then putting the plastic bag back into the corner of the tent again, as Alan shines the torch on the head piece of his sleeping sack, he notices his cellular is missing.

Turning himself around and literally having his rear pointing in the direction of the headrest to Paul's sleeping sack, as he turns around and crawls for the exit, he loses his balance on a concave groove to the ground that's underneath the tent and nearly falls flat onto Paul's sleeping sack, which he quickly notices is lumpy.

"Oh, shit sorry about that, Paul didn't fill me in on him havin' brought a date back from Mixtures." Alan says quietly as he quickly removes his hand from the sleeping sack.

"Are you okay?" Alan says quietly again with getting no reply.

Still getting no reply, Alan starts to push his luck as he quietly turns himself around to see if he can get a glimpse at Paul's date. So quietly crawling back up to the headrests of the sleeping sacks, Alan shines the torch on Paul's sleeping sack, where it's plain to see there's an individual in the sack, as their body is completely covered from head to toe.

As Alan's hand slowly goes down to unzip the top part of Paul's sleeping sack a bit, just to get a peek in on Paul's date, he quickly removes his hand from doing so and shakes his head side to side as his lip movement can be seen saying the word, 'No', but is completely silent. Suddenly putting a little grin on his face as if he's come up with a good idea, Alan says, "Hi, I'm Alan, d'you wanna come and join me an the guys in the other tent, it looks like Paul could do with a bit've company."

Still remaining silent with no movement coming from the sleeping sack at all, Alan shines the torch on the head piece of the sleeping sack, where as he unzips it he quietly says, "Whatta you think, huh?"

Still getting no reply and acting all silver-tongued, Alan slowly takes hold of the zip to the sleeping sack and says, "Paul could do with a little bitta warm lovin', huh?" Where quickly and carefully opening the sleeping sacks head piece so smoothly, Alan smiles and says, "Whatta you think?" But inside the sleeping sack as Alan shines the torch on in, an old ladies ghostly dead face pops out, with her jaw bone opening automatically and scaring the shit out of Alan, where looking at the dried intensity of her pale tongue coming into view, it's plain to see she's been dead for some time.

"**WHAT THE, HOLY SHIT, FUCKIN' HELL, GUYS .., HOLY MOTHERIN' FUCK**!" Alan shouts as he pelts out of the tent and starts vomiting.

"Don't tell me, he's found your shitty underwear?" Chris says as he looks at Paul.

"It's more than likely all the poisonous creatures you've attracted with your shitty attempt on cooking earlier." Ryan says to Chris.

Suddenly Alan's hand holding the first aid cream comes through the entrance of Ryan and Chris's tent, where Paul takes hold of it and hands it to Ryan, though in the process Alan's hand quickly disappears and vomiting noises kick off again.

"Was your ride really that bad tonight?" Chris says. Then Alan's hand appears again in an uppercut fist format, where he suddenly starts moving his forefinger back and forth giving them the signal to come and see as to what he's vomiting for, to which his hand disappears like a flash of lightening and more vomiting noises kick off.

"Come on, let's go and see what this nutter's barfing over," Chris says to Paul.

As the two of them get out of the tent Chris says, "Okay, what's all this non-stop spewin' for, huh?" Where Alan points to the tent, but quickly turns around and vomits again.

"Come on," Chris says as he taps his hand on Paul's shoulder.

"My bet's is that Paul's brought a packet of used durex that are more than likely filled to the brims." Ryan squirts out from the tent.

As Chris and Paul arrive at the tent, Chris pulls open half of the entrance that's unzipped.

"After you," Chris says as he waves Paul on into the tent whilst holding it open for him.

"Shit there's someone in my sack." Paul says.

"I take it it's that pussy that was tryin' to make out with you earlier, huh?" Chris says.

"Ha, huh," Paul says as his cocky mannered laugh turns to a startled finish.

"Well, what is it?" Ryan shouts from the tent.

"Well?" Chris says as he looks for an answer from Paul, but Paul is unresponsive.

"Here throw us that torch of yours Alan," Chris says. Where catching the torch Chris looks into Paul whose light from his watch is shining down on the dead figure.

Not being able to see it the best, Chris bends down and crawls up to Paul, where shining the torch down on what Paul's looking at, Chris takes one look at the old ladies dead face and darts out of the tent.

"Crap, crap, crap," Chris says, "I could've done without this kinda shit, my babe's nightclub would've kicked this killer of a camps fuckin' ass for six."

"What's up?" Ryan queries, where opening the flap to Ryan and Chris's tent, Chris looks in on to Ryan.

"It's another dead body, which this time has been stuffed in Paul's sleepin' sack." Then quickly looking back to Alan and Paul's tent he can see there is no sign of Paul.

Heading over to the tent and looking inside, Paul hasn't moved a muscle.

"Bro, get outta there, are you after her cell phone fuckin' number or somethin'. Cuz personally I can give you a little hint, she ain't gonna answer it," Chris says as he drags Paul's frozen figure out of the tent.

"Whatta we gonna do, whatta we gonna do, whatta we gonna do," Paul says getting all hysterical as he turns left to right continuously like he's going insane.

"Come on bro you're stronger than that, hang in there." Chris says as he holds Paul still by getting a grip of his shoulders.

"This would put any guys off wanting to pull some pussy," Paul says.

"Are you okay Alan?" Chris says. Where as Alan holds up his forefinger giving Chris a sign to wait a second, Alan quickly turns his head and vomits again.

"Right let's get packin' and get outta here." Chris says as he has hold of Paul whilst looking at Alan and waiting to hear if he gets any reply from Ryan. But everyone remains quiet.

Five minutes pass by.

"Well, this is all I'll be taking from the tent," Alan says as he gets into the van with a plastic bag in his hand as he closes the door behind him.

"Whattabout you man?" Chris says as he looks at Paul.

"Whether I need it or not man it's stayin'. I mean would you want the sleepin' sack that some old ladies dead bodies been stuffed in? Or would you even think of leanin' over the body and grabbin' any other bags that your gears been left in?" Paul says.

"Well I guess when you put it that way I suppose you've gotta point." Chris says.

"**Suppose**?" Paul says.

"And how are you feelin'?" Chris says to Ryan.

"Like shit, but I'm just thinkin' of it as a free travel memorabilia." Ryan says.

"Well fuck if I never get a chance to forget mine ..., ooh ..., shit!" Paul says with shivers running up his back.

"And whattabout you Alan?" Chris says.

"I just hope all this shit clears over night and we can get outta here." Alan says.

"Well here's what we're gonna do." Chris says.

39.

With three cop cars and an unmarked car arriving at Samantha's house, as they all get out and cover the area, Steve and Jake slowly head towards the rear of the house.

Arriving at the back of Samantha's house there's no sign of Jack again, where this time his lead has been shredded apart.

Taking a glimpse at the rear door, where there's blood on the floor, Steve quickly vaults from one side of the doorway to the other, pointing his gun into the house in the process, where as he lands safely on the other side of the doorways entrance he gives Jake the signal to point their guns into the house at the same time. So quickly aiming their guns into the house at the same time, having their firearms cover the surroundings indoors, noticing the entrance is all clear the two of them enter on into the house and keep each others backs covered.

In the living room there's smashed glass and blood all over the floor, but there's no sign of any life or danger.

"Put it this way, they sure like hide and go seek." Steve says as he steps out of the house that's been searched through thoroughly.

"Who knows what they've got lined up for us next?" Jake says.

"Either way from what they've left here," Steve says looking at the blood on the floor, "The evidence handling crew are sure gonna have their work cut out for them this night."

"Huh! What about our hairy asses?" Jake says.

"Speak for yourself."

"Just think on the amount of paper work we're gonna be crammed with that needs sorted out. I mean we've nearly got a whole filing cabinet on this case and we've still no leads on the killer other than a photo of Jamie-Lee Walters and some so-called ID of Jo Walters." Jake says.

"Well these sure ain't love letters gettin' left for us, that's for sure."

Steve says as he holds up the evidence handler's bag containing the cut out of a photo.

40.

In at the tatty abandoned house the Stranger is standing in front of the photo of Jo and his Mum, Veronica Walters, who are up in a frame on the wall. Where over at the corner of the room where Naomi Layne's dead figure once sat, is Amy Waterson, adhesively taped. Yet over at the two-seat settee is the same sized figure of Samantha's body which is completely rapped up in the big thick adhesive tape, with only the closed eyes, nose, hand and part of her mouth sticking out as her figure remains motionless.

Stroking the picture, the Stranger turns around and walks towards Amy, where picking her up and placing her over their shoulder, they head for the front door and walk on out.

With the Stranger out of sight altogether and the door closing over behind them, making a big bang, looking over towards Samantha her eyes start to open slowly, looking very scared, shocked and confused.

41.

"How are you feelin' bro?" Chris says to Ryan.

"Quit worryin', I'll be fine. Plus it's quite luxurious watchin' you guys do all the work anyway, I could get used to this." Ryan says.

"Well are we gonna need much more of this?" Alan says as he holds a branch in his hand.

"Yeah, I wanna see the whole van covered, I don't want be able to see any of it. And we'll keep covered up till the'morrow." Chris says.

"Have you been in this kind've shit before?" Alan says.

"No, why, what on earth gives you that idea?" Chris says.

"It's just the way you drove the van down to the concrete road, reversed back, then brushed over the tire marks that were bendy and leading up to here." Alan says.

"That's to have anyone thinkin' the van went down to the busy road and just drove off. I got it off the undercover cop tips." Chris says. "Now less talk and get coverin' up."

With fifteen minutes having past by, the van is completely out of sight, where with Alan being the last person to get into the van, Chris assists him by taking hold of the branch that's going to be connected to the inside part of the door, so with the door closing over it can keep the rear door camouflaged as well.

"That's us guys. Now are you sure you're gonna be okay?" Chris says to Ryan.

"You're starting to sound like my Pop man, quit the worryin' I'll be fine." Ryan says. "Plus look on the bright side there's still over half a bottle of cream that Alan, I mean Simon packed for us." Ryan says quickly correcting his sentence.

"Yeah, he's got more brains than all four of us put together." Alan says.

"Well I dunno about you guys but I could do with a few vibes to relax the mind," Paul says.

"Keep the volume low though." Ryan says.

"Well, duh." Paul says all cocky mannered.

Climbing into the front of the van with a bit of struggle, Paul turns on the radio.

"That fat ass of yours near got stuck dude," Chris says as he takes a puff of a fresh cigarette.

"And you, get rid of that smoke, whatta you tryin' to do give me an infection or somethin'?" Ryan says.

"Yeah, that's probably due to the amount of shit that's still up my whole after what's happened to us this night." Paul says answering Chris's last sly remark as he tries to get some decent songs on the radio. Then suddenly the news comes on.

"Leave that on man," Ryan says as he notices Paul is about retune it for more music. "Let's see what the fucks happenin'."

NEWS

..., the main people the cops are looking
to speak to at the moment are a group of
men that were at Mixtures bar earlier on,
as one is believed to be a Jo Walters.
Walters is thought to have been Killed
in a serious crash with his father Jamie-
Lee Walters 18 years ago, where it has
been brought to our attention that Jo's
Mother, Veronica, was also found buried
in her backyard after having been
scrupulously murdered on the same day.
So be warned, he should not be approached
in anyway shape or form, as the female
employee to Mixtures, Samantha Molar, to

who ended up taking Jo Walters back to her house, is also now reported missing.

"What the fuck? Gimme your lighter," Alan says to Chris whose still trying to put out his last cigarette.
"What for man?" Chris asks.
"JUST GIMME THE LIGHTER," Alan shouts.
"Okay, keep your hair on man." Chris says strangely as Alan reaches into his pocket and takes out his wallet. Where taking something out of his wallet and lighting the lighter, it reveals the details of his ID, with the name Jo Walters on it. Where as the radio continues giving information about Jo Walters personal details, all of them match with Alan's ID as he scrolls down it as they are read out.
"You mean you got me the fake ID of a fuckin' killer?" Alan says angrily as he jumps towards the front of the van and starts punching Paul in the face, where Paul just sits there taking them, not even attempting to fight back.
Quickly taking hold of Alan with a muscular grab, Chris fires Alan back on his butt.
"Alan, wind your fuckin' neck in and take a fuckin' seat. Paul knew nothing about the ID's." Chris says.
With a sorry facial expression Paul just sits still with his face completely battered and beetroot red.
"Now let's think about this," Chris says.
"Think about it, you mean like on what we're gonna do, huh? What is it, that we're gonna stay here for the next twenty fuckin' years hidin' out or what?" Alan angrily says.
"Let's just see what the'morrow brings, huh?" Chris says.
"Oh, so the cops have more to throw in my face? Oh, that's good and what about Samantha, huh? If it wasn't for us none of this would've happened." Alan says whilst throwing a punch into a bag that's on the floor as he lowers his head in shame.

"I'll be on the look out first, now let's get some shut eye." Chris says.

42.

"Hay, Steve," Jake says as he watches Tracey run towards the direction of their unmarked car, as Robert is seen a good bit behind her packing away the camera supplies. "It looks like she either has more news for us or she's looking to give you another slap across the face." Jake says. Where Steve's facial expression isn't impressed.

"I bet you ten to one that you're gonna get another smacking." Jake says.

"Give it a rest ass wipe." Steve says as he turns away from looking at Jake, slows down the car and winds down the window.

"I'm tellin' you, I'll even bet it's your right cheek too." Jake says.

"You know you've a real gamblin' problem dude." Steve says. Then arriving at Steve's window, Steve looks at Tracey, "What?" Steve says arrogantly as he can still barely look in her direction.

"We've gotta talk." Tracey says whilst trying to catch her breath.

"Why what's happened?" Jake says busy thinking it's some more news on the case.

"No as in me and you." Tracey says as she points towards Steve and then herself.

"Uh, do you not notice we're at the scene of a crime here?" Steve says. "It'll have to wait," Steve says as he manages to look into her eyes.

"Whattabout later?" Tracey says with love wrote all over her face as she looks at Steve.

"We're gonna be up to our eyes in fillin' out report forms more than likely." Steve says.

"Well if you manage to get a bit of time out, behind you, if you take your first right, the first house you come across is my grandma's house that I'm stayin' at for a couple of weeks. I should be around there about 12:30 a.m. after the midnight news." Tracey says.

Though with Steve remaining silent, Tracey lowers her head

slightly, but gradually being able to lift her head up again she looks at Steve once more. "And Steve, with havin' found out on why you've been hittin' the drink hard lately it's completely understandable. As if anythin' like that happened to you I'd more than likely be the same, if not worse." Tracey says. "But it's somethin' I'd rather talk about with you, other than keep tucked in."

Still remaining silent, Steve looks like he's busy wondering on how she's found out about it.

"Like I said, my Gran's house is the first right behind you, then the first house you come across." Then Tracey turns around and slowly walks off while Steve remains speechless.

Leaning over Steve like he's trying to stick his head out of Steve's window, Jake shouts, "He'll be there." Then Steve gives him a good forceful punch in the arm.

43.

In the pitch black woods the only light that gives any kind of brightness is the moon that's only a stone throw away from being a full one, where dodging in and out of the trees and branches very slowly, up ahead there looks like there's one hefty heck of a sized bush. Though getting up close to it, it's just a pile of branches containing their leaves that have been piled up on top of each other. Then suddenly noticing a bright reflection coming from in between the leaves and branches, heading up close to it, it's plain to see it's the window to Ryan's Dad's van.

Inside the van with loud snores literally sucking in the roof, Chris stands up from doing guard and heads to the back of the van where the snoring sounds are coming from.

"Right, who's on guard now?" Chris says at a half decent tone. Though the snores continue as if he's standing there talking to himself.

"Right, who's doing guard now?" Chris says a bit louder, to which Paul wakes up.

"I'll do it." Paul says with a depressing voice.

"Give Alan a shout in a couple of hours." Chris says.

"Do I have to?" Paul moans.

"Well come on you don't expect me to do it again do you. And I don't think Ryan's in any fit state on doin' it, huh?" Chris says quietly.

"Oh, I suppose so!" Paul says.

As Paul slides past Chris and makes his way to the front of the van, Chris being the big Daddy longlegs he is just lays down on the centre part of the floor, in between the two occupied seats. As the seats in the back of the van are like big long rectangular seats on both sides of the van, literally like you'd get in a cop van. Where just about to knock out on the floor, Chris sits up and takes a peek at Ryan to see if he's okay.

With all being quiet and Chris already on cloud nine and snoring slightly, Paul, not really being able to see overly much is just twiddling his thumbs and forefingers around in circles as he listens out for anything unusual. But quickly making Paul freak out, a bit of branch on the front window beside him makes a loud squeaky noise as it slides down then suddenly stops, then quickly letting off another miner squeak as it slides down a little bit more it stops altogether.

As a few minutes pass by, Paul's eyes look like they're ready to come to a close, but all of the sudden the silence is broken by strange moving sounds coming from outside the van, having Paul bounce up to being one hundred percent aware again.

Trying to remain still the noises outside continue with loud thumping noises sounding like it's coming from the floor.

"Shit, did you hear that?" Paul silently says.

"Hush up." Chris says as if he hasn't got a care in the world.

Then suddenly from the other side of the van there's a noise that sounds like lighter foot steps making it's way around to the other side of the van, to which the noise from the leaves being trampled on are being heard.

With Alan and Ryan still sleeping, they are promptly awoke from the loud dog barks coming from outside. Though with the loud dog barks having made them jump out of their sleep, Alan rolls off the seat he's lying on and lands strait on top of Chris, banging their heads together, where with Ryan swinging himself around to the sitting up position with his soar leg, he isn't able to keep it up, where as it drops towards the floor he kicks Chris strait in the balls with force.

"Oooh." Whimpers Chris.

"Shit, soz man, the leg just dropped." Ryan says.

"You don't say," Chris says with his hi pitch whimpering voice.

Suddenly from outside the van, loud dog whimpers are heard going off, though as the whimpering continues they sound like they're getting further away and end up stopping altogether with outside going back to complete silence.

"What the fuck was going on out there?" Alan says.

"It was probably some mutt fighting some fox or wolf man, but as for in here I'm getting my balls fuckin' ripped off. I'd probably have been safer out there for Pete's sake." Chris says.

"Soz about that man." Ryan says.

"So you should be, as I'm near in the mood to rip that fuckin' leg off and ram it up your ass." Chris says.

Turning himself back into the lying position to enable Chris's groan to get some lee-way, Chris pushes Alan off him as Ryan goes back into raising his leg up a bit.

"Now come on let's get some shut eye." Chris says as he rolls over to lying on his front, "And I think I'll lye like this before my nuts are ripped into shreds."

"Soz man." Ryan says again.

"Ooh, just you wait till you're better dude, you'll get what's comin'." Chris says.

44.

Sitting as quiet as can be with their eyes hanging out of their head from the tiredness wrote all over their faces, Jean and Rachel are sitting side by side, to which Jean comforts Rachel by giving her a motherly loving cuddle as the two of them watch the horrifying news over Naomi Layne's body having been found in the rear dumpster to Mixtures.

"Mom, I hope Amy's alright. If she's not I'll never forgive myself for leaving her alone." Rachel says as she tucks her face into her Mum to hide her tears.

"Now come on," Jean says as she places her forefinger under Rachel's chin to lift her head up from looking at the floor so the two of them can see eye to eye. "I don't want you ever talking like that, okay?" Jean says in a very well controlled manner with love and concern wrote all over her face as she looks into Rachel's eyes.

"I'm sorry Mom," Rachel says. Then she starts to cry uncontrollably.

"Don't be silly my little angel, you have nothing to be sorry about." Jean says as she puts both her arms around Rachel whilst kissing her on the forehead.

Outside of the waiting room as Rachel and Paula remain cuddled up to each other, there's a big corridor to which the lights have been dimmed for to enable patients to get a nights sleep, though also in the corridor on the left hand side there seems to be private wards with a brave gap in between each door. Though opposite to the private wards there are open wards that have approximately eight beds in each ward, with mosey baskets on the left hand side of the beds, where the curtains to most of them are closed over.

Back towards the entrance door to the private wards, on the left hand side of the door there is a little box outside each room, though out of all the boxes that can be seen, there's only one of the boxes that contains a bright red light.

With the light suddenly disappearing, the door opens with a nurse and Pete walking out of the room, where after a quick conversation the nurse heads one way and Pete head the other, which is in the direction of the waiting room.

Arriving at the waiting room which has no door to it, and is only big enough for a wheel chair to get through, Pete looks at Jean comforting Rachel. Though seeing the tears that are rolling down Rachel's eyes as Jean lifts her head up and notices Pete, her choice of words don't seem to be leaving her lips.

"What's up?" Pete says. But then noticing that they've been watching the television, he looks at Jean as he points to the box, "It's not ..,"

"No, no," Jean says quickly reassuring him, "If we heard anythin' from the box you'd be first to know." Jean says.

"I take it she's cryin' over Amy still missin'?" Pete says.

"Yeah, though she's got it in her head that it's all her fault due to not stayin' with Amy."

Sitting on the other side of Rachel Pete takes hold of Rachel's hand like it's an inner part of a sandwich due to both of his hands covering her hand from the top and bottom.

"Now I don't want to hear that kind've nonsense, you hear me?" Pete says as he tries to remain strong.

"But I could've stayed with her till she got the bike back home at least." Rachel says as she starts to cry again.

"Now come on, promise me you won't ever think of anymore nonsense like that. As after all if I recall your plans were on behalf of Amy as well, huh, to get settin' up the computer games and see if it was alright with your Mom that Amy could stay at yours for the night, am I right. And that way you'd have all ready for her coming." Pete says trying to be strong for everyone's sake. "To my knowledge that's true friendship if ever I've seen it." Pete says as he gives Rachel a little kiss on the forehead. "Now you be a big strong girl and we'll find Amy soon enough, huh?" Pete says.

"Okay," Rachel says lifting her head up from leaning on her Mum.

"Thanks," Jean says as she pats Pete on the shoulder.

"We've all gotta be strong in these kind've circumstances," Pete says as he gives Jean's hand a little squeeze. "Now here, do you lovely ladies wanna head on home and get some shut eye?" Pete says.

"Ah no, Mom, can we stay, please?" Rachel says.

"It looks like the boss has spoken." Jean says as she stands up at the same time as Pete. Where with Rachel about to stand up as well, Jean says, "You just sit here for a minute and keep an eye on the box for us while I have a little talk with Pete, alright?"

"Okay, okay Mom." Rachel reassuringly repeats.

Heading out to the hallway, Jean takes hold of Pete's hands and says, "You seem to be stronger than anyone considering what's been happenin'."

"Personally," Pete whispers, "If I wasn't I'd crack. Plus I've gotta be strong for Barbara and Amy's sake."

"Well as Rachel's made it clear we're stayin' here." Jean says.

"Thanks," Pete says as he gives her a cuddle.

"Think nothin' of it," Jean says as she closes her eyes as they cuddle, like she's praying for everyone's sake, though out of nowhere walking around the corner a man looks at Jean and Pete, slightly unimpressed. Where as they finish their cuddle Jean says, "Be strong," as she wipes a tear from Pete's face, then as they both turn in the direction of the man looking at them they walk up towards him.

"Matthew," Pete says with new tears starting to appear, "Your two lovely ladies need meddles for everythin' they've done for my family this night."

"Yeah, I heard what was on the news and got on the first flight back." Matthew says.

"So that's why I couldn't get you on the cellular." Jean says.

"Must've been," Matthew says, "So has there been any sign of Amy yet?" Matthew asks as he pats Pete's shoulder.

"No, though the cops have been a great help this night and have told me they'll keep us posted." Pete says.

"And how's Barbara copin' through all this?" Matthew says.

"Very hard, as when I was out lookin' for Amy, Barbara blacked out while I was gone, where if it hadn't of been for your two quick thinkin' ladies, who knows what the outcome would've been." Pete says.

Suddenly peeking her head around the corner from the waiting room Rachel looks towards her Dad, where quickly running up to him she bounces up to him and raps her arms around him so tight.

Suddenly, with them all standing outside the private room Barbara's in, some nurses come running from the entrance direction Matthew came from, where all of the sudden the red light to Barbara's room brightens up. Where as the nurses open the room it's plain to see why, as Barbara's having an epileptic fit on the bed.

As Pete runs into the room lastly, trying to act as strong as can be for Barbara's sake and stop his tears from appearing, Matthew puts his arms around Rachel and Jean so lovingly as the door closes over, where it's like he's thanking God the boat that Pete's in isn't happening to him.

"Come on let's head down to the waiting room. We don't wanna get in the way." Matthew says as Rachel starts to cry again due to having noticed the state Barbara's in.

45.

At the FBI branch Steve is sitting at his table busy writing away with the entire branch near enough completely pitch black, as the only light shining a bit of brightness around all the unoccupied tables and chairs that surround the room is the light coming from Steve's desk, the fire exit lights and the television, which is on low volume.

Coming to a halt with his writing as he takes a peek up towards the television at the same time, Steve takes hold of the control and turns the volume up to hear of the news.

NEWS
With the shocking news that has gone on today over a young girls body having been found in a dumpster at a bar called Mixtures, which is on the outskirts of Boston City, the young girl has now been identified as Naomi Layne….,

"Yo boss, how's the paperwork goin'?" Jake says busy startling Steve.

"What the fuck are you doin', tryin' to give you partner a heart attack or somethin'?"

"You have a heart, yeah right. Well come on what's the crack are you finished or what? Jake says.

"Yeah, but hold up and check this out, as I was also checkin' out what kinda shit was goin' on around the time that the Walter dudes were supposed to have gone off the cliff in their land rover too." Steve says.

"So, what did you come across?"

"On the day that they went off the cliff, the mother of the young dude, Jo, was buried in her back yard." Steve says.

"Yeah, I knew that man."

"Yeah, but also on the same day after the land rover went off the cliff, the headmaster of Jo's school went up in flames in his own house."

"Well accidents happen."

"Yeah, but again, conveniently on the same day there was three students in the same year as Jo, beat to a pulp and killed, where even one of them was stabbed to death on his front door step."

"So?" Jake says.

"So, if we get settin' up a news report on the box, we can get joggin' a few memories and see if anyone can give us any details of the Walters family that can be of any help. Cuz personally the same shit has been happenin' every year for the past eighteen, with my Angelina bein' one of them." Steve says.

"You're tellin' me, though this has been the worst year he's done so far." Jake says.

"Well it ain't the worse year for me. That's for sure." Steve says.

"Soz man, you know what I mean." Jake says.

"Yeah, I know, but for some reason I'm gettin' this hunch that whoever it is, they just ain't gonna stop this time." Steve says.

"What makes you think that? As it usually lasts a month then doesn't start somewhere else until the followin' year around the same time." Jake says.

"Just call it a hunch." Steve says.

"You and your hunches man," Jake says as he looks at Steve weirdly.

"I'd even bet my life on it." Steve says.

"Well you can count me out on the bet." Jake says.

"Why's that?" Steve questions.

"Cuz you've fuck all else to leave but bills you little prick." Jake says. Suddenly the television blackens. "See, it's even happening hear man, you've got the top dogs clampin' down on you dude."

196

"Ah, it's probably some camera error," Steve says. Then suddenly a voice can be heard.

"Tracey, we're on the air." Robert's voice is heard saying as the camera swings around in the dark trying to find her.

"Tracey, we're on." Robert's says again as the camera is aimed on a couple of cops doing guard outside Mixtures.

"If that pricks left her alone I'm gonna rip him apart," Steve says with his eyes peeled on the box and not one bit impressed.

Then suddenly continuous dog barks are heard coming from a distance in the wood lands, to which one of the cops seen on camera takes hold of his radio and looks like he's calling for a back up due to looking into the woods.

Suddenly appearing from the dark road leading up to Mixtures, Tracey walks up towards the camera, though before she has a chance to get up to the camera Steve looks at Jake, "Come on, let's head on down to the scene and see if anythin's changed."

"Why, don't tell me, you've got another hunch somethin's up this time, huh?" Jake says.

"Yeah, somethin' like that, it looks like I've caught what you seemed to have been bugged down with earlier." Steve says.

"Well as long as it's just a bug that's fine by me," Jake says, "Providing it ain't a bug where you're gonna rip a head off of a certain cameraman for havin' left Tracey on her own, huh?" Jake asks.

"Don't worry, I'm not gonna do anythin' crazy," Steve says.

"Yeah, that's what scares the shit out of me, as you'll more than likely flip out due to usin' your brain for a change." Jake says.

In at Ryan's Dad's van everyone is out for the count and sleeping away, though as Paul's head drops forward he quickly wakes up all startled, where opening his eyes as if he's seen a ghost he quickly catches on where he is. Though remaining still with no snores coming from the back of the van at all, as he winds the car window down so minor he can hear more dog barks, but they must be coming from some distance as they can vaguely be heard. Though Paul, still scared stupid just sits still where he is and leaves the guys in piece.

Heading out to the country with the Boston City lights disappearing in the distance, a cellular suddenly rings.

"Hello." Jake says as Steve drives on, where listening for a few seconds Jake brings his call to a closure and says, "We'll be there in a few minutes." Then he closes over his cellular.

"What's all that about?" Steve says.

"The cops on guard tonight heard some dog barks comin' from in the woods from behind Mixtures, where when one of them went to check out what it was, while the other stayed on guard at Mixtures, he was away longer than expected, where when his partner who called for back up and went to check out what was taking him so long, he found his partners body in a tent in the woods, but not only that, as he was lying on top of the corpse of an old lady who's body was in the sleepin sack too." Jake says.

"Ah shit, I think I'll give Pete a call, as I did state he'd be notified of any changes, and the last place I'm sure he'd wanna find out the news is on the box." Steve says.

"Personally man, this ain't lookin' to good for Amy." Jake says, where Steve replies by shaking his head side to side due to having the cellular ringing up against his ear.

Arriving at the T-Junction to take a left turn to Tracey's Aunt's house, strait ahead at Mixtures the place has more evidence handlers and cop cars swarming the place.

"And you thought you had the paperwork finished." Jake says.

"Hmmm!" Steve hums.

"And personally out've all the people I thought would've been first on the scene is Tracey and Robert." Jake says.

"Let's just hope she hasn't heard yet. In fact drop me down at the house she's stayin' at and you head back up to Mixtures, I won't be long behind." Steve says.

"It's good to see you two're gettin' back man. You're definitely comin' back to your good old self, huh?" Jake says.

"Old? Speak for yourself man." Steve says as they arrive at Tracey's Gran's house, where as Steve quickly gets out of the car, Jake speeds off.

With the sound of the FBI car disappearing out of sight, Steve looks over at the news van, where there's music coming from, but he can't see anyone in the front of the van. So taking the advantage of being in the house with Tracey on her own he gives the door a knock, where with it opening on it's own and Steve not liking the look of it, he quickly pulls out his gun from the rear of his pants.

"Tracey," Steve says as he enters the house and keeps himself covered, busy looking everywhere.

Though a minute later, walking out of the house, Steve looks over towards the van that is wobbling with a slight thumping noise being heard.

"Oh, I get it," Steve says as he walks towards the van, "Let's have a quick ride before Steve comes, huh?" Steve says as he opens the rear door to the van, where lying there in front of him covered with blood that's starting to rapidly drip out of the vans rear door and onto the rear step of the van is Robert, dead.

"HOLY FUCKIN' SHIT, TRACEY," Steve shouts thinking that Tracey's dead body could be somewhere around the house, like Robert's that's bleeding away in the van, but as he turns around to start looking, **smack**,

"DON'T DO IT," says the Stranger as they stand there holding the rusty metal poll in their hands, then suddenly they start to continuously kick Steve in the back and in the head, where at the same time Steve's also getting smacked with the poll too, and all that can be heard are the cracks of Steve's bones.

Eventually stopping and dropping the poll, the Stranger walks towards the corner of the house and disappears, then suddenly reappearing, he's seen carrying another adhesive taped body over his shoulder, where walking off with the body he scatters what looks like torn up card and paper to the floor as he eventually disappears into the woods, leaving Steve and Robert either dead or close to it.

46.

With the morning having arrived and the summers sky being bright blue, Steve is lying fast asleep in his own private room with a drip attached to his arm, but awakening him out of his sleep a tray on wheels bangs into the door as a nurse enters on into his room, though quickly getting behind the nurse and assisting her on keeping the door open is Jake entering the room at the same time.

"Good morning sir, have you any idea what day it is?" The nurse says.

"Lady, I can barely keep track of what day it is when I'm workin'. And as for that little prick, keep him away from me," Steve says.

"Why's that?" The nurse says quite concerned.

"Cuz he's nothin' but a frickin' jinx."

"What're you talkin' about?" Jake says.

"Let's have a little recap over what you said yesterday, huh."

"Like what?" Jake questions.

"Uh, let's see. 'Well let's go and kick some balls', huh?" Steve states to Jake.

"Yep that's my Steve, he knows what he's talkin' about." Jake says.

"Well how are you feeling today?" The nurse says.

"Personally, oh shit...," Steve says painfully as he tries to sit himself up a bit, "..., it feels like I was lyin' on a bed of nails while someone was usin' me as a trampoline, whilst using my head as their golf ball."

"That's not bad compared to some of the stories I've heard." The nurse says.

"Well all screwin' aside, when am I gettin' outta here?" Steve says.

"At least a week with three work free weeks to follow," the nurse says.

"Work free, it's like we work for free anyway." Jake says.

"Let me rephrase that, after a week of doing nothing here, you head home and do nothing at home, at work or anywhere else for three more weeks. Now open wide," the nurse says demandingly as she checks inside Steve's mouth then places the thermometer in it, "Close over."

"And while that's got you quiet I thought I'd let you know there's still no sign of the little girl Amy, Samantha or Tracey, though the usual newspaper and postcards were found from where you were left for dead last night," Jake says as he takes out an evidence handlers bag.

"Well your temperatures slightly high, but it's not too bad," the nurse says as she removes the thermometer from Steve's mouth. "There should be no more need for this anymore," the nurse says as she quickly dismantles the drip from Steve's arm. "Now you get some food and fluid down you, and you make it short and sweet," the nurse says busy ordering Jake to pay heat as she walks out of the room.

"Put it this way I wouldn' wanna be in her bad books," Jake says as she disappears.

"Now come on less of the shit, what's happenin' now?" Steve says.

"Well even though Amy, Samantha and Tracey haven't been found, we near enough have all the guys searchin' the woodlands while the helicopters are coverin' from above too." Jake says.

"Well I'm just prayin' that they're okay, as If anythin' is repeated as to what happened to Angelina, I won't sleep till I find the little mother fucker." Steve says speaking his mind. "By the way, did Robert make it by any chance?"

"He was pronounced dead when we ended up findin' you both in the state you's were in. Now come on, like the nurse said for now, get this stuff in you and keep the phone handy and I'll keep you posted, right bro?" Jake says as he heads for the door.

"Will do man, now watch your back, you hear me?" Steve says.

"Will do, and that's a promise." Jake says as he opens the door to Steve's room, where just about to knock is Pete.

"Huh, you and your promises, yeah right." Steve says.

"Is this the room for Steve, the FBI?" Pete says.

"He's kinda busy at the mo." Jake says.

"Is that Amy's Pop, Pete?" Steve says. Pete nods at Jake.

"Yeah," Jake says.

"Well let the man in you frickin' prick." Steve says.

"Now like I said you take it easy and get that food down you, you hear me?" Jake says as he lets Pete in.

"Get outta here and do a bit've work." Where thinking Steve's talking to him, Pete nearly turns around. "No not you Pete. Come on in man, take a seat." Steve says, where with Pete looking like he doesn't know what to say, Steve kicks the conversation off.

"So how's your wife keepin' since last night?"

"She's had a couple of epileptic fits and the doc's have said it's too early to introduce her." Pete says.

"Well if you haven't had a chance to hear any news, my partners just after tellin' me that near enough all the cops and FBI are searchin' for Amy, Tracey and Samantha and tryin' to hunt down the prick who's kidnapped them, excuse my French." Steve says.

"Don't worry about it, as I've got plenty of other words that would describe them." Pete says.

"Not only that man but there's also helicopters surfin' the area non-stop too." Steve says.

"Well it looks like you were one of the lucky dudes to get away from them." Pete says.

"I know, I'm just prayin' Amy, Samantha and my Tracey are found safe and unharmed." Steve says.

"I hope you're right man." Pete says.

"I take it you haven't heard about what happened to the camera man last night?" Steve says.

"No, why's that?"

"He was my partners work colleague who was found battered to death in his news van when I went down to see my partner Tracey last night. And that's when the fucker bounced on me." Steve says.

"Shit man, this ain't lookin' to good at all?" Pete says as he lowers his head.

"You know yourself, for your wives sake you've gotta keep strong, especially with the circumstances the two of you are in, and if there is any changes in the circumstance I'll be the first one to let you know, okay man?" Steve says.

"Thanks a lot for everythin'. And I hope you get better soon," Pete says with the tears nearly appearing from his watery eyes, obviously due to thinking of the worst.

"Don't worry about me Pete, and like I say keep your head up high for Barbara's sake, and I'll keep you posted personally on any changes that occur, okay?" Steve says.

"Thanks. Sure I'll head on and leave you to get on with that food before it freezes over and see how Barbara's gettin' on." Pete says.

"Pete." Steve says.

"Yeah," Pete says.

"Anytime you wanna talk bro, I'll be a stone throw away, and I mean anytime, that goes for your Barbara too, okay?" Steve says.

"Thanks man," Pete says as he walks out of the room looking like he still has more to say.

47.

As Simon gets escorted on the bus, his Mum Charlotte gives him a little tug and says, "I thought you said Alan's friend was supposed to be meetin' you down here?"

"No Mom, he said he'd meet me at a stop off called Village Everette Road." Simon says as he steps onto the first step of the bus.

"Uh, there's been a slight diversion on stoppin' off there, I didn't get hearin' the news as to why, but I can always give your son directions to it if you want, as the other drop off point is a stone throw away from it." The bus driver says.

"See Mom, I'm in good hands," Simon says busy walking up another step with Charlotte still having hold of his bag.

"I dunno." Charlotte says.

"Look I'll even sit at the front of the bus and the bus driver can give me all the details." Simon says.

"I'll keep him right." The bus driver says.

"See," Simon says breaking free from his Mum and taking a seat at the front of the bus.

"You ain't makin' the decisions to easy man." Charlotte says to the bus driver. Then the bus driver pretends to zip his mouth shut.

"Now I wanna hear from you as soon as you get there, hear me?" Charlotte says walking up the steps and giving Simon a kiss.

"Mom," Simon says as if his reputation is flashing before his eyes.

"Don't Mom me Mr. Now I expect a call pronto, k, k?" Charlotte says busy pointing at him for an answer.

"Okay, okay." Simon says quickly agreeing with her orders so the bus can get moving.

Quickly taking hold of his cellular, which only has one bar of battery life left, Simon, as the door closes quickly holds it up to the window to show his Mum, where as the bus starts moving, it's plain to see her lips and hand movements are giving him the signal to turn it off, though as he attempts to do so it automatically does it itself due to the battery being completely drained out. Not wanting to work his Mum up, Simon gives her the thumbs up as he shows her his battery-less cellular, making out that it's turned off, where she smiles over the outcome and waves as the bus drives off.

48.

"So is everyone agreeing to this or what?" Chris says as he looks at Ryan, Alan and Paul.

"I don' think we've any choice." Ryan says whilst starting to look a little worse for ware.

"And you's?" Chris questions again as he looks at Alan and Paul's sad faces, where with the two of them not answering Chris shouts, "**WELL**?"

"Yeah," answers Paul all miserable and even scared to look at Alan.

"Whatever," Alan whines, "I mean what the heck, I'll see you in forty years."

"Well good, thank fuck that's finalized. Now asses out and get clearin' the sticks. And you two," Chris says as he takes hold of Paul and Alan by the necks, "You's better start gettin' along, as we don't want years of friendship fucked up over one fuckin' night."

Opening the rear door with one jumping out after the other, they start to remove the sticks off the van, but as Chris remains at the rear of the van to take the sticks off of the top of it, Paul heads around to the left hand side of the van and Alan heads around to the right, with their faces looking like a wet weekend.

"Fuck knows what it's gonna take to get them two back to normality," Chris says to Ryan.

"**SHIT, SHIT, SHIT, SHIT, SHIT, YOU SEE WHAT I FUCKIN' MEAN!**" Alan is heard shouting like crazy. "I'll be lucky if I don't get the chair for this man. I mean which stuffed up sick mother fucker would do this kinda stuff to a human bein', huh?" Alan says as he looks at the wrapped up dead body figure.

"Alan, calm down." Chris says.

"Calm fuckin' down, *calm fuckin' down*, look at the circumstances we're in here, do you blind mother fuckers not see that?" Alan says hysterically.

"Alan you're tryin' my patients." Chris says.

"Ah, fuck you man, you're just wantin' off lightly, I know your game?" Alan says as he's near nose to nose with Chris, where Chris Pushes Alan for six, having him nearly land on the dilapidated still figure.

"You see what I fuckin' mean, you see, huh, huh, it's all me, me, me, and for all we fuckin' know you could've been the one who did this while we were sleepin'." Alan says, though looking at him in the face Chris can tell rightly Alan doesn't mean a single word he's saying. Though looking at Paul, he looks as if he's having his doubts on Alan's thoughts.

"Fuck this I'm outta here." Alan says.

"You're only gonna make yourself look worse off with runnin' away man." Chris says.

"Are you not gonna stop him?" Ryan says as he looks at Chris and Paul.

"Ryan we have nothin' to worry about, absolutely nothin'." Chris says, "He'll be back, he's just worked up over what's been happenin', and it was plain to see he didn't mean a word of what he was just sayin'."

"I'm just prayin' he won't do somethin' stupid," Ryan says.

"Oh fuck this," Paul says as he runs after Alan.

Eventually catching up on Alan, Paul gets a few punches in the face, though managing to grab hold of him Paul gives him a hefty shake, where Alan breaking down in tears throws an effortless punch at Paul, where with Paul grabbing hold of him, Alan just breaks down. Then they start to slowly walk back to the van with their heads lowered, with Paul having his arm around Alan for comfort.

"Chris, sorry man, I didn't mean a word I said," Alan says.

"I know bro, it's plain to see it was a heat of the moment, but just outta curiosity how the fuck did Paul manage to get you back, huh?" Chris says.

"I bet it was for half of the winnings he got." Ryan says messing around.

"No, it's a lot more important than money." Alan says. "Samantha needs our help."

"Shit, good point." Ryan says.

"So come on what the fuck are we gonna do." Alan says looking clueless.

"How about I head back to Mixtures, phone the cops or talk to them if they're still there, tell them and show them where we got the fake ID's from. Then if they accept that's where we got the fake ID, I'll inform them we need an ambulance for you before I show them where we are." Paul says.

"Do you think they'll take it?" Ryan says.

"Once they know it's a fake ID they're bound to give us some leeway." Paul says.

"Yeah, but the way they'll more than likely look at it is that we got the fake ID to do all the killings." Ryan says.

"Well fuck it man, it's a chance we'll have to take, as the last thing we want is your leg gettin' that fucked up that it needs ripped off, or Samantha remainin' in serious shit, huh?" Paul says.

"Hmmm, you've got a good point." Ryan says.

"So who's in," Chris says busy placing his hand out waiting for the others to pile on. Where piling his hand on first is Ryan, then Paul, then hesitantly Alan, to which Paul for pure friendship places his other hand on top of Alan's.

49.

"Well it looks like this'll be the closest I'm gettin' you." The bus driver says to Simon.

"Thanks a lot." Simon says as he takes hold of his bag.

"Now you see this more or less x-junction that's up ahead, after this first left I'll be taking?" The bus driver says as Simon walks up to him.

"Yeah." Simon says staring in the direction the bus driver's pointing towards.

"You take the first left at the X-Junction and walk about eight hundred meters or so, then the first T-Junction you'll come across is where you're meeting point is. Though just to be on the safe side lay low behind some tree's, and if you're bro don't turn up, just keep walkin' in the same direction you've came from and you'll come across a bar, which I'm sure wouldn't decline you on using their pay phone to call your Mom," the bus driver says. "It's called Mixtures."

"Thanks a lot for your help." Simon says.

"Don't worry about it," the bus driver says, "Happy campin'."

Getting off the bus the bus driver lets Simon cross the road before he takes his required turn off, where Simon waves at him as the bus turns and drives off.

Like guided, Simon comes up to the obscure X-Junction, takes his first left and walks on down the single filed country road, which is barely big enough for two cars.

Taking his cellular from his pocket and turning it on, it quickly beeps that the battery is about to collapse, so as fast as lightening he turns it off, swings the rucksack off of his shoulder and places it into a small zipped pocket at the front of his back pack.

Also as he continues to walk he unzips a different part of his rucksack, where extra clothes and appliances have been packed, to which he takes hold of a bottle of Pepsi. Then zipping his rucksack back up and swinging it onto his shoulder again, he continues to walk as he slurps away. Putting the lid back on the bottle as he continues to carry it in his hand, swinging it back and forth, quicker than expected, which is noticed by the look on his facial expression, Simon is only 20 meters from the T-Junction he was advised to head for.

Quickly running down to the T-Junction Simon can't see any sign of Alan anywhere. So again taking the advice of the bus driver, Simon heads into the woods to hide behind some tree's that are in front of the T-Junction itself.

Hiding behind the tree's, to which there is even more tree's right behind them Simon's stuck right in the middle of them, keeping himself well hid as he looks towards the T-Junction.

With five minutes past and the T-Junction still empty, not even being noticed due to quietly walking a little bit deeper in the woods, Paul continues to walk past Simon towards Mixtures.

With another five minutes having past by, Simon takes another look at the T-Junction for a few seconds, where noticing a few big branches starting to move hastily, Simon notices a grubby dressed long haired individual walk out onto the road holding a cellular in his hand. So quickly taking his cellular out of his bag, Simon turns it on, gets Alan's name in view and quickly presses the call button, where looking strait at what looks like the Stranger, the cellular starts to ring in their hand. So again, quickly turning his cellular off and putting it back into the zip part of the rucksack, Simon jumps out from behind the tree's and heads towards the Stranger, who has their face covered by their long hair as they look towards Alan's cellular.

"I take it Alan sent you to come and get me so the pussies can sober up, huh?" Simon says to the Stranger whilst looking at them weirdly, but the Stranger keeping their face hid doesn't reply. Then Simon looks at the Stranger again, looking quite unimpressed over the state of their clothes they're walking around in.

"I take it you're on this so called campin' spree too, huh?" Simon says, "As personally, I'm havin' second thoughts already, I think I was safer where I was with hidin' behind them trees than walkin' with you to meet up with the guys." Where only managing to see the lips of the Stranger due to the leafs playing camouflage as he walks into the woods, they don't look like they're impressed in any shape or form, as the Stranger just blasts through the big thick fully dressed branches, with Simon walking behind them and nearly getting smacked in the face from the ricochet of the branch.

"Watch what you're at dude," Simon says. Then trying to make conversation, Simon says, "So how come you didn't kick Alan's ass to come and get me himself, huh?" But quickly showing a sign of madness followed up with anger, the Stranger snaps a thick stick off a tree, smacking anything with force that's in front of them. Where answering his own question Simon follows up with a closure, "Don't tell me, the little pricks on his third round of drink already and you're pissed off that it's not you gettin' as drunk as a skunk?" Simon says to the Stranger as they continue to walk through the big bulky woodland.

Noticing he's not getting a single reply from the Stranger, Simon, nearly gets another branch fired into his face as they walk deeper into the woods.

"You're not exactly the talkative type dude, what's up, you sufferin' from a hangover or somethin' too man?" But not replying the Stranger continues to walk approximately another twenty steps, then stops, bends down slowly with their face still not being unveiled and picks up their mucky styled rucksack with the handle piece of their knife sticking out, where they don't even take the slightest peek back and just walk off, nearly having a branch fire in Simon's face again.

"Whatta prick," Simon says very quietly to himself.

50.

"And what would you two lovely ladies like to order?" A young waiter says to Charlotte and her friend, as if they're royalty.

"I dunno about you Diane, but with the amount've running around I've been doin' with my Simon since last night, I could literally eat a horse." Charlotte says.

"Uh, sorry to be a bearing of bad news, but that doesn't seem to be on the menu," Diane says as she looks at Charlotte to make another realistic decision.

"It looks like I'll just have to settle with your all day breakfast," Charlotte says messing around like she's the queen.

"And what would you like to drink with that, Mam?" The waiter says.

"I'll take a black coffee thanks," Charlotte says, where looking at the table as if she's after sugar, it's already there in the little square packets in a bowl.

"And how about you Mam," the waiter says to Diane.

"To make things easy I'll just have the exact same," Diane says.

"Oh, you two can come here anytime," the waiter says shaking his head happily whilst collecting the menus.

"Oooh, we will," Diane says as she watches his muscular figure walk off.

"I needn't ask what your taste buds are droolin' over," Charlotte says, "But I can tell you one thing it ain't the breakfast."

"Couldn't you just eat him all up?" Diane says.

"I dunno," Charlotte says, "Would you like me to ask him if he supplies the sauce or mayonnaise?"

"Don't you dare," Diane says frowning as the waiter is already heading in their direction.

"Now, there's one for you and one for you," the waiter says as he lays the two mugs of coffee in front of them. "If you would like or need anythin' else, anythin' at all, don't be afraid to hollow." He says. Then he walks off to another table.

"And don't forget that's hollow he said." Charlotte says.

"The dirt is literally drippin' outta you lady." Diane says.

"Yeah, see what happens when I'm left on my own," Charlotte says.

"Ha, ha, ha, huh, well how long are they gonna be gone for anyway?" Diane says.

"I'm near sure it's long enough so that they're not here for when their examination results come through, either that or for when their bucks run out." Charlotte says.

"Let's just hope they're havin' a good time then, huh?" Diane says to Charlotte. But Charlotte glares towards a window to the café due to sitting at a table outside, where she looks like she's in a world of her own.

"Charlotte, what's he at?" Diane says to Charlotte busy thinking she's looking at the waiter.

"Charlotte," Diane repeats due to getting no reply as she looks at Charlotte's hand starting to shake.

"Charlotte, are you okay?" Diane says, "You're startin' to scare the shit outta me lady."

Getting up from the table and walking up to the window, all Charlotte can see glaring at her from the television is a picture of her ex-lover from a long time ago, being the one and only, Jamie-Lee Walters.

"Who the heck's that that's got your attention?" Diane says looking back and forth from the television to Charlotte.

"That's Jamie-Lee." Charlotte says in disbelief.

"Who?" Diane says literally querying for more information.

"My Alan's biological father." Charlotte says all flabbergasted.

"Shit, you've never told me about him, where does he live?" Diane says.

"He's dead."

"Oh, shit sorry," Diane says as if she doesn't know whether to stop or continue with the conversation.

"Apparently from what I found out after him and his son were killed in a crash, that had their land rover go of the edge of a very steep mountain, due to the neighborly chit chat of course, is that he was nothing but an alcoholic wife beater, which on the day of his death I found out from experience." Charlotte says.

"What, no he didn't?" Diane says.

"If only." Charlotte says.

"Here, let's not talk about it here," Diane says, "As you wanna have a good time while the boys are away instead of having non-stop worries over this shit that the news is goin' on about, huh?" Diane says trying to make Charlotte feel a bit better.

Though still looking at the television Charlotte can see a quick glimpse of Jo, who Alan is a spitting image of, then suddenly a news reporter is seen standing at a scene.

"Here you don't mind if I fit the bill and cancel our order, as somethin's just cropped up." Diane says to the waiter.

"Sure, I'll only take for the two coffees, that's three dollars," the waiter says. "It's nothing serious I hope," the waiter says as Diane takes out a five dollar bill from her purse.

"I hope not. Sure keep the change there," Diane says looking at Charlotte whilst handing the five dollars to the waiter.

"You don't mind if I go in for a minute do you?" Charlotte says to the waiter as she points at the television flabbergasted.

"No, not at all," the waiter says. Where heading on into the café with Diane following her, Charlotte stops to have a listen to the news.

NEWS REPORTER
In this quiet little country area, which
I'm sure some of you may know about
from last nights news reports, so far

there's been two bodies found, two people recently killed and one critically injured around this location. One who's body was found in the rear dumpster to a country bar called, Mixtures, has been identified as the missing girl Naomi Layne, to who's family has been informed about, where she was reported missing approximately 13 days ago. The other one is that of an old lady to who is still to be identified. Though only since last night when the poor old lady was found rapped up in a sleeping sack inside a tent by a Police Officer, Mr. Scott Dixon, upon Mr. Dixon's find, he was stabbed in the back and left for dead lying on top of the poor old ladies corpse. Also the other person that was found dead near the crime scene in his news van, is Robert Grey, who was the camera assistant to one of our well known news reporters, Tracey Lewis, where he was found stabbed to death in the rear of his news van by a well known FBI Officer, Steve Hughes, to who after finding the body was ruthlessly bounced on and nearly beat to death, where at this present moment in time he's critically ill in hospital.

Not only is it the killings and attempted murders that's scaring the members of the public around this area, it's also the reports of three people who've gone missing as well, one being a young girl who lives around this location called, Amy Waterson, the other being our well known news reporter, Tracey Lewis. And finally a member of staff from the Mixtures bar called, Samantha Molar too. So please if you know anything of their whereabouts or even know anything about Jamie-Lee, Veronica or even Jo Walters past, or have any news that can be of any help or assistance to assist the Police and FBI on solving this case, please phone 1-80 ....,

With the news's cameras lens zooming back to have the news reporter being seen from a distance, as the reporter walks towards the camera, which has a T-Junction in view, as the reporter gets closer to the T-Junction a sign comes into view reading, 'Village Everette Road.'

NEWS REPORTER
Now I'd like to hand you back to Anna for our latest news up dates.

"Ah, no way." Charlotte says.
"What's up?" Diane says.
"Village Everette Road, did you not see it on the news?" Charlotte says.
"What about it?" Diane says.
"That's where Simon's meetin' Alan."

"Come on, we better head down to the cops and get filling them in." Diane says, "Come on," she says taking Charlotte by the arm.

"I hope all's alright." The waiter says all concerned.

"So do we man," Diane says giving him one last glimpse.

"The next coffee's on me ladies." The waiter shouts to them as they run off.

51.

With Mixtures being swarmed with cops, Paul quickly hides behind a tree and says, "Shit," as he kicks the floor looking all confused as to what to do. Though knowing rightly he has to approach the cops for Ryan's sake, he comes out from behind the tree and heads towards the direction of the cops that are guarding Mixtures.

"Excuse me, can I speak to one of the officers in charge please," Paul says to the cop who's guarding the barriers that Mixtures is cordoned off with.

"And your name is?"

"Paul."

"May I ask what for?" The cop says.

"It's regarding the killings that have been happening lately," Paul says as Jake pulls up in his unmarked FBI car. Though walking out of Mixtures as Jake gets out of the car, Lee looks towards the cop and Paul and shouts, "THAT'S THE MAN, THAT'S ONE OF THE LITTLE PRICKS THAT WERE HERE LAST NIGHT."

"Freeze, get your hands in the air and get down on your knees, now." Jake says as he points his gun at Paul.

"He was the one that was waving the big bucks everywhere last night, while his friend went back to Samantha's house. Who knows he was probably causing a diversion." Lee says.

"Get the cuffs on him." Jake says to the cop, where as the cop gets Paul's hands cuffed behind his back, the cop quickly searches Paul for anything dangerous or illegal as he reads him his rights.

"Right you, back on in there." Jake orders Lee as he points for him to get back on into Mixtures. "And you start talkin'." He says to Paul.

"There was another body found outside our van while we were tryin' to lay low last night." Paul says.

"Do you realize how much shit you're in?" Jake says, "You'll be lucky if you don't get slammed into the chair for what you've done."

"But we were only on a campin' spree man, and somehow this shit has been landin' in our face none fuckin' stop. I mean me and the guys only came here for to pull some pussy, but the dead bodies seem to be appearin' everywhere we fuckin' look." Paul says hysterically.

"Oh, so you and your so called guys just land in this quiet little area, yet dead bodies suddenly appear all over the place?" Jake says.

"Yeah, I mean take, take last night for example when we set up camp. We end up comin' down here for a few drinks, yet end up gettin' shot at over a body found in the dumpster. Then to top it all we arrive back at our campsite and find a dead body in my frickin' sleepin' sack. Though this morning when we all wanted to hand ourselves in, when we get out of the van a young girls body's found outside our fuckin' van too. I mean wouldn't this kind've shit screw up your mind as well?" Paul says frantically.

"Okay and the other dudes with you are?"

"My best buddies, Alan, Chris and Ryan." Paul says.

"We were also informed there's a Jo Walters with you too, which fits the description of a young boy that was killed in a crash 18 years ago." Jake says.

"That's Alan," Paul says trying to reach for his fake ID with difficulty due to the handcuffs.

"You might wanna go nice and slow there." Jake says drawing out his gun as fast as lightening.

Slowly trying to reveal his ID to Jake as it comes into view from the right hand side of Paul's behind, he finishes his last sentence, "As I myself got some fake ID's for us all from the key shop that's opposite the hospital in the centre of Boston City, as we've only just finished our final exams and didn't wanna be home for when the results come through the door." Paul says as he hands Jake his ID.

"DID YOU ASK HIM ABOUT ALL THE MONEY HE WAS WAVING

AROUND?" Lee says busy shouting outside Mixtures front door and pointing away at Paul.

"You get in and stay in or I'll have you arrested." Jake says to Lee, who disappears back into Mixtures, though just as Jake's about to continue with Paul, his cellular rings.

"Well what's up?" Jake says as he answers his cell phone. Where remaining silent for a few seconds he says, "I'll get that checked out and get back to you." Then looking towards the cop Jake says, "Could you check out the whereabouts of the bus that was supposed to come down this direction and check if there's a young boy on it called Simon, as his Mom rang after she seen what was on the news and is getting quite concerned."

"Shit, shit, shit. It's just like I fuckin' predicted," Paul says.

"What's his surname," the cop says to Jake.

"Simon Woods." Paul answers before Jake gets a word in edgeways, where Jake nods at the cop to elucidate that Paul's correct, then the cop continues with his radio call.

"You're right, how'd you know that?" Jake says.

"It's just like I predicted to Alan, as the same mother fucker that's been causin' all this aggravation got hold of Alan's cellular when we were at Mixtures and dumped the dead body in my sleepin' sack, where like I was stating to Alan, with Simon contacting Alan all the time they've obviously managed to get hold of him, that's the main reason why I'm down here to get this matter sorted and get Simon safe. And I take it that was Simon's Mom Charlotte on the phone?" Paul says.

"Yeah, you're right." Jake says.

"If necessary I can always show you where I got the fake ID's from." Paul says.

"I think our main concern at this precise moment is identifying the dead bodies and bringing your friends into custody to see if their stories add up with yours." Jake says.

"Not forgettin' Simon I hope." Paul says.

"That's being dealt with as we speak." Jake says.

"Uh, you may wanna phone for an ambulance too," Paul says.

"Why's that?" Jake questions.

"As the barman managed to shoot a hole in Ryan's leg last night. That's why we didn't hand ourselves in, as we were scared shitless."

"And you didn't think it would've been a good idea to have called for an ambulance for your friend?" Jake says.

"From the shit we heard on the radio last night it didn't exactly boost the moral with everything pointing at us." Paul slowly says.

"Well just think if you had've, your little dude Simon wouldn't have ended up on the bus." Jake says. Where Paul's facial expression is virtually saying, 'Oh, shit'.

Directing Paul over to the cop, as the cop puts down his phone Jake says. "D'you wanna get a few of your guys together, call for an ambulance and let the evidence handlers know that another bodies been found." Jake says to the cop.

"Will do," the cop says with his deep voice.

"I'll take him with me for the time bein'," Jake says, where the cop just gives the thumbs up and gives the other cops a briefing.

Arriving at his unmarked FBI car, Jake opens the passenger door for Paul.

"Mind your head," Jake says, where Paul ducks down and tries to get seated, but finds it quite awkward due to having the cuffs behind his back.

Getting into the drivers side and starting up the engine, as he starts driving off his cellular rings, "Well," Jake says busy listening for a second, "Has the bus been searched?" Where with a couple more seconds of silence Jake says, "For all we know he could've been layin' low." Then busy listening away Jake's face doesn't look overly impressed as he says, "Shit. Well I wanna see more people down here searchin' these woodlands inside and out."

Hanging up his cellular Jake starts to dial more numbers as Paul says, "I take it there's no sign of Simon on that bus then, huh?" But Jake remains irresponsive due to waiting for his call to be answered.

"Yo Steve, from what I've been told today it ain't lookin' so good for Amy's parents, cuz as we speak I'm spinnin' on down to where a young girls bodies been found." Jake says.

- -

"Ah, shit." Steve says, where with his door being open Pete notices the emotional impact that's heating up in the room.

"Well keep me posted." Steve says as he hangs up his cellular.

"What's that about?" Pete says.

"My partner, he's just after tellin' me that a young girl's been found this mornin'."

"Dead?" Pete says trying to hold back his tears from appearing.

"Yeah," Steve says.

"It's not is it, Amy?" Pete says getting all worked up and nearly starting to cry uncontrollably.

"It's too early to say at the moment Pete, and I know it's even to hard to say with the situation you're in, but you're gonna have to be as strong as you possibly can for Barbara and your newborn's sake." Steve says.

"I don't know how I'm gonna cope if it's Amy, she's like a little piece of my soul that I've had all my life. I must've been a right mean mother fucker in my last life to deserve this kinda shit," Pete says.

"Yeah, well you're not now, which was plain to see when you were down at Mixtures, huh?" Steve says quickly reassuring him.

Interrupting Pete and Steve from talking a nurse quickly arrives beside Pete.

"Mr. Waterson?"

"Yeah." Pete says worryingly.

"You're wife, there was no other option than for to allow her to start delivering, as with just havin' taken another fit, she's now eight centimeters dilated...," the nurse says.

Pete barely being able to get a word out to Steve literally gives the signal that he has to go.

"Hang in there Pete and be strong like I said, I'll keep you up-to-date on any news, keep me posted." Steve hollows as the door to his private room closes over slowly with no sign of Pete or the nurse anymore.

"Well, I take it there was no sign of Simon then, huh?" Paul asks Jake again.

"No, apparently he got off at a different stop due to the buses regular road having been diverted from the crime scene." Jake says.

"I hope the little dudes okay." Paul says looking all depressed as he glares out of the window. Where Jake looking out of the corner of his eye knows rightly Paul is not putting on an act for sure.

Coming up to the turn off to the short country road that Ryan's van is not to far away from, behind the unmarked FBI car, there's three cop cars and the evidence handling van, though coming towards them on the other side of the road is an ambulance to which Jake signals them to slow down as he holds his FBI badge out the window and circles it around, giving them the signal to stop, where coming inline with his window Jake says to the ambulance driver, "Follow me."

Giving way for the ambulance to reverse back and follow the unmarked FBI car, the cop cars follow on after it.

"It's up here and on your left." Paul says.

As the cars pull over, the cops get out of their vehicles with barely having any space to carry out a maneuver due to the tree's being so close together on both sides of their car doors, where with broken branches lying everywhere, along with the branches camouflaging the van being tightly together, it's like one big squashed up mess.

As all the cops have their guns pointing at the van Jake shouts, "Your vehicle is surrounded, now open the rear door slowly and get your hands where I can see them."

"We wanna hear Paul," Ryan is heard saying, "We wanna make sure he's alright."

So heading to his back passengers door Jake opens the door and pulls Paul out half decently.

"Let them know all's okay." Jake says.

"Guys, do as the say, they're here to help." Paul says, where looking at the rear door to the van it's opened slowly by Alan, while Chris and Ryan have their hands in the air.

"Now keep your hands where we can see them and get out of the vehicle slowly with your hands in the air." Jake says.

"Well I'd like to man but my leg's screwed. I got shot from that dude at the bar last night." Ryan says.

"So your friend was saying." Jake says.

"Do you want us to get him out?" Chris says busy lowering his hands to pick up Ryan.

"Just keep your hands where I can see them thank you." Jake says. "Now is anyone else in the car?"

"No," Ryan says, "Hopefully!"

"And whatta you mean by that?" Jake says.

"Well the way our lucks been goin', we seem to be comin' across a dead body wherever we end up. I'm just prayin' there's none we don't know about!" Ryan says.

"Yeah, I've been told about that too." Jake says, "Now you two keep your hands in the air and step out of the vehicle slowly." Where with all guns pointing in their direction they do as they're told.

"Alan, it looks like my prediction was right man. The mother fucker has contacted Simon." Paul says as Alan slowly steps off the back of the van, with Chris slowly following.

"He was on the bus headin' this way, but when the cops stopped the bus there was no sign of him."

"Hay you, get in the car," Jake says to Paul.

"It was your Mom that called to see of his whereabouts," Paul says as he tries to keep his head out a little bit as he's getting pushed into the back passenger seat to Jake's car.

With Alan seeing a gap in the trees and the cops giving Jake cover as he tries to cram Paul back into the FBI car, Alan quickly dives for the gap and a cop opens fire, to which the bullet ricochets off of Chris's shoulder as he turns around from getting out of the van.

"HOLD YOUR FIRE," Jake shouts.

"Oh, shit man," Chris says as he takes hold of his shoulder. Then looking at the blood on his hand he says, "Shit."

"Welcome to my club big man," Ryan says, where with the gap and the tightness of the trees that Alan's managed to escape through, the cops aren't able to follow him as he's heard fighting through the branches.

"He's not gonna get very far, now search them two and get them a medic. Preferably in a different location as to where Pete and Steve are. As I think if they know you're close by, they'll probably do somethin' we'll all regret." Jake says.

Arriving down at Mixtures, Jake automatically locks the car behind him, leaving Paul in the back passenger seat. Then heading over to Mixtures and entering on in, Lee is seen standing behind the bar sorting out some glasses.

"Well, any luck on catchin' them?" Lee says as he notices Jake walk up to the bar.

"I've one in the car at the mo, and the cops are dealin' with the other guys." Jake says.

"I hope they get put in the chair," Lee says.

"Well one is at this precise moment." Where looking at Jake weirdly, Lee has a look of disbelief on his face. "He's in the chair in the back of my car. Where if you end up in the car also, I'm gonna have to put you in cuffs for your own safety." Jake says.

"But I've done jack shit." Lee says.

"Yeah, but it's your help we're after." Jake says.

"Like what?" Lee questions.

"Would you be able to identify what the little girl Amy Waterson looks like?" Jake says.

"Yeah, her Pop brings her down here on the odd occasion during the day to play a few games of nine ball." Lee says.

"That's good enough for me. Now place your hands behind your back." Jake orders.

"What the heck for?" Lee says busy doing as he's told as Jake walks up to him.

"We've found a young girls body that needs identified."

"Shit." Lee says.

"Are you up for identifying it for us?" Jake says.

"Yeah, but I don't know how I could break the news to Pete and Barbara." Lee says.

"Don't worry, that's our job." Jake says.

"But what's with the cuffs?" Lee questions.

"So you don't kick the shit outta him in the car," Jake says as he walks Lee towards the car.

"Oh, look at him, it's like butter wouldn't melt in his mouth." Lee says as Jake opens the front passenger door. "You murderous mother fucker." Lee says as he takes his seat and gets strapped in the front by Jake.

"Now less of that or I'll take you in for miss conduct." Jake says before he closes the front passenger door whilst Paul remains silent.

Walking up the side of Ryan's van, an unzipped body bag can be seen. Where as Lee and Jake get closer Lee takes one look then quickly steps back and says, "Holey shit, which sick fuck could do such a thing?"

Giving Lee a chance to recuperate himself, Jake says, "Well, do you recognize her?"

"I don't know how on earth Pete and Barbara's gonna live without her." Lee says.

"So I take it this is Amy?" Jake says.

"Yeah, that's her man," Lee says all watery eyed.

"Well come on, I'll drop you back up at the bar." Jake says.

"Personally I couldn't get back into the car with that murderous mother ....," Lee says managing to control his wording.

"Think of Barbara and Pete man, they have to be informed about this also, after all they are the parents." Jake says where Lee suddenly starts to walk slowly towards the car.

Staying silent as he is driven back to Mixtures, letting him out of the car and removing the handcuffs, Jake says, "You don't mind keepin' a hush to this till the parents are informed," where Lee just nods to agreement.

Though as Jake gets in the car and starts to drive off, Lee quickly turns around and runs after it for ten steps shouting, "IF YOU'VE DONE ANYTHIN' TO SAMANTHA YOU'RE DEAD MOTHER FUCKER, YOU'RE DEAD."

Inside the car and being able to hear Lee take out his anger, Paul says to Jake, "But we've done nothin' wrong man, I swear," where Jake remains silent as they drive off.

52.

Walking out of a room where Paul is seen in the background sitting at a table, with a guard in the corner of the room, Jake closes the door behind him and takes hold of his cellular and dials a few numbers.

"Hi Steve," Jake says, "Bad news, the body that was found today has been identified as, Amy Waterson."

"Holey shit man," Steve says as he pushes the table on wheels in front of him, containing his dinner, out of the way due to losing his appetite, "How the fuck am I gonna break the news man?"

"Give it some time." Jake says.

"And have them hear it on the box or some news paper man, come on!" Steve says.

"Well filling you in with the news, one of the little shits escaped earlier when his friend told him his brothers gone missin' from the bus that was makin' it's way towards a bus stop near Mixtures, but personally he's a bit of a look a like to Jo Walters, but it couldn't be him man, as he's a lot younger for sure," Jake says.

"So whatta you doin' with the dude that's in custody now?" Steve says.

"Lettin' him sweat it out a bit while I get down to this key shop with a search warrant, as he told me that's where the fake ID's were got. Then I'll head back to the Mixtures direction and see if there's any sightings of that little dude Alan that escaped." Jake says, where walking in his direction is another FBI looking for his attention.

"Well gotta go man." Jake says hanging up.

"What's up?" Jake says to the other FBI officer.

"There's a lady at the reception lookin' to talk to you."

- -

"And how can I help you Mam?" Jake says as he arrives at the destination the other FBI officer pointed him to, which is towards Charlotte.

"I've just come to query as to whether there's any word of my son, Simon Woods, who was headin' by bus in the direction of a crime scene today?" Charlotte says, "As he was supposed to be meetin' up with his brother Alan and his friends who are on a campin' spree."

"Come with me Mam," Jake says, where Charlotte is guided to a room that Paul can be seen through the glass.

"Do you recognize this man Mam?" Jake says.

"What the hell's he doin' here?" Charlotte says, "He's supposed to be campin' with my Alan and his friends Ryan and Chris." Then thinking the worst as she looks at Paul, Charlotte says, "Why if they've been roamin' the town and havin' had my Simon put on a wild goose chase I'm gonna tare them a new rear end."

"No Mam, they've been on their campin' spree, but your son was given the fake identification of Jo Walters." Jake says.

"As in *the* Jo Walters that was killed 18 years back with his so called Pop, Jamie-Lee?" Charlotte says.

"Yeah, you sound like you know them."

"Well that's the other thing I wanted to talk to you about." Charlotte says.

"Why's that?"

"Eighteen years ago I was havin' an affair with his father, Jamie-Lee Walters, who's Alan's biological Pop by right."

"As in father?" Jake says.

"I'd prefer not to look at it that way. As when I told him I was pregnant he lost the plot altogether by shakin' me about like crazy, to which he finally threw me up against the wall, where I fell to the floor scared shitless. Then ordering me, or should I say threatening me to get an abortion, he just charged outta my house slamming the door behind him. Where only half an hour later when I was watchin' the box, a news flash came up, which was over the finding of his wife havin' been buried in their backyard, along with details about his land rover having went flying off the edge of a cliff, which had his son and himself in it. But personally I've always had this gut feelin' that the bastard's still about. You know what I mean?"

"Personally Mam, I think you've just helped us out big time," Jake says.

"I hope so for my two boys' sakes," Charlotte says. "Is it okay if I go and talk with Paul?"

"He's still up for questioning at the moment Mam, so it can only be for a few minutes." Jake says.

"Please find my boys." Charlotte says as Jake opens the door to escort her into Paul.

"We're onto it as we speak Mam."

"Please forget the Mam, I'm Charlotte." Charlotte says, then opening the door and seeing Paul having his forehead touching the table, as the guard stands behind him, Jake looks over at him.

"Two minutes," Jake says. Then he lets Charlotte in.

"Oh, Paul are you okay?" Charlotte says quickly giving him a kiss on the forehead.

"*Charlotte*," Paul says nearly bursting into tears, "This whole campin' spree has been one big frickin' nightmare."

"Don't worry I'll let your Mom know as soon as I get outta here," Charlotte says as she gives Paul a kiss on the head and takes a seat.

"I'm mean Chris and Ryan are even in hospital too, due to havin' been shot." Paul says.

"Don't worry about it now, the cops are doin' their best to find out who the real culprit is over all this mayhem. Plus I'll contact their parents and let them know what's been goin' on also."

"I'm really sorry about Simon havin' gone missin'."

"Don't worry the cops have got it all under control. They'll be bringin' this to an end soon enough." Charlotte says as the door closes over with Jake disappearing out of sight.

- -

    Knowing rightly that heading back to the scene of where Amy's body was found to find Alan is more important than checking for where the fake ID's were made, Jake gets on into his car and spins off.

53.

With severe pain Steve tries his hardest to get out of bed and stand up.

"Hay, nurse, NURSE," Steve says with his volume increasing as he watches a nurse pass by his door, where keeping his eyes peeled on the doors entrance, the nurse comes back into view in a moonwalk mode.

"Are you not supposed to be lying down sir?" The nurse says.

"I need to get up, could you get me a wheel chair please?" Steve says.

"Just stay there a minute," the nurse says giving her orders as she quickly runs off.

Coming back into the room with the senior nurse that took Steve's temperature when Jake was visiting, the two of them head to either side of Steve's bed and maneuver him back in, where taking his temperature as he's in the lying position again, the senior nurse says, "I take it you're that little bit confused with my advise on doing no work here, huh?"

"No, I need a wheel chair now." Steve very seriously says.

"Sir, you are in no fit state to go anywhere." The nurse says.

"Listen up Mam, there's one loving couple in this hospital who have been put through non-stop shit all of last night and today. Where to make the shit even thicker, I've just been informed by my main partner in crime that their daughter's body has been found." Steve says.

"But sir ...,"

"Never mind the 'but sir', what would you rather them have, huh? Have them hear it on the news or over hear some dude talkin' about it without them not even knowin' Jack about it, come on, huh?" Steve says.

"Could you do me a favor?" The senior nurse in charge asks the other nurse, "Could you get this man a wheel chair and don't let him outta your sight, cuz if he was to hear of another crime scene, he'd be gone, am I right?" The nurse in charge asks Steve.

"I promise, I'll stay in bed after this, I'll even eat all my greens," Steve says.

"You eat all your greens anyway, your plates are always empty," the nurse in charge says.

"See, I'm a man of my word." Steve happily says as the other nurse comes back with a wheel chair.

- -

Getting pushed down the maternity ward and listening to a few baby cries as three of the red lights to the private maternity rooms are glowing, it's plain to see it's one busy morning.

"Thanks for helpin' me out on this," Steve says to the nurse.

"Ah, think nothin' of it sir." The nurse says, "Personally my heart goes out to them."

"Well it looks like they're a little occupied with their light on at the mo, you don't mind leavin' me on down to the waitin' room, huh?" Steve says.

"No, not at all," the nurse says, though as they come in line with Barbara's room the light suddenly goes out.

"Talk about timin'." Steve says, "But either way, I think it's better to drop me on off to the waitin' room and send Pete on in."

"Okay," the nurse says, where bringing Steve on into the waiting room she heads back to Pete and Barbara's room.

In the waiting room Steve is the only one occupying it, to which he looks around at all the pictures and leaflets of the newborn babies on the wall, then Pete all tired with watery eyes walks on in.

"The amount've times I've read them over and over again since I've been here has been crazy." Pete says.

"There's any God's amount've info on babies." Steve says as Pete sits on the chair beside the wheel chair.

"Well how's Barbara keepin'?" Steve asks.

"She's been clear of taking any fits for a few hours anyway." Pete says.

"And how's the circumstances with your newborn?" Steve asks.

"We've had a little baby boy," Pete says busy struggling to get his words out and stop himself from crying.

"All okay I hope, considering what Barbara's gone through and all?" Steve says.

"He's in an incubator, as Barbara's virtually drained out." Pete says, "If only my little angel Amy was here to see her new brother." Pete says busy struggling with his words.

"That's what I needed to talk to you about Pete." Steve says.

"What? No, no, don't tell me." Pete says crying uncontrollably.

"I'm sorry man, but it was your Amy's body that was identified at the scene earlier." Steve says as he places his hand on Pete's shoulder.

"Ah, no, no, no," Pete says barely being able to pronounce the words with his unstoppable breathlessness as he breaks down.

"I'm really sorry Steve," Steve says to Pete as he strokes his back.

"So am I," Pete says crying out his words, "So am I."

With a few minutes having past by Pete eventually lifts his head up, where his face and eyes are as read as can be while his tears look like waterfalls.

"What am I gonna do, huh?" Pete says.

"In regards to tellin' Barbara I take it?" Steve says knowing rightly Pete had a little bit more of that sentence to cover.

"Yeah," Pete says silently.

"You know yourself man, you're gonna have to tell her sooner or later, but it may be better to let her recuperate from the fits she's been havin' before you tell her the news. I'll personally make sure no newspapers get a hold of this and the doctors and nurses don't speak a word about it." Steve says.

"Thanks Steve, for everythin'." Pete says with tears rolling down his eyes.

"Are you sure you're gonna be okay man?" Steve says.

"Yeah, I just need a little bit of time to myself before I head on into Barbara." Pete says.

"Well Pete here's my card, and if you or Barbara when you's are all outta here need any help, I'll make sure you get all the help and support you need, okay?" Steve says.

"Thanks, you're a good man you know that." Pete says busy trying to stop himself from crying.

"If you need to have a talk Pete, I'm still here for another week or so, so you know what room I'm in, huh?" Steve says.

"Yeah." Pete says.

"Well I'll see you later, okay." Steve says as he strokes Pete's back then takes hold of the wheels to the wheel chair and starts wheeling himself out of the waiting room slowly.

"Here, wait up. Let me help you there man, I think I need to go out for a bitta fresh air anyway." Pete says.

"Sure there's no need, the nurse is gonna be back any time."

"I see, there she's comin' now," Pete says as he walks Steve up towards the nurse.

"Now like I said, let her recuperate from the ....," suddenly Barbara's door opens as Steve not noticing continues. ".., fits before you let her know."

"Know what?" Barbara says. Then raising her voice she repeats, "Know what?" Where inside Barbara's room she's lying on the bed holding her newborn son as a nurse stands by her side. Then coming in line with her door in the wheelchair, Steve takes a glimpse in with Pete appearing after him, revealing his blustered up beetroot face, then suddenly Barbara starts to shake her head side to side.

"Here, let me put your little angel back in the incubator there for a bit more oxygen." The nurse says as she takes hold of the newborn. Where as Pete walks up to Barbara she starts to go into another uncontrollable fit, where with the nurse already having the newborn in the incubator she quickly rings the bell for assistance as Steve and the other nurse disappear out of sight.

"Hang on in there my little angel." Pete is heard saying as the door closes over, but running around the corner and reopening the door two other nurses run on in to assist aid.

"I hope she's gonna be okay," Steve says as the other nurse wheels him outta of the maternity ward.

"Don't worry I'll keep you posted, providing you stay in your pit this time, huh?" The nurse says as she wheels Steve off.

"Cops honor." Steve says.

54.

"Holey cow, you mean to tell me you wasters have been hiding out in this hell hole, what's up you couldn't be assed to set up camp or somethin'?" Simon says to the Stranger as they both walk closer to the abandoned house.

"I've seen cleaner crap than this," Simon says acting all hard, "If this is the waste of space you guys have been sleepin' in, I'd hate to see the puke you've all be eatin', uh?" Simon says as he follows the Stranger into the abandoned house.

With Simon walking on in and the Stranger standing at the door, Simon quickly stops, looks at the bodies and shape of the place and says, "Where's the guys?" But the Stranger closes the door with the darkness covering their face and puts on the bolt.

"Right enough of the playin' around, where's Alan?" Simon says, "Where's my bro you heap of shit." Simon says as he pushes the Stranger back as they walk closer to him. Though quickly grabbing the stick part from a rejected brush that just slides out of the attachment part it's supposed to remain in, the Stranger quickly raps Simon across the head, where just about to continue beating Simon the Stranger's suddenly distracted by dog barks, which suddenly stop as the Stranger heads for the door. Though turning around to continue with Simon, the photo distracts the Stranger completely, as they just walk up to the photo and start stroking away at the picture.

----

18 YEARS AGO

Startling Veronica and Jo out of their sleep unexpectedly with all the noise, Jamie-Lee storms swiftly into the living room appearing a lot more worse for wear, more than likely due to the air hitting him as he walked out of the bar, which seems to have changed his form of manner into being one very angry tipsy individual.

"*I need money.*" Jamie-Lee angrily informs Veronica in a desperately drunken shook up manner. Then storming up to Veronica and Jo with his temper running high, violence is getting the better of him as he grabs a tight grip to Veronica's coat, pulls her up from the settee, shakes her back and forth like crazy, then throws her back onto the settee beside Jo, who's shocked over witnessing what's happening in front of him.

"I NEED MONEY! NOW WHERE IS IT BITCH?" Jamie-Lee shouts, nearly coming in nose to nose contact with her.

"I don't have any." Veronica replies, scared lifeless.

"Don't gimme that shit lady, now where is the fuckin' money?" Jamie-Lee says furiously as he grabs hold of Veronica and pulls her up from the settee.

"You took the last of the money with you." Veronica replies with tears rolling down her battered and bruised face. Where looking at Jo as Jamie-Lee has hold of Veronica, he gets up from the settee and sprints to the entrance of the kitchen that's connected to the living room, busy looking at his Mum helplessly in despair.

Slapping Veronica around the face vehemently, to which some blood from her recent beating is seen landing on the wall behind her, Jamie-Lee shouts, "YOU'RE HIDING IT FROM ME BITCH, YOU'RE HIDING IT FROM ME." Then suddenly noticing the suitcase poking out from the back of the settee, Jamie-Lee's head drops and shakes side to side slowly, to which there's complete speechlessness. Though quickly breaking the atmospheres silence, Jamie-Lee throws an unsuspected uppercut towards the right hand side of Veronica's jaw bone, causing her to plummet to the floor.

"YOU AIN'T GOT ANY MONEY. YOU AIN'T GOT MONEY, SO WHATTA THESE FOR THEN, HUH, HUH?" Jamie-Lee angrily shouts as he notices from down the back of the settee that a suitcase and rucksack has been attempted to be hid, where taking hold of the suitcase he throws it on top of Veronica.

"NOW LESS OF THE LYING BITCH I NEED SOME MONEY NOW, NOW. NOW WHERE IS IT?" Jamie-Lee angrily shouts as he grabs Veronica by the hair and pulls her up to the sitting position then fires her back onto the settee. Where looking behind Jamie-Lee, Jo's face is drowning with tears as he stands shaking like a leaf.

"I haven't got any," Veronica chokingly says, "I swear." She says like it's her last gasp of breath being used.

Then Jamie-Lee looking towards a stereo system notices an empty bottle of beer. Where grabbing hold of it he walks over to Veronica and waves it in front of her face that is poring with blood.

"You see this." Jamie-Lee says pointing at the label stuck on the bottle, "This is the only thing worth fuckin' livin' for, but without money I can't get any. **CAN YOU NOT DRILL THAT INTO YOUR FUCKIN' HEAD?**" Jamie-Lee shouts as he smashes the hefty glass bottle over Veronica's head, where with the glass shattering everywhere, in slow motion Veronica plummets sideways to the floor with no sign of eye movement at all as her body crushes to the ground, where Jo is literally in shock watching everything happen in front of him.

Kicking her in the belly while she's down, Jamie-Lee waves the remainder of the smashed bottle at Veronica's dead eyes and says, "You'll never fuckin' change will you?" Where looking at her in disgust for a response, Jamie-Lee's question is answered abruptly by the voice of Jo, as he cries the words, "**NO, NO, NO, NO, NO, NO, NO.**" To which each time Jo's voice expresses the word '**NO**', Jamie-Lee's facial expression looks ever so painful. Slowly descending forward, Jamie-Lee's body plummets towards the ground, where landing on top of Veronica his face smacks forcefully onto the smashed glass, though standing near where Jamie-Lee once was, Jo is completely in shock and distressed as he continues to hold the knife in a stabbing mode, as lying in front of him which he isn't even looking down towards, is the dead bodies of his Mum and Dad.

- -

Thunderous noises are close by as Veronica's face is as still as can be as the rain pelts down on her body as she lies still in a little mucky ditch. Then suddenly small heaps of muck start getting thrown on top of her body bit by bit as the rain gets heavier, where drifting back a little bit, a small figure being covered by the darkness is seen shoveling muck that is disappearing down a hole as it leaves the spade.

- -

As the engine to the land rover is running, all the doors are closed as the rain pelts down on it. Where sitting on the front passenger seat facing towards the drivers side, Jo's eyes are poring with tears as his body shakes unstoppably. Soaking wet from top to bottom, his clothes are also plastered in an unaccountable amount of muck, with bloodied patches all around his clothing too. Where looking away from the drivers side Jo lowers his head in shame and starts crying, "What've we done, w, w, w, what've we done," Jo struggles to say as his tears uncontrollably surge from his eyes. Though strapped into the drivers seat with his hands stuck to the steering wheel with adhesive tape, is Jamie-Lee, whose forehead on the headrest, as well as his feet on the peddles, which look automatic, have been stuck together with adhesive tape too.

With the driver's door opening and Jo appearing, Jo removes the foot from the brake pedal, puts the clutch into automatic, then taking hold of what looks like a large heavy object, he throws it on top of Jamie-Lee's foot that is stuck with the adhesive tape to the accelerator pedal and slams the door. Suddenly the land rover starts moving at a crazy pace as the rear wheels spin like mad, literally burning the wheels before it zooms off.

Flying down the country road like there's no tomorrow the land rovers barely driving strait, as with it speeding down the hill and getting faster beyond belief, it's narrowly missing oncoming traffic by millimeters, plus the window screen wipers aren't even on either, where as the rain pelts down on the land rovers front window and the lightning suddenly striking, Jamie-Lee's face can't even be made out due to the blurriness.

With the lightning striking again and brightening up the edge of the mountain a lorry can be seen coming around the corner, but not even slowing down the right hand side of Jamie-Lee's land rover has the front of a lorry crashing into it with force. Where flying over the metal barrier, Jamie-Lee's land rover tumbles down the side of the steep mountain as the lightning strikes again, and upon landing upside down with force the land rover blows up something shockingly, making the lightning look like a little match stick.

Walking on the side of the road Jo is getting soaked by both the rain and the puddles he has no choice but to walk through, where with his face getting drenched it's hard to make out if there are any tears, but it's plain to see he's still in major shock.

Passing Jo in the van is Sam, but this time his mother's the main driver, where Sam puts his hand behind his mothers head rest and gives Jo the middle finger.

"Isn't that a disgrace, look at that kid, some parents just don't give their kids the support they need, huh?" Sam's Mum says.

"Yeah, tell me about it. Plus in this time of life you wouldn't even take a chance on giving the dude a lift, huh?" Sam says knowing rightly his Dad wouldn't think twice about picking him up.

"I know you just can't be too sure with the amount've things you hear on the news." Sam's Mum says.

"Yeah, you're right there." Sam says busy smirking.

Looking back at Jo he's continuously staring at Sam's van driving off in the distance as he continues to walk through the puddles whilst carrying a rucksack in his hand.

- -

"Sam, stick the empty milk jugs out front for the'morrows collection like a good man will you?" Trevor says finishing off the dishes.

"As long as I don't get any thank you kisses!" Sam says. "Cuz I don't think you took that medication you required to take earlier when we got home from school, did you?" Sam says busy messing about.

"Ah, you know me; medication wouldn't help my brains either way, as the brain cells are few and far between." Trevor says.

"But what the heck you're still my half acceptable Pop anyway," Sam says as he opens the front door and bends down to set the milk jugs on the floor.

"Yeah, and who knows you could turn out just to be like me some day, huh," Trevor's voice is heard saying.

"Ooh, that's spooky." Sam says. But as he raises himself up from putting the milk jugs on the floor, standing right in front of him and staring him blue in the face is Jo.

"Whatta you want Mr. Waste-a-Space?" Sam says as he looks at Jo with a sympathetic cocky mannered facial expression. "Have you come to give your praise or somethin' for your little lift from earlier?" Sam says.

"Who's that at the door Sam?" Trevor's voice is heard questioning from the kitchen. But as Sam turns around to answer whilst looking away from Jo, before he gets a chance, all that can be seen is Jo raising a knife and continuously stabbing Sam in the back whilst silently crying the words, "No, no, no, no, no, no, no," where with Jo standing in the frozen stabbing position like he did with his Dad, Sam's body plummets to the carpet in the hallway while Jo slowly walks off.

Lying there stone dead, with Jo disappearing out of sight, Sam's Mum walks down the stairs and notices Sam covered and lying in his own pool of blood.

"AAAAAAAAAAAAAAAAGH!" She screams. Where running from the kitchen to see what all the commotion's over, Trevor, looking at the state Sam's been left in, dives for the front door, but there is no sign of anyone.

Quickly darting back into the house Trevor feels for Sam's pulse, and tries to listen to see if he's still breathing.

"*Call an ambulance, call an ambulance.*" Trevor says to his wife as he starts with the compressions, though Sam's Mum just stands in complete shock, knowing rightly he's not going to be able to give any compressions due to the stab wounds. Standing up Trevor takes hold of his Wife, picks up the phone and dials for an ambulance.

Walking towards the woods with the rain still belting down, Jo's face is in complete shock over what's happened in such a short period of time. And with him wearing dirty dark clothes and there not being a speck of brightness coming from the sky, the only light that is about is coming from a little cottage house in the distance, that Jo is walking towards.

Inside the house which is quite historically laid out with old time decorations and furniture, the electricity suddenly glitches in Mr. Connery's living room, causing the lights to flicker as he sits on his one seat settee which has a sturdy looking table beside it, though as he continues to read away at what seems to be school work, the way it's stacked and separated with quite a few names poking out from the pages, as if there markers, the lights abruptly clank out altogether. Though the only thing that's giving him any assistance over seeing anything in the living room is the lovely blazing fire he's got sizzling away.

Setting the work down on the table, the tiresomeness on Mr. Connery's face as he stands up and heads for the hallway is crazy looking, as his eyes are virtually dangling out of his head, from all the reading and homework correcting more than likely.

Arriving in the pitch black hallway, Mr. Connery manages to find the cloakroom door, where as he opens it two seconds pass by and a torch light's suddenly turned on out of the blue, where shining it deeper into the cloak-room the electricity boxes can be seen, where Mr. Connery starts pushing the buttons to an upwards position, then gradually as he pushes the last button upright, light is seen coming from the living rooms direction.

Placing the torch back on its shelf and heading out of the cloak-room, as Mr. Connery closes the door, behind the door and in the direction of the kitchen a small dark figure can be seen.

"Hay, what the fuck are you doin' in my house?" Mr. Connery blurts out.

"What've we done, what've we done?" The small figures voice cries out. But before Mr. Connery can even get a word out, a plastic bottle that seems to be open is fired in his direction and poring out everywhere, eventually landing in the living room.

"What the fucks the meanin' of this you little prick?" Mr. Connery angrily asks, but just as his question is asked another open bottle splashes everywhere and lands at Mr. Connery's feet.

"You see what you've done? You see what you've done?" The small figures voice cries out. Then all that can be seen coming from the kitchen is the strike of a match that glows up the small figures waste, where as the match is let go of, a slight piece of the kitchen, the whole of hallway with Mr. Connery in it, and the living room literally bursts out into flames, with two slight explosions coming from the bottles that were thrown. Where back in the kitchen as Mr. Connery is screaming in the hallway like mad, the kitchens completely unoccupied.

Sitting on the settee watching an advertisement finish on the box, charlotte looks down at her belly with grave concern as she holds it with her right hand whilst closing her eyes like she's getting some serious pains, but quickly taking her mind off of it a news report appears on the television, along with flashing lights that can be seen passing her window.

>**NEWS REPORT ON TELEVISION**
>As you can see a body of a young man, Sam Graham has been found stabbed to death at his front door by his devastated father Trevor Graham only twenty minutes ago, and is currently being taken away as we speak.

At Trevor's house flashing lights are all over the place, and standing outside his entrance Trevor is so taken back over what is going on, along with his wife who is bursting with tears as the police start to barricade the area up.

Looking at the news reporters who are at the roadside of the scene doing their live news report, they have a policeman walk up to them as they cut off from doing a piece of news, and as the policeman finishes whispering to the female news reporter, the news reporter shouts to the cameraman, "Get us back on the air now!"

Still all worked up from Jamie-Lee's visit earlier, as Charlotte stands up from the settee another news flash suddenly appears, catching her attention.

NEWS REPORT ON TELEVISION
It has just been brought to our attention that this is not the only incident that has happened tonight, as I am just after getting informed by the Police that two deaths have also happened on the road tonight, that isn't too far away from here. They are believed to be the bodies of a father and son, called Jo and Jamie-Lee Walters ....,

Charlotte's eyes rise open, looking like she doesn't know whether to laugh or cry, and putting her two hands together, caressing her inner arms against her chest and resting her chin on top of her hands like she's just about to say a prayer, she continues listening to the rest of the news.

NEWS REPORT ON TELEVISION
.., and not only that but with the Cops also having checked around Jamie-Lee's property, at the rear lawn to Jamie-Lee's house, his wife's body, Veronica Walters was found berried under a pile of dirt.

From the part of the settee that Charlotte was last seen, there is no sign of her, but heading into the hall and seeing a door half open and light coming out of it, all that can be heard are continuous vomiting noises coming from that direction, with Charlotte shouting, *"NO, NO FUCKIN' WAY, NO WAY,"* with crying and more sounds of vomiting noises following.

- -

BACK TO THE PRESENT TIME

Outside the abandoned house Alan is seen walking in between the trees and coming closer to the house, where taking a stop pit and kneeling down behind a little bump on the ground, Alan looks over towards the abandoned house, where appearing from the side of the house on all fours is Jack. Acting quickly, Alan does a little whistle to get Jack's attention. Where noticing him strait away Jack heads in his direction.

"Jack, there's a good boy." Alan whispers as Jack walks towards him, though with getting closer and closer, Jack starts to gradually put on an angry face, revealing his sharp teeth.

"Jack what's the matter. You know it wasn't me that's done any of this shit." Alan says, where thinking he's just about to get his balls bit off, Alan closes his eyes so tightly and places his hands over his balls, though as a few seconds pass, Alan slightly opens his eyes and notices Jack's not in front of him anymore, even though he's still growling. Slowly taking a peek over his shoulder in case Jack's just about to bight his rear end off, Alan notices he's growling at Jake who was creeping up on Alan with a gun in his hand.

"Call the dog off," Jake says.

"You might wanna put the gun away first," Alan says.

"I know all about what's been goin' on." Jake says.

"Yeah, like me and the guys on a campin' spree with fake ID's and getting sucked into this hellhole." Alan says.

"Yeah, but I know more," Jake says as he puts his gun away, where the teeth on Jack are getting sharper by the second. "You're Mom's told me all about it down at the station."

"Told you what?" Alan questions.

"About you guys headin' on a campin' spree so you's won't be around for the exam results, then your little bro receivin' a message on his cellular that he could join you." Jake says.

"So Paul was fuckin' right, the little ass wipe that's got my cellular has been contactin' Simon, and has been doin' all these killin's too." Alan says.

"But that's not all." Jake says.

"What else is there then, huh?" Alan queries.

"Well for one he's got your brother, and two, you see the fake ID you have of him, your Mom's confirmed it's the fake ID of your step brother." Jake says.

"Are you sure you're in the right job?" Alan asks.

"Whatta you mean?" Jake questions.

"Because you're head is full of shit! Now how the fuck is he supposed to be my step brother, huh?" Alan arrogantly says.

"I'll let you discuss that part with your Mom," Jake says. "Now call the dog off and let's go, as you've wasted more police time on findin' you when we could've been searching for your brother." Jake says.

"Good boy Jack," Alan says as he strokes Jack and stands up, where getting all hyper for having been called 'good', Jack starts barking, "That's a good boy now enough of that." Alan says, where Jack does what he's told then lets off a little whimper. Though just as Alan, Jack and Jake are about to head off, banging noises are heard coming from the door to the abandoned house, where quickly taking cover behind the mound, they look towards the abandoned house to which the door opens and Jo Walters, all confused walks out of.

Taking hold of his gun slowly, Jack starts to growl in the direction of Jake, but Alan quietly says, "It's alright boy, it's alright," though as Jake starts to point his gun at Jo, distracting him from taking a shot Simon bounces out of the house and onto Jo, busy throwing punches, kicks and pulling hair.

Not being able to get a clear shot Jake quickly grabs hold of his cellular and calls for back up as Jo carries Simon back into the abandoned house with Simon still trying to throw continuous kicks and punches

"Now you stay put." Jake says to Alan.

"While my brothers in there with that maniac," Alan says, "Don't you think two dudes are better than one?"

As the door is kicked open with no movement whatsoever coming from Simon on the floor, Jo having made his way over to Samantha is just about to stab Samantha in the direction of her heart until Jake shouts.

"FREEZE, THE GAMES OVER JO, NOW PUT DOWN YOUR WEAPON."

"Can't you see what he's doing to her?" Jo says all scared and confused. "The bastards constantly beating my Mom while she's down, can you not see that?" Jo says as he looks at Samantha's adhesive taped figure all rapped up, as if it's his Dad he's looking at, "That's why I've gotta kill him."

"No, please," Samantha's voice cries through the little air holes of her adhesive taped mouth that hasn't been properly covered over, as Jack is seen entering into the house slowly.

"Mom is that you?" Jo says helplessly.

Quickly catching on that he's not completely with it, Samantha acts fast to play along with Jo's game.

"Yes." Samantha says.

"You're the only one that means anything to me Mom." Jo says whilst looking at Samantha as if he pictures her rapped up body being his Mothers.

"Now Jo, put down the knife," Jake says.

"But can you not see he's killing her." Jo cries with confusion.

"Who is? Who is?" Jake repeats to see if he can get through to Jo.

"My Pop, he's just killed my Mom, look can't you see," Jo says pointing at Samantha, "Can't you see she's just got the bottle rapped over her head and he's still kicking her while she's down. That's why I've gotta kill him. It's all my fault we should've left when we had the chance, but I had to fall asleep, that's why I've gotta kill him." Jo says all worked up.

"Now calm down Jo, we know it was your Pop that killed your Mom, we're only here to help you and put your Pop behind bars," Jake says.

"No, no, no, no, no, no." Jo says as he pictures his Mum getting the bottle rapped over her head and falling to the floor. "**I'VE GOTTA KILL HIM BEFORE IT'S TOO LATE!**" Jo screams.

With everything going into slow motion, Jo is just about to stab Samantha, though as Jack jumps up to dig his teeth into the wrist of Jo's hand holding the knife, Jake takes a shot at Jo at the same time, where with both Jack and Jo falling to the floor all that can be heard is a whimpering noise with a loud thump to the floor following.

With everyone's shocked facial expressions scared silly over what's just happened, everything goes back to the speed of normality, where lying on the floor with a bullet in his head is Jo who has Jack lying on top of him with no movement at all.

Quickly arriving at the scene more cops with an ambulance park up outside the abandoned house.

"Simon, Simon. Are you okay?" Alan says as he leans down to the ground to take hold of his little brother whose face is completely still, then suddenly slight whimpering noises are heard coming from the direction of Jo and Jack, where limping his way towards Alan as he holds Simon in his arms is Jack busy whimpering on every move he makes as he limps in their direction. Arriving up to Alan and Simon, Jack starts licking Simon's face as he whimpers in the process. Then suddenly Simon starts to move ever so slightly and slowly opens his eyes.

"What's happened?" Simon says with his voice sounding very painful to talk.

"It's a long story, now try not to move bro," Alan says as he gently cuddles Simon and Jack simultaneously.

With the back up arriving into the abandoned house and making sure as to whether Simon, Samantha and Tracey are injured in any form before they start to lift or remove the adhesive tape from them, Jack starts to make his way over to Samantha as Jake makes his way over to Tracey to which the ambulance crew have the adhesive tape taken off her head already.

"Are you okay Tracey, you're not hurt anywhere are you?" Jake says to Tracey.

"Where's Steve, why's he not with you? Is he okay?" Tracey says to Jake all horrified.

"He's okay. He's sitting up in hospital for a week, by order of the nurse in charge." Jake says.

"Yeah, there's one slight problem though." The nurse says as she enters into the abandoned house, "He doesn't listen," she says as she points to Steve in the wheelchair. "No come on get her in a bed, and I'll personally make sure you both have a private room together. As I think that's the only way I'm gonna be able to keep him in the hospital." The nurse says.

With Tracey's stretcher getting in line with Steve's wheelchair, Steve takes hold of Tracey's hand and gives it a kiss.

"Tracey, I'm sorry, but Robert didn't make it." Steve says.

"Ah, shit, what happened?" Tracey says in disbelief.

"I found him in the back of the news van stabbed to death," Steve says.

"Oh, no way." Tracey says as she takes hold of Steve's hand when her stretcher comes in line with his wheelchair.

"Are you hurt anywhere," one of the ambulance crew members says to Samantha as he lowers the stretcher down with his partner.

"I don't think there's any broken bone's if that's what you mean." Samantha says as Jack whimpers away beside her.

As Simon is getting taken out in a stretcher, Alan lets go of his hand, "I'll catch up with you down at the hospital okay my little bro?" Alan says, "Be strong, huh?"

"Will do." Simon says as he pretends to show off the muscles on his right arm then goes strait into agony and lies back down on the stretcher.

With Alan walking up to Samantha and Jack licking away at her face due to the ambulance crew having removed the thick adhesive tape from her head so far, Alan looks at her face being all beetroot red from the adhesive tape.

"Are you looking for someone to look after this little savior while you are in the hospital?" Alan says.

"He seems to have taken to you rightly, huh?" Samantha says.

"You've heard the good old saying the pets are like their owners. Though all joking aside he's been helping us out all the way." Alan says, "If it wasn't for him who only knows how far it would have ended up."

"Well if you don't mind looking after him that is?" Samantha says.

"After all that's happened, it's the least I could do." Alan says.

Noticing rightly that Alan is trying to reassure Samantha that all is okay now, Jake walks up to the two of them as she is placed on the stretcher.

"You see if it hadn't of been for Alan and his crew being here, who only knows how long the killings would lasted. As it's been eighteen years this has been going on for now." Taking hold of Alan's hand and playing along with his roll as he shakes his hand, Jake follows on and says, "If you're ever looking for a place in the FBI, don't hesitate to contact me and I'll get a good word in for you." Then Jake walks off and out of the abandoned house.

"Alan." Samantha says as she's hoisted up in the air on the stretcher.

"Yeah," Alan says.

"Do you believe in love at first sight?" Samantha says, where lowering his lips towards Samantha's and giving her a kiss with love wrote all over it, his question is answered, followed up with the jealous whimpers of Jack in the back ground.

55.

With Alan and Samantha's lips still kissing like crazy, as their mouths depart they look into each others eyes with love wrote all over them. Where looking all around the place, they are sitting in Barry's Ravenswood Nightclub, where other than Ryan sitting on the table with them, the rest of them are partying away.

As the music comes to a short stand still, everyone ends up taking a seat around the table, where with them all taking a seat, Barry walks up to them.

"Thank God you guys are back. I was nearly runnin' outta business." Barry says messing around.

"Well just keep them drinks coming," Paul says as he hands Barry a couple of fifty dollar notes.

"Don't tell me you actually charged the guys for those free fake ID's you got?" Barry says. "Did he actually charge you guys?" Barry questions Ryan, Alan and Chris as they look at Paul very angrily.

"Come on look on the bright side," Paul says as all the angry faces look at him, "At least on our next killer of a camp we've got our lovely babes to take with us!"

"**WHAT, ANOTHER CAMPING SPREE? AND FREE FAKE ID'S.**" They all shout.

Knowing rightly he's in for it, and being lucky enough to be sitting on the outside of the table, Paul gets up and starts to run like crazy around the dance floor as the music starts, with Chris and even Ryan whose on his crutches chasing him.

Glaring into Samantha's eyes as Alan gives her a lovely long kiss, the screams from Paul can be heard in the background.

"Samantha, I love you so much." Alan says.

"I love you too Alan." Samantha says as she strokes his face.

"Now just keep that thought in mind and I'll be right back." Alan says as he gives Samantha another kiss. Then he starts chasing after Paul with Chris and Ryan, to which Ryan in a pretending manner is swinging his crutches at Paul.

"*Grab that stupid little fucker.*" Ryan shouts giving his orders.

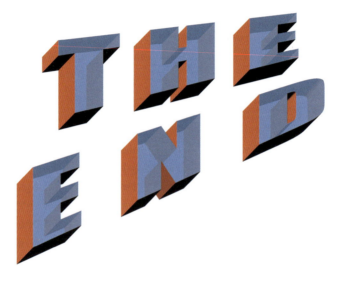